Brenda Jackson is a *New York Times* bestselling author of more than one hundred romance titles. Brenda lives in Jacksonville, Florida, and divides her time between family, writing and traveling. Email Brenda at authorbrendajackson@gmail.com or visit her on her website at brendajackson.net.

Books by Brenda Jackson

Harlequin Desire

The Westmoreland Legacy

The Rancher Returns
His Secret Son
An Honorable Seduction
His to Claim
Duty or Desire
One Steamy Night

Westmoreland Legacy: The Outlaws

The Wife He Needs
The Marriage He Demands
What He Wants for Christmas
What Happens on Vacation...
The Outlaw's Claim
Second Time's the Charm

Visit the Author Profile page
at Harlequin.com for more titles.

TAMING A HEARTBREAKER

BRENDA JACKSON

HARLEQUIN
SPECIAL
EDITION

Recycling programs for this product may not exist in your area.

ISBN-13: 978-1-335-59466-2

Taming a Heartbreaker
Copyright © 2024 by Brenda Streater Jackson

Husband Material
Copyright © 2010 by Harlequin Enterprises ULC

For questions and comments about the quality of this book, please contact us at CustomerService@Harlequin.com.

TM and ® are trademarks of Harlequin Enterprises ULC.

Harlequin Enterprises ULC
22 Adelaide St. West, 41st Floor
Toronto, Ontario M5H 4E3, Canada
www.Harlequin.com

Printed in Lithuania

MIX
Paper | Supporting responsible forestry
FSC® C021394

CONTENTS

TAMING A HEARTBREAKER

Prologue

Sloan and Leslie Outlaw's wedding...

"Sloan definitely likes kissing you, girlfriend."

Leslie Outlaw couldn't help but smile at her best friend's whispered words. "And I love kissing him."

She'd married the man she loved, and she'd had her best friend Carmen Golan at her side. Leslie followed her friend's gaze now and saw just where it had landed—right on Redford St. James, who was being corralled by the photographer as Sloan took pictures with his best man and groomsmen.

Unease stirred Leslie's insides at her friend's obvious interest.

Leslie had known Redford for as long as she'd known Sloan, since she'd met both guys the same day on the university's campus over ten years ago. Redford had been known then as a heartbreaker. According to Sloan, Redford hadn't changed. If anything, he'd gotten worse.

"Carmen, I need to warn you about Redford," Leslie said, hoping it wasn't too late. She'd noted last night at the rehearsal how taken her best friend had been with Redford. She'd hoped she was mistaken.

"I know all about him, Leslie, so you don't need to warn me. However, you might want to put a bug in Sloan's ear to warn Redford about me."

Leslie lifted a brow. "Why?"

A wide smile covered Carmen's face. "Because Redford

St. James is the man I intend to marry. Your hubby is on his way over here. I will see you at the reception."

Leslie watched Carmen walk toward Redford. Marry? Redford? She had a feeling her best friend was biting off more than she could chew. Redford was not the marrying kind. He'd made that clear when he'd said no woman would ever tame him.

Chapter One

Two years later...

Redford St. James froze, with his wineglass midway to his lips, when he saw the woman walk into the wedding reception for Jaxon and Nadia Ravnell. Frowning, he immediately turned to the man by his side, Sloan Outlaw. During their college days at the University of Alaska at Anchorage, Sloan, Redford, and another close friend, Tyler Underwood, had been thick as thieves, and still were.

Redford had been known as the "king of quickies." He would make out with women any place or any time. Storage rooms, empty classrooms or closets, beneath the stairs, dressing rooms …he'd used them all. He had the uncanny ability to scope out a room and figure out just where a couple could spend time for pleasure. He still had that skill and used it every chance he got.

Although he, Sloan and Tyler now lived in different cities in Alaska, they still found the time to get together a couple of times a year. Doing so wasn't as easy as it used to be since both Tyler and Sloan were married with a child each. Tyler had a son and Sloan a daughter.

"Why didn't you tell me Carmen Golan was invited to this wedding?"

Sloan glanced over at Redford and rolled his eyes. "Just

like you didn't tell me Leslie had been invited to Tyler and Keosha's wedding three years ago?"

Redford frowned. "Don't play with me, Sloan. You should have known Leslie would be invited, since she and Keosha were friends in college. In this case, I wasn't aware Carmen knew Jaxon or Nadia."

Sloan took a sip of his wine before saying, "The Outlaws and Westmorelands consider themselves one big happy family, and that includes outside cousins, in-laws and close friends. Since Carmen is Leslie's best friend, of course she would know them." Sloan then studied his friend closely. "Why does Carmen being here bother you, Redford? If I recall, when I put that bug in your ear after my wedding, that she'd said she intended to one day become your wife, you laughed it off. Has that changed?"

"Of course, that hasn't changed."

"You're sure?" Sloan asked. "It seems to me that over the past two years, whenever the two of you cross paths, you try like hell to avoid her. Most recently, at Cassidy's christening a few months ago." Cassidy was Sloan and Leslie's daughter. Redford was one of her godfathers, and Carmen was her godmother.

"No woman can change my ways. I don't ever intend to marry. Who does she think she is, anyway? She doesn't even know me like that. If she did, then she would know my only interest in her at your wedding was getting her to the nearest empty coat closet. The nerve of her, thinking she can change me."

"And since you know she can't change you, why worry about it?"

"I'm not worrying."

"If you say so," Sloan countered.

Redford's frown deepened. "I do say so. You of all people should know that I'll never fall in love again."

Before Sloan could respond, his sister Charm walked up and said the photographer wanted to take a photo of Jaxon with his Outlaw cousins.

When Sloan walked off, leaving Redford alone, he took a sip of his wine as he looked across the room at Carmen again. Sloan's words had hit a nerve. He *wasn't* worried. Then why had he been avoiding her for the past two years? Doing so hadn't been easy since he was one of Sloan's best friends and she was Leslie's, and both were godparents to Cassidy. Whenever they were in the same space, he made it a point to not be in her presence for long.

He could clearly recall the day he'd first seen Carmen at Sloan and Leslie's wedding rehearsal two years ago. He would admit that he'd been intensely attracted to her from the first. It was a deep-in-the-gut awareness. Something he had never experienced before. He hadn't wasted any time adding her to his "must do" list. He'd even flirted shamelessly after they'd been introduced, with every intention of making out with her before the weekend ended.

Then he'd gotten wind of her bold claim that he was the man she intended to marry. Like hell! That had wiped out all his plans. He was unapologetically a womanizer, and no woman alive would change that.

Carmen wasn't the first woman to try, nor would she be the first to fail. Granted she was beautiful. Hell, he'd even say she was "knock-you-in-the-balls" gorgeous, but he'd dated beautiful women before. If he'd seen one, he'd seen them all, and in the bedroom they were all the same.

Then why was he letting Carmen Golan get to him? Why would heat flood his insides whenever he saw her, making him aware of every single thing about her? Why was there this strong kinetic pull between them? It was sexual chemistry so powerful that, at times, it took his breath away.

Over the years, he'd tried convincing himself his lust for

her would fade. So far it hadn't. And rather recently, whenever he saw her, it had gotten so bad he had to fight like hell to retain his common sense.

Although Sloan had given him that warning two years ago, Carmen hadn't acted on anything. Was she waiting for what she thought would be the right time to catch him at a weak moment? If that was her strategy then he had news for her. It wouldn't happen. If anything, he would catch *her* unawares first, just to prove he was way out of her league…thanks to Candy Porter.

Contrary to her first name, he'd discovered there hadn't been anything sweet about Candy. At seventeen, she had taught him a hard lesson. Mainly, to never give your heart to a woman. Candy and her parents had moved to Skagway the summer before their last year of high school. By the end of the summer, she had been his steady girlfriend, the one he planned to marry after he finished college. Those plans ended the night of their high school senior prom.

Less than an hour after they'd arrived, she told him she needed to go to the ladies' room. When she hadn't returned in a timely manner, he had gotten worried since she hadn't been feeling well. He had gone looking for her, and when a couple of girls said she wasn't in the ladies' room, he and the two concerned girls had walked outside and around the building to find her, hoping she was alright.

Not only had they found her, they'd found her with the town's bad boy, Sherman Sharpe. Both of them in the backseat of Sherman's car making out like horny rabbits. The pair hadn't even had the decency to roll up the car's window so their moans, grunts and screams couldn't be heard.

Needless to say, news of Candy and Sherman's backseat romp quickly got around. By the following morning, every household in Skagway, Alaska, had heard about it. She had tried to explain, offer an excuse, but as far as he'd been concerned, there was nothing a woman could say when caught with another man between her legs.

Heartbroken and hurt, Redford hadn't wasted any time leaving Skagway for Anchorage to begin college that summer, instead of waiting for fall. That's when he vowed to never give his heart to another woman ever again.

That had been nearly nineteen years ago, and he'd kept the promise he'd made to himself. At thirty-six, he guarded his heart like it was made of solid gold and refused to let any woman get close. He kept all his hookups impersonal. One-and-done was the name of his game. No woman slept in his bed, and he never spent the entire night in theirs. He refused to wake up with any woman in his arms.

Redford knew Carmen was his total opposite. He'd heard she was one of those people who saw the bright side of everything, always positive and agreeable. On top of that, she was a hopeless romantic. A woman who truly believed in love, marriage and all that bull crap. According to Sloan, she'd honestly gotten it in her head that she and Redford were actual soulmates. Well, he had news for her, he was no woman's soulmate.

When his wineglass was empty, he snagged another from the tray of a passing waiter. When he glanced back over at Carmen, he saw she was staring at him, and dammit to hell, like a deer caught in headlights, he stared back. Why was he feeling this degree of lust that she stirred within him so effortlessly?

There wasn't a time when she didn't look stunning. Today was no exception. There was just something alluring about her. Something that made his breath wobble whenever he stared at her for too long.

He blamed it on the beauty of her cocoa-colored skin, her almond-shaped light brown eyes, the gracefulness of her high cheekbones, her tempting pair of lips, and the mass of dark brown hair that fell past her shoulders.

Every muscle in his body tightened as he continued to look

at her, checking her out in full detail. His gaze scanned over her curvaceous and statuesque body. The shimmering blue dress she wore hugged her curves and complemented a gorgeous pair of legs. The bodice pushed up her breasts in a way that made his mouth water.

"Now you were saying," Sloan said, returning and immediately snagging Redford's attention.

"I was saying that maybe I should accommodate Carmen."

That sounded like a pretty damn good idea, considering the current fix his body was in.

"Meaning what?" Sloan asked.

A smile widened across Redford's lips. "Meaning, I think I will add her back to my 'must do' list. Maybe it's time she discovers I am a man who can't be tamed."

Sloan frowned. "Do I need to warn you that Carmen is Leslie's best friend?"

"No, but I would assume, given my reputation, that Leslie has warned Carmen about me. It's not my fault if she didn't take the warning. Now, if you will excuse me, I think I'll head over to the buffet table."

He then walked off. At least for now, he would take care of one appetite, and he intended to take care of the other before the night was over.

"I wish you and Redford would stop trying to out-stare each other, Carmen," Leslie Outlaw leaned over to whisper to her best friend.

Carmen Golan broke eye contact with Redford to glance at Leslie and couldn't help the smile that spread across her lips. "Hey, what can I say? He looks so darn good in a suit."

Leslie rolled her eyes. "Need I remind you that you've seen him in a suit before. Numerous times."

"Redford wore a tux at your wedding, Leslie, and he looked

good then, too. Better than good. He looked scrumptious." Carmen watched him again. He definitely looked delicious now.

She knew he was in his late thirties. He often projected a keen sense of professionalism, as well as a high degree of intelligence far beyond his years. But then there were other times when it seemed the main thing on his agenda was a conquest. Namely, seducing a woman.

Carmen knew all about his reputation as a heartbreaker of the worst kind. She'd witnessed how he would check out women at various events, seeking out his next victim. He had checked her out the same way, the first time they'd met.

She'd also seen the way women checked him out, too and definitely understood why they fell for him when he was so darn handsome. His dark eyes, coffee-colored skin, chiseled and bearded chin, hawkish nose, and close-to-the-scalp haircut, were certainly a draw.

Then there was his height. Carmen was convinced he was at least six foot three with a masculine build of broad shoulders, muscular arms and a rock-hard chest. Whenever he walked, feminine eyes followed. According to Leslie, although he made Anchorage his home, his family lived in Skagway and were part of the Tlingits, the largest Native Alaskan tribe.

Since their initial meeting two years ago, he'd kept his distance and she knew the reason why. She'd deliberately let it be known that she planned to marry him one day, making sure he heard about her plans well in advance. And upon hearing them, he'd begun avoiding her.

"Granted, it's obvious there's strong sexual chemistry between you and Redford," Leslie said, interrupting Carmen's thoughts. "Sexual chemistry isn't everything. At least you've given up the notion of trying to tame him. I'm glad about that. You had me worried there for a while."

Carmen broke eye contact with Redford and looked at Leslie. "Nothing has changed, Leslie. I'm convinced that for me it was love at first sight. Redford is still the man I intend to marry."

Leslie looked surprised. "But you haven't mentioned him in months. And at Cassidy's christening you didn't appear to pay him any attention."

Carmen grinned. "I've taken the position with Redford that I refuse to be like those other women who are always fawning over him. Women he sees as nothing more than sex mates. Redford St. James has to earn his right to my bed. When he does, it will be because he's ready to accept what I have to give."

"Which is?"

"Love in its truest form."

Leslie rolled her eyes. "I've known Redford a lot longer than you have, and I know how he operates. I love him like a brother, but get real, Carmen. He has plenty of experience when it comes to seducing women. You, on the other hand, have no experience when it comes to taming a man. Zilch."

"I believe in love, Leslie, and I have more than enough to give," Carmen said softly.

"I believe you, but the person you're trying to give it to has to want it in return. I don't know Redford's story, but there is one. And it's one neither Redford, Sloan nor Tyler ever talks about. I believe it has to do with a woman who hurt him in the past, and it's a pain he hasn't gotten over."

"Then I can help him get over it," Carmen replied.

Leslie released a deep sigh. "Not sure that you can, Carmen. Redford may not ever be ready to accept love from you or any woman. You have a good heart and see the good in everyone. You give everyone the benefit of the doubt, even those who don't deserve it. I think you're making a mistake in thinking Redford will change for you."

Carmen heard what Leslie was saying and could see the worried look in her eyes. It was the same look she'd given her two years ago when Carmen had declared that one day she would marry Redford. She understood Leslie's concern, but for some reason, Carmen believed that even with Redford's reputation as a heartbreaker, he would one day see her as more than a sex mate. He would realize she was his soulmate.

"I'm thirty-two and can take care of myself, Leslie."

"When it comes to a man like Redford, I'm not sure you can, Carmen."

Carmen shrugged. "I've dated men like Redford before. Men who only want one thing from a woman. I intend to be the exception and not the norm." Determined to change the subject, she said, "I love June weddings, don't you?"

The look in Leslie's eyes let Carmen know she knew what she'd deliberately done and would go along with her. "Yes, and Denver's weather was perfect today," Leslie said.

"Nadia looked beautiful. This is the first wedding I've ever attended where the bride wore a black wedding dress."

"Same for me, and she looked simply gorgeous. It was Jaxon's mom's wedding dress, and she offered it to Nadia for her special day."

Nadia not only looked beautiful but radiant walking down that aisle on her brother-in-law Dillon Westmoreland's arm. Both the wedding and reception had been held at Westmoreland House, the massive multipurpose family center that Dillon, the oldest of the Denver Westmorelands, had built on his three-hundred-acre property. The building could hold up to five hundred people easily and was used for special occasions, family events and get-togethers.

Carmen glanced around the huge, beautifully decorated room and noticed the man she had been introduced to earlier that day, Matthew Caulder. He'd discovered just last year that he was related to the Westmoreland triplets, Casey, Cole and Clint. It seemed the biological father Matthew hadn't known was the triplets' uncle, the legendary rodeo star and horse trainer, Sid Roberts.

It seemed that she and Redford weren't the only ones exchanging intense glances today. "You've been so busy watching me and Redford stare each other down, have you missed how Matthew Caulder keeps staring at Iris Michaels?" Carmen leaned in to whisper to Leslie.

Leslie followed her gaze to where Matthew stood talking to a bunch of the Westmoreland men. Iris was Pam Westmoreland's best friend. Pam was Nadia's sister and was married to Dillon. "No, I hadn't noticed, but I do now. Matthew is divorced, and Iris, who owns a PR firm in Los Angeles, is a widow. I understand her husband was a stuntman in Hollywood and was killed while working on a major film a number of years ago. I hope she reciprocates Matthew's interest. She deserves happiness."

Carmen frowned. "What about me? Don't I deserve happiness, too?"

"Yes, but like I told you, I'm not sure you'll find it with Redford, Carmen, and I don't want to see you get hurt."

"And like I told you, I can take care of myself."

At that moment, the party planner announced the father-daughter dance, and Dillon stood in again for Nadia's deceased father. While all eyes were on them, Carmen glanced back over at Redford. As if he'd felt her gaze, he tilted his head to look at her, his eyes unwavering and deeply penetrating.

Like she'd told Leslie, she didn't intend to be just another notch on Redford's bedpost. Their sexual chemistry had been there from the first. It was there now, simmering between them. He couldn't avoid her forever, and no matter what he thought, she truly believed they were meant to be together. She had time, patience and a belief in what was meant to be.

She would not pursue him. When the time was right, he would pursue her. She totally understood Leslie's concern but Carmen believed people could change. Even Redford. His two best friends were married with families. She had to believe that eventually he would want the same thing for himself.

Was he starting to want it now? Was that why he'd been staring tonight after two years of ignoring her? Her heart beat wildly at the thought.

When everyone began clapping, she broke eye contact with Redford and saw that the dance between Nadia and Dillon had ended. Now the first dance between Jaxon and Nadia would start. As tempted as she was, she refused to look back at Redford, although she felt his eyes on her. The heat from his gaze stirred all parts of her.

When the dance ended, Jaxon leaned into Nadia for a kiss, which elicited claps, cheers, and whistles. As the wedding planner invited others to the dance floor and the live band began to perform, Jaxon and Nadia were still kissing.

Carmen smiled, feeling the love between the couple. She wanted the same thing for herself. A man who would love her, respect her, be by her side and share his life with her. He would have no problem kissing her in front of everyone, proclaiming she was his and his only. He would be someone who would never break her heart or trample her pride.

How could she think Redford St. James capable of giving her all those things when he was unable to keep his pants zipped? Was she wrong in thinking he could change? She wanted to believe that the same love and happiness her sister Chandra shared with her husband Rutledge, the same love Leslie shared with Sloan, and Nadia shared with Jaxon, could be hers. Even her parents, retired college professors now living in Cape Town, were still in love.

People teased her about wearing rose-colored glasses, but when you were surrounded by so much love, affection and togetherness, you couldn't help but believe in happily ever after. She was convinced that everyone had a soulmate. That special person meant for them.

Unable to fight temptation any longer, she glanced back at Redford. His eyes were still on her and that stirring returned. He smiled and her heart missed a beat.

Then her breath caught in her throat as he began walking toward her.

Chapter Two

Easy-breezy. That thought ran through Redford's mind as he moved toward Carmen. He felt her response all the way across the room. He saw it in her light brown eyes and noted it in the way she stared back at him. Granted, he doubted she would agree to a quickie in one of the closets somewhere in Westmoreland House, but as far as he was concerned, she was ripe for the picking.

She'd had two years to change her mind about that marriage foolishness. Other than acknowledging her presence whenever he saw her, he had not given her any reason to think he supported that nonsense. If the meaning behind him avoiding her for two years hadn't been clear, then that was her problem, not his.

Sloan had reminded him that Carmen was Leslie's best friend. He loved Leslie like a sister, but like he'd told Sloan, Leslie should have talked her best friend out of her foolishness long ago. According to Sloan, Leslie had tried, so as far as Redford was concerned, Carmen had been dutifully warned. There was nothing left for Leslie to do but stay out of his and Carmen's business. They were both adults and old enough to do what they wanted to do.

The people Carmen had been standing with earlier were out on the dance floor and she'd been left alone. Coming to a stop in front of her, he extended his hand. "May I have this dance, Carmen?"

He wondered if she was aware that her smile contained a spark of sexual energy. She placed her hand in his. "Yes."

The moment their hands touched that energy increased, and a ball of need burst to life inside his stomach. He wasn't surprised by the reaction, just by the magnitude of it. Blood pounded at his temples and for the life of him, he couldn't stop staring at her face…especially that smile. It was as if her beauty was hitting him up close and personal, and had him spellbound. How was that possible when he'd never let a woman get to him?

They reached the dance floor where others were moving to a slow song. Drawing her into his arms, he said, "I think us dancing together is long overdue." From the look he saw in her eyes, it was obvious she agreed. Her next words confirmed it.

"You're the one who's been avoiding me, Redford."

There was no need to deny it when she was right. "I had my reasons for putting distance between us."

She lifted a brow. "You *had* your reasons? Does that mean they aren't there anymore?"

"It means I've abolished any misgivings I had in the past." She could take that to mean he'd surrendered to her foolishness, if that's what she chose to believe. However, that's not what he'd said. What he meant was any misgivings about sharing her bed were gone.

"I'm glad you're open to change, Redford."

Open to change? Did she honestly think that one dance with him meant that? If she did then she was totally wrong. Just like he didn't expect her to change her optimistic, cheerful attitude, she shouldn't expect him to change his "bed as many women as you can" frame of mind.

"When it comes to change, Carmen, I've heard it's the one constant." No need to tell her that's why he'd changed his mind and added her back to his "must do" list. Life was too short not to do those things you enjoy. His pleasure was bedding women.

"I understand you're a college professor," he said, starting a different line of conversation.

She smiled proudly. "Yes, I am. I come from a long line of them. My grandparents on both sides, my parents and my sister. I guess you could say education is in our blood."

He also knew from Sloan that she and Leslie had met when Leslie had left the University of Alaska Anchorage to attend Howard University in Washington, DC, where the two had become roommates. Carmen was an economics professor at Georgetown University. "You like teaching?"

The way her smile brightened gave him her answer, but he wanted to hear it anyway. He liked the sound of her voice. "Yes. I love teaching. I started out being an elementary school teacher while working on my PhD. Once that was done, it took me two years before I was hired as part of Georgetown's faculty. That was four years ago. I love it there and hope to get tenured in a few years. My home is right in the neighborhood. That makes it convenient, and I don't need a car."

"Tell me about your family." He knew from Sloan that she had a sister and her parents were alive.

"My parents are retired college professors who moved to Cape Town five years ago. My sister Chandra is also a college professor. So is her husband, Rutledge. They both teach at Georgia State University in Atlanta." She paused and then added, "Then there's Elan, my twelve-year-old nephew. He's adorable."

Redford lifted a brow. "Adorable at twelve?"

She threw her head back and laughed. "I know, right? That's the age when they begin getting beside themselves. So far, Elan is still as lovable as ever. However, he has informed us he intends to break family tradition since he has no intention of being a college professor. His love of trains overrules such a notion."

Redford smiled, recalling the days when he loved trains.

Like his father and grandfather, he'd wanted to become an engineer for the Skagway Railway System.

"Both my father and grandfather retired as engineers for the Alaska Railways. Dad was one of their best. Even now he occasionally works as an engineer for the train tours in Skagway. It's such a scenic route through the mountains, glaciers and waterfalls."

He watched her eyes light up. "I can't wait for Elan to meet you. He will be thrilled to know the son of a train engineer."

Redford was just about to ask her what made her think he and her nephew would ever have a reason to meet, when the dance came to an end. "Want something to drink before we dance again?"

"Yes, and will we be dancing again, Redford?"

He smiled down at her as he led her off the dance floor. "Yes."

No need to tell her he intended to keep her in his arms on the dance floor—and later tonight in his bed.

Carmen couldn't believe that instead of avoiding her like he normally did, Redford had stuck by her side the rest of the night. He was being very attentive, dancing with her for every dance, whether fast or slow. Even after the newlyweds left to start their honeymoon, the party continued well into the night.

The Westmorelands had been gracious enough to make sure all the attendees at the wedding had a place to spend the night on the grounds of Westmoreland Country. Some of the traveling family members would be guests in several individual homes, and others would be staying at Bella's Retreat.

Bella was the wife of Dillon's brother, Jason. Years ago, Bella inherited land connected to the Westmoreland property from her grandfather. When the ranch house burned down, she rebuilt it into a beautiful fifteen bedroom guest house for family, friends and associates of the Westmorelands. Over the years, as the Westmoreland family continued to grow, Jason and Bella added numerous guest cottages on the property. Carmen had been invited to stay in one of them.

"Well, it's certainly been a wonderful day," Carmen said, glancing up at Redford. "The newlyweds are on their way to their honeymoon in the Maldives."

Redford chuckled as they danced to what the DJ had announced would be the last song. "Not quite. When they left, unknown to Nadia, they headed straight to Jaxon's ranch in Virginia to stay the night. He has a special surprise for her there."

Carmen couldn't help but smile, wondering what the surprise could be. She started to ask Redford but changed her mind. According to Leslie, the Outlaw and Westmoreland men and their friends often exchanged confidences they didn't share with anyone when asked not to. At times, not even with their wives. She figured it was no different from when women kept each other's secrets. "That's wonderful."

When the dance came to an end, Redford asked, "So how long are you staying here?"

"I fly out tomorrow evening after dinner. What about you?"

"I plan to hang around for a few days. There are several card games happening, and I plan to participate."

Carmen often heard how the Westmoreland and Outlaw men, along with their friends, enjoyed playing poker whenever they got together. "I wish you the best of luck."

"Thanks."

At the sound of a baby crying, Carmen glanced over to where Bane and Crystal Westmoreland were surrounded by six kids. Two sets of triplets. One set, around six years old, and the other set, all three in diapers, were boys they'd named Raphel, Ruark and Rance. All six of Bane and Crystal's kids had their father's hazel eyes and were adorable.

"Sounds like someone isn't happy," Redford said, removing his tie and unbuttoning the top button of his shirt but keeping his jacket on as they reached the elegant hallway that led outside. Why at that moment did he have to look so sexy?

"Yes, sounds like it," she said, trying to concentrate on what he was saying and not on how sexy he looked. "Do you like kids, Redford?"

"Yes, I like kids. However, I don't plan to ever have any of my own."

His words surprised her. "Why?" she asked like she had every right to know. In a way she did. When they married, she wanted at least four.

"Because I just don't want any."

He'd spoken with such finality that Carmen couldn't help wondering why he would feel so strongly. She knew from Leslie that he was an only child, but she hadn't heard anything about him not having a good family life to the point where he wouldn't want a family of his own one day. In fact, she could hear the love in his voice when he'd spoken of his father.

His not wanting kids would definitely be a subject they would need to address again. She suspected there was a reason he didn't want any children, just like she knew there was a reason he never wanted to share a serious relationship with a woman.

When they headed out of the building, which was decorated with greenery and lanterns, she asked, "Is there a card game tonight?"

He glanced down at her. "Yes, but it won't start until after midnight. I understand Nadia's sisters, Pam, Jillian and Paige, will be hosting a wedding after-party for the ladies and expect the men to make an appearance for at least an hour."

"Are you going to the after-party?"

"No. I've had enough partying for one day."

She nodded. "Like you, I've partied enough today, too."

"So, what are your plans for tonight?" he asked her.

"I don't have any."

He slowed his pace. "I have a suggestion."

"What?"

She wondered if this was where he would suggest that they go to her cottage or his. If that was his plan, she had news for him. It wouldn't happen. Although she would admit that just being near him had desire like she'd never felt before twisting inside her. This was all new to her, but regardless, she wouldn't lose her common sense over it.

"A wine and cheese moonlight picnic by the lake," he said.

She stared at him. Why had he suggested something so romantic? The smart response would be to decline. Now that he seemed to be showing interest in her, she should set a pace that wasn't too fast.

"Carmen?"

She was about to say she wasn't interested in such a picnic, when instead she said, "A moonlight picnic sounds wonderful." He smiled and she wished that smile didn't stir her insides the way it was.

"Good. How about we meet at the gazebo in about thirty minutes? I need to get everything."

She lifted a brow. "Get everything?"

"Yes, the food, wine and blanket."

Blanket? Right. They would need one to sit on. "Okay. I need to change out of this dress anyway."

His gaze roamed over her. "No, don't change. I like seeing you in that dress. It looks nice on you."

Why did his compliment make her heart skip a beat? "Thanks. I'll see you in half an hour."

"And I'll be waiting."

Chapter Three

Redford watched Carmen walk away while thinking he wanted to be the one to take that dress off her tonight. There was something about her that brought out the primitive male in him. It had been nearly too much for his heart to take, while they'd been dancing, to focus on her face and not her cleavage.

And whatever perfume she wore was also doing a number on him. The scent made him want to growl at the moon instead of sitting on a blanket beneath it. Why in the hell had he suggested a picnic instead of proposing they go to her cottage and have their own party?

When Carmen was no longer in sight, Redford released a deep breath, stunned by the degree of desire he felt for her. They'd danced to every single song, and he had loved it. Seeing how she'd moved her body during the fast songs, and then the way she felt in his arms during the slow ones, had fired up his libido even more. There had been something about holding her in his arms while their bodies were close that made him think of sharing even more intimacies.

He glanced at his watch again. Carmen would be back soon, and he didn't want her waiting. Leaving the area, he went back inside Westmoreland House and approached Alpha, who was married to Riley Westmoreland, and who'd been the wedding planner. She assured Redford there was more than enough food left for a picnic. After telling her he only wanted a bottle of wine and an assortment of cheeses, she left and returned within minutes with a basket for him. She'd even brought a blanket.

Redford was glad he hadn't run into Sloan or Leslie. Leslie had watched him like a hawk when he and Carmen had been on the dance floor, and he'd deliberately ignored her stare.

With the picnic basket in hand, Redford rounded a corner and saw a crowd standing around Bailey Westmoreland Rafferty. She and her husband Walker were the proud parents of a newborn son they'd named Thomas, after Bailey's father.

Before reaching the exit door, he ran into Maverick and Phire who were pushing their son, Legend, in a stroller. Following not far behind the couple were Cash and Brianna Outlaw with the newest member of their family, a son they'd named Brian.

Babies seemed to be everywhere. He recalled the look on Carmen's face when he'd stated he didn't want kids. Like he told her, he liked kids. After all, he was godfather to Sloan and Leslie's daughter, who he adored. However, that ordeal with Candy had shattered his life in so many ways. Her betrayal had cut deep, right into his heart. After that, nothing else mattered in his life other than succeeding in college and career. It was then that he'd vowed to remain a bachelor for life and dismiss all the things that went with loving a woman. Such as marriage, children and a house with a white picket fence.

Tucking the blanket firmly under his arm while he carried the picnic basket, Redford continued walking to where he and Carmen were to meet. So far none of those he'd passed had asked about the basket and blanket. They seemed in a hurry to get to the after-party.

He rounded the corner of Westmoreland House. The surrounding area was lit by beautiful torches, but the yard was empty. He figured most people were inside attending the party. From the sound of things, it had already started. Those Westmorelands and Outlaws were definitely in a festive mood. Well, he was in one hell of a horny one.

"It's kind of late for a picnic, isn't it?"

He rolled his eyes, figuring it had been too much to hope he could avoid seeing Sloan again tonight before the midnight card game. Smiling humorlessly, he said, "It's never too late to do anything you've set your mind to doing."

Sloan frowned. "I hope you know *what* you're doing, Redford."

"I always know what I'm doing when it concerns a woman, Sloan."

Shaking his head, Sloan walked off and Redford was glad that he had. Carmen was an adult. As long as he kept things honest and didn't make promises he didn't intend to keep, there was no reason for him to feel guilty about anything.

Redford looked at his watch when he reached the gazebo, and when he glanced back up at the yard, he saw Carmen walking toward him. Like he'd requested, she kept on that dress, although she'd replaced her stilettos with more comfortable shoes.

He was intensely aware of everything about her, especially the way she was looking at him. Suddenly, feeling somewhat weak in the knees, he propped against one of the gazebo posts. Why did seeing her do that to him?

"I hope I didn't keep you waiting, Redford," she said, cheerfully, when she came to a stop in front of him.

"No, you didn't keep me waiting," he said, fighting to regain control of his senses and his body. "Ready for our picnic?"

"Yes. Since you got the basket, I can carry the blanket," she offered.

"That will work," he said, handing the blanket to her. Their hands touched in the process and he heard her sharp intake of breath. As they walked toward Gemma Lake, he thought about what Sloan had said earlier… *"I hope you know what you're doing, Redford."*

At that moment Redford hoped like hell that he knew what he was doing as well.

As they walked the length of the yard that led to the lake, Carmen tried switching her thoughts away from the man beside her. That wasn't an easy thing to do. In fact, she doubted there was anything about Redford St. James that was easy. Except for falling in love with him. Even with his less than desirable reputation, she truly believed he was the man she'd been waiting for.

When she'd gone back to her cottage to change shoes and freshen up, she'd given herself a serious pep talk. If she could feel the strong sexual vibes between her and Redford, then she was certain he could, too.

The last thing she wanted was for him to think that was a cue for sex since it wouldn't be happening. Granted, she was curious to find out if all those wild and passionate stories she'd heard about, read about in romance novels, and even dreamed about a time or two, were anything close to the real thing. But she refused to be a notch on any man's bedpost, even the man she intended to marry one day. There was more to a relationship than the physical. If no other woman had gotten that point across to him, then she didn't mind being the first.

Deciding to kick-start conversation between them, she said, "I understand you own a number of successful resorts." According to Leslie, his business was a multi-billion-dollar enterprise consisting of fishing, hunting and ski resorts spread out from the Gulf of Alaska to the Yukon.

He glanced down at her. From his expression she could tell she'd caught him during a moment of deep thought, and it took him a second to process what she'd said. "Yes, that's right. People would be surprised at the number of tourists that visit Alaska each year. And that number is increasing tremendously."

Why did the sound of his voice caress her skin? Every part of it. "I can believe it. Although I'm not a fan of cold weather, I'm glad I get to visit Alaska to see Sloan, Leslie and Cassidy. It's amazing how much land there is in Alaska. Developed and undeveloped."

"I heard your first time to Alaska was when you attended Tyler and Keosha's wedding with Leslie as her plus-one."

It happened again, his voice and her skin's reaction to it. She had controlled it while they danced together but was having a hard time doing so now. "Yes, it was. When Leslie lived in DC, her father would come spend most of the holidays with her and her aunt, so she wouldn't have to return to Alaska."

"And run the risk of her path crossing with Sloan's," he said.

Since it was a statement and not a question, she figured he knew firsthand about Sloan and Leslie's breakup in college that had sent her from the University of Alaska at Anchorage to finish college at Howard in DC. For years, Sloan hadn't known where she'd gone. It had taken ten years for their paths to cross again and for Sloan and Leslie to discover their breakup had been based on a lie, one deliberately orchestrated by her ex-roommate. Now Sloan and Leslie were back together and happily married.

"I understand that you, Sloan and Tyler were roommates in college."

"Yes, we were. Those were the good old days. Tyler and Sloan had steady girls, namely Keosha and Leslie. I was the odd man out—their fun-loving, nonserious, won't commit to any woman friend."

Was he telling her that for a reason? Had she read the signs he was putting out tonight all wrong? Although a leopard couldn't change his spots, she wanted to believe the right woman in Redford's life could make a difference, and she intended to be that woman.

"I think this is a good spot, don't you, Carmen?"

Instead of looking at him, she glanced around. The last thing she needed was to get caught up in the beauty of his dark eyes again. "Yes, it's perfect."

Carmen spread out the blanket and then eased down onto it and stared out at the beauty of the lake. Like she'd told Redford, this spot was perfect. It was far away from Westmoreland House where the noise from the after-party could not be heard, but the lights from all those torches around the property, as well as the full moon in the sky, were a shimmering glow across the waters.

Out of the corner of her eye, she watched as Redford placed aside the basket and eased down onto the blankct beside her. When she had left her cottage to meet him at the gazebo, she debated the idea of going through with sharing a moonlight picnic with him. However, in the end she had pushed her misgivings aside. What harm would being alone with him cause?

When it came to staying in control of any situation, she was an ace. No amount of desire, passion or attraction could change that. Her family often said she was the most in-control person they knew. She didn't try to control others, but when it came to herself, she had the ability to maintain a level head. Being a thirty-two-year-old virgin was proof of that.

"Anything else in the basket besides wine and cheese?" she asked him.

"You sound hungry."

"No, just curious," she said, grinning.

"Alpha prepared it for me, and I told her just cheese and wine. However, I didn't look to see what was inside." He pulled the basket toward them. "Let's take a look, shall we?"

In addition to the bottle of wine, wineglasses, a container of assorted cheeses, and the necessary eating utensils, Alpha had included slices of wedding cake. Carmen glanced over at Redford. "I guess we won't go to bed hungry tonight."

He chuckled. "No, I don't think we will."

Chapter Four

The night was perfect. While pouring their glasses of wine, Redford realized he'd never had a moonlight picnic before and he rather liked it. There was something about being alone with Carmen on this lake at night, sharing a blanket and wine, that had sexual energy hitting him low in the gut.

So far everything about it spelled seduction in big bold letters and being here with her aroused him in a way he hadn't expected. Anticipation for what he hoped would take place later had his pulse beating way too fast to be normal. On top of that, his brain was filled with salacious ideas for making love to her.

In an attempt to get his mind and body under control, he forced his thoughts from Carmen to his surroundings. Gemma Lake, which sat smack in the middle of Westmoreland Country, was beautiful and even more so at night. The lighted, colorful water fountains in the middle of the lake were a spectacular sight.

There was a full moon in the sky and the stars dotted around it like a majestic court. The night's temperature was perfect, and as far as he was concerned, so was the woman with him. He rarely thought of any woman as perfect. What he wanted from all women was the same. There could never be any exceptions.

He doubted she'd known what he'd been thinking when she'd mentioned them not going to bed hungry tonight. There was a totally different type of hunger invading his body. One that had nothing to do with food.

"I thought I was full after eating that dinner at the reception, but there's nothing like wine and cheese. And I can't wait to get into the cake since I passed on it earlier," she said.

He took a sip of his wine. "Why did you pass on it?"

"I was full from eating and didn't have room for dessert. Now I do."

He grinned. "I had room for dessert then and I do so again now. I love cake."

She nodded. "What's your favorite?"

Redford chuckled. "Cake."

She threw her head back and laughed. He liked the sound of it.

He chuckled too. "I've never encountered a cake I didn't like. I inherited a love for cooking from my mom. But not for baking. Mom made the best cakes. For a while she ran a bakery out of our home since Dad preferred she didn't work outside the home until I was in junior high school."

Redford wondered why he'd told her that. Usually, he didn't share any personal information about himself or his family with any woman. His only excuse for doing so now was that he was trying to make sure Carmen felt relaxed with him.

"I rarely cook. Leslie says I need to buy stock in every fast-food place in the city. However, I do enjoy baking cakes and even took a cake-baking class in college. My specialty is carrot cake."

"That's one my mom never made."

"Well, one day I intend to bake a carrot cake just for you."

He didn't say anything. Instead, he took another sip of his wine. This was the second time tonight that she'd hinted at them seeing each other again. Of course, that wouldn't be happening unless their paths crossed because of their friendships with Sloan and Leslie.

Wanting to change the subject, he asked, "Have you lived in DC long?"

"Close to fifteen years now. I moved there for college from Atlanta."

"That's where you're from? Atlanta?"

"Yes, born and raised. My father attended Morehouse and my mom attended Spelman College. They liked Atlanta and thought it would be a great place to live, marry and raise a family."

Redford took another sip of his wine and began eating some of the various cheeses. He was easing Carmen into a steady stream of conversation to get her relaxed. Experience had shown him that a relaxed woman, especially one who was trying to fight an intense attraction, was more open to seduction. He had it down to an art form. His approach was so smooth, usually the woman didn't know what was happening until she was captivated to the point of no return.

"Do you ever star watch?" he asked her, easing to lie flat on his back on the blanket to stare up into the sky.

His question made her switch her gaze from the lake to the sky. "All the time. I've got a good view from my bedroom window. I enjoy ending my days by lying in bed and staring at them before drifting off to sleep. However, I don't claim to have my own personal star up there like Canyon."

Canyon Westmoreland was one of Dillon's brothers. Canyon said he recognized one particular star from childhood that he still claimed as his. "I guess you heard about Flash," Redford said.

He liked the sound of her chuckle. "Yes, I heard about Flash. I understand Canyon and Keisha had a nighttime wedding just so Flash could attend, and that Canyon wouldn't let the wedding begin until he saw it in the sky," she said.

"I heard that as well." When things got silent between them, he said, "Make a wish upon one of those stars up there, Carmen."

"A wish?" she asked, looking down at him.

Redford felt heated lust the moment their gazes connected. "Yes, a wish. I heard whenever you make a wish upon a star there's a chance it might come true."

She glanced back into the sky and closed her eyes. When she reopened them she looked at him. "Now it's your turn."

He nodded and did the same thing. He wished she would be an easy conquest tonight. And more than anything, he wished for a night of intense pleasure in her bed.

Glancing back at her, he said, "I hope both of our wishes come true, Carmen."

She stared at him. "So, what did you wish for?"

He could say their wishes could not be shared. But then he thought, what the hell, why not tell her? In doing so, she would know just what he wanted.

Easing into a sitting position, he reached out and took her hand in his. Trying to ignore the intense sexual hunger stirring inside him, he said, "My wish was for you, Carmen."

He watched her blink before asking in a soft voice, "For me?"

Redford nodded, holding her gaze steadily. "Yes. My wish is for you to be mine."

Carmen forced back a gasp of surprise at such an admission from Redford. Her heart swelled with love for him. Were his words his way of letting her know she had somehow eased her way into his heart? The mere thought of such a thing had joy flowing all through her.

"What did you wish for, Carmen?"

She had wished for a couple of things. For him to accept that he was her soulmate, like she'd accepted that he was hers. For them to live a long and happy life together. Instead of breaking down every single detail, she summed it up by saying, "My wish was for you to be mine, too, Redford."

From the smile that spread across his lips, he obviously liked her answer. "Then let me grant your wish." He reached out and pulled her into his arms.

Carmen was convinced her body went into a pleasurable shock the minute Redford took possession of her mouth. She hadn't been given time to think and already her tongue surrendered to his. She'd been kissed before by men who thought they were experts. She'd thought so, too.

Until now.

Redford's mouth mated with hers in a way she'd never experienced before. She'd always enjoyed the art of kissing as long as it didn't go any further. She could handle even the most passionate of kisses. However, when Redford deepened the kiss, she moaned. No man's kiss had ever made her moan before.

Then he wrapped his arms around her and his fingers stroked the length of her spine. She felt them through the material of her dress. It took everything in her to retain control of her senses. When she heard herself moan again, she knew she was about to lose them.

When her mouth could barely take any more bold strokes of his tongue, she eased her hands up to his shoulders. Instead of pushing him away, though, like she should do, her fingers traced his upper arms, loving how powerfully male they felt. Then her breasts pressed firmly to his chest. She could actually feel the hardened tips of her nipples poking into him.

Suddenly, he released her mouth, but just long enough for them to inhale and exhale. Then his mouth reclaimed hers again, deepening the pressure. He was giving her something she'd never had before—full contact, wet tongue, unapologetic, raw. This was the kind of kiss she'd read about. She always thought she could tell fantasy from reality. Now she wasn't sure.

Presently, she wasn't certain of anything other than how his kiss was making her feel. Redford was not holding himself in check. He was going at her mouth with toe-curling determination and hot abandonment.

Needing to breathe, she was the one who ended the kiss this time. Heat stirred in her stomach, and before she could say they were moving too fast, he began feathering kisses around her mouth, corner to corner. His hands were no longer at her back. Now his fingers tunneled into her hair, and she loved the feel of it. His fingers' magic touch steadily broke down her defenses and zapped her control.

"Redford..."

He captured her mouth again, with even more intensity. He was creating a physical need within her that she hadn't known could exist. One she hadn't known she could feel.

Breaking off the kiss, he cupped her face in his hands. Carmen noted he was breathing just as hard as she was. Staring into her eyes, his gaze seemed to melt into hers. Then he claimed her mouth yet again, his tongue taking hers in long, hard, and devouring strokes.

When she felt herself ease down on the blanket, she relished the feel of his strong thighs when he placed his body over hers. He had slid his hand beneath her dress—and then suddenly, he broke off the kiss and sat up. Droplets of rain sprinkled down her face.

"Come on, let's go before it starts raining harder," he said, standing.

When he extended his hand to her, she took it and stood to her feet, trying to ignore the sensations still rushing through her. They quickly gathered the blanket and put the wine bottle and glasses in the basket. With her hand held firmly in his, they quickly moved toward the guest cottages.

Carmen knew she should appreciate the rain coming down when it had. She didn't want to imagine what they would be doing if it hadn't. His hand had been under her dress just inches from the waistband of her panties. How had she allowed him to get that far? To take liberties she hadn't ever given any other man?

"Which one of these cottages is yours?" he asked.

"That one." They moved in that direction. Moments later they stood in front of the door.

"Sorry our picnic got interrupted, Redford." With that, she knew she should thank him for a nice picnic and go inside.

"Carmen?"

Redford saying her name held her still. "Yes?"

"May I come in so we can finish off the wine?"

For some reason she couldn't discard from her mind what he'd told her about looking into the stars and wishing for her. Whether he knew it or not, that meant everything to her. His wish had been for her to be his.

Her mouth still reeled from the effects of his kisses. She still felt the intensity of them through her entire body. Even now, while they stood facing each other, the sparks were still flying between them. It was raining harder now. She couldn't send him away to get totally drenched, could she?

If he came inside, would the storm brewing between them, turbulent and tempestuous, get out of control? No. She would admit his kisses had almost done her in while on that blanket, but now she was in full control of her faculties.

"Carmen?"

She drew in a deep breath and said, "Yes. Come in so we can finish off the wine."

Chapter Five

As Redford poured the remainder of the wine into the glasses, out of the corner of his eye he could see Carmen move around the cottage. It was identical to the one he was using, with a spacious living room, bedroom and bathroom.

Redford tried forcing his concentration back to what he was doing. That was hard, especially when thoughts of the kisses they'd shared ran rampant through his mind. The kisses had been expected. Gone according to plan. What had not been expected was the impact her taste had on him.

It was as if the moment their tongues tangled, something had come over him that was deeper and stronger than mere desire. It was something that had caught him off guard. A rational part of him wanted to believe there was a first time for everything, but the irrational part could not accept he'd let go of his smooth moves with this particular woman.

For a short while, all the legendary exploits he was known for had been eradicated from his brain. His focus had been only on her. Mainly, how she made him feel, the way she tasted and his desire to connect their bodies in the most primitive way. He ached to get inside her, and even now he could feel her heat.

Turning with both wineglasses in his hand, he saw Carmen now stood at the window, peering out. It was raining even harder and the sound of it beating on the cottage's roof was almost deafening. He wondered if she knew that the weather could affect a person's sex drive, especially when it was raining like it was now.

He could feel it. And seeing her in that dress wasn't helping matters. He almost regretted having asked her to keep it on.

"Here you are," he said, moving toward her.

She turned and smiled. "It seems Denver's weather is so unpredictable. There was no sign of rain when we were watching the stars."

"Yes, I would say it surprised us," he said, handing her the wineglass. Not only had the rain surprised him, but it had angered him. His hands had made it under her dress, and he'd been about to slide his fingers under the waistband of her panties, when he had felt the first droplets.

"Thanks."

Meeting her gaze, he said, "You're welcome."

After taking a sip of wine, he moved to stand beside her and look out the window. "It's coming down pretty hard." That meant even if he finished his wine, she wouldn't send him out in the storm. At least, he hoped she wouldn't.

"Do you want to sit on the sofa and talk?" he suggested, turning from the window to look at her.

She arched a brow. "Talk about what?"

"Anything." Conversation was part of his strategy for tonight. Sexual chemistry crackled in the air. Some due to the rain, and some due to the lust flowing between them. He had no problem with all the arousal consuming them both.

"Okay, we can sit and talk," she said. "Hopefully the rain will stop soon."

Redford watched as she moved to sit on the sofa. She'd made sure the side split in her dress didn't show too much thigh. He was tempted to tell her not to bother because he intended to see her naked by morning.

He moved to sit down as well. However, he didn't take the wing-back chair across from the sofa, but eased his body down beside her. Other than the lifting of her brow in surprise, she said nothing. Instead, she took another sip of wine like she really needed it.

"Tell me about your classes, Carmen."

"What classes?"

"The ones you teach at Georgetown." Redford figured talking about something she was passionate about would relax her, and he wanted her as relaxed as she'd been by the lake.

Leaning back against the sofa, he slowly sipped his wine while listening. He had honestly thought he would find the subject of economics boring, but quite the contrary. The way she broke it down made it relatable to his business model regarding his resorts.

Talking made the shape of her mouth even more alluring, and the sound of her words was like a soft caress. Suddenly she chuckled about something. Whatever had been amusing, he regretted missing the punchline. When she asked about his resorts, and how he determined when to buy or build, he knew it was his time to talk.

The last thing he wanted to do was discuss business, so he decided to make it quick. He'd gotten comfortable enough to remove the jacket he had slid back on when it had begun raining. And she'd relaxed to the point where she'd kicked off her shoes to sit with her legs tucked beneath her. It was such a sexy pose. She was obviously listening to what he was saying.

He wondered how long it would take for her to notice that he'd shifted positions and now they were sitting closer than they had been before. When she leaned over to place her empty wineglass beside his on the coffee table, he took her hand in his and entwined their fingers.

"I enjoyed listening to you, Carmen."

"And I enjoyed listening to you as well. I find your work fascinating, Redford."

He glanced down at their empty wineglasses and then over at the window. "We finished the wine, but it's still raining."

"So I hear."

"Do you plan to send me out in it?" he asked, tempted to bring her hand, the one he was still holding, to his lips to kiss it.

"Surely a little water won't hurt you," she said. At that moment he knew she'd realized how intimate their positions were.

"It might."

"Do you think you're made of sugar, Redford St. James?"

He tightened his hold on her hand and eased closer to her. "You've tasted me, Carmen. What do you think?"

When she unconsciously licked her lips with the tip of her tongue as if remembering his taste, he got hard. He doubted she knew that seeing her do such a thing made him want her with a vengeance. He'd never wanted any woman with a vengeance before.

"Well, what do you think, Carmen?" he asked again when she'd yet to answer.

Their gazes locked. When he heard the sound of a moan, he wasn't sure if it had come from him or her. What was there about her that convulsed his body with such sexual need? His body was on fire. Dazed to the point that just being this close to her was pure torture.

"I think you tasted kind of sweet," she finally said.

He inched his mouth closer to hers. "You know what that means, Carmen?"

She shook her head. "No, what does that mean?"

"It means," he said, inching even closer to her. "I need to share my taste with you again so you can be certain."

And then he captured her mouth.

Redford took Carmen's mouth with a ferociousness that made everything inside of her feel his possessiveness. This kiss was even more torrid than the others. She could actually feel her veins throb.

At present, her veins were the least of her worries. This kiss was making it hard for her to think…at least logically. All she could concentrate on was his delicious, all-consuming taste. And it *was* sweet. The sweetest flavor she'd ever consumed. However, she couldn't say it had anything to do with sugar. It had everything to do with the man himself.

He tightened his arms around her as his mouth continued to devour hers in a way she wasn't used to. Everything about Redford was seductive and intense. Just the thought that she was the one he'd wished for, the one he wanted to make his, had her falling in love with him even more.

Something else was increasing as well. Need. And it was creating a sexual longing within her, making her think things, do things and want things. Her brain, which she could usually count on to be logical, dependable and reliable, was letting her down in the most salacious way.

Without breaking contact with her mouth, he stood, drawing her up off the sofa in a pair of strong, powerful arms. That's when she felt him. He was aroused. Totally and fully. He wanted her. A man's erection couldn't lie. She'd felt an aroused male body pressed against her before, but at the time she'd known it was a waste of time and effort on the guy's part.

Why wasn't she thinking that way now? Instead, she wanted to do something that she'd never done before in her life—touch it. How illogical was that? But at that moment, under the onslaught of his tongue, logic was being tossed out the window and getting rained on.

Lightning crackled the sky, followed by a boom of thunder that shook the earth. As far as Carmen was concerned, neither could compare to the tempestuous desire that was taking her over.

Redford suddenly broke off with a half-strangled moan. The

lamp light behind him flickered when thunder and lightning fought for dominance of the storm outside. Inside, there should be another fight going on, but there wasn't one. How could she fight this? Feelings and sensations so new and unique, they had her craving them instead of rebuffing them.

"I think we have on too many clothes, Carmen."

Redford's words should have knocked some sense into her. Instead, she felt the erection pressing against her middle get harder. It was as if that part of him was calling out to her. Pleading for release from its confinement. Was that why she agreed they had on too many clothes?

Expelling a breath, not of frustration but of need, she tipped her head back to stare up at him. This was the man she loved, had loved from the moment she'd laid eyes on him. And tonight, after two years of avoiding her, he had admitted to wishing for her on a star and saying he wanted to make her his. No man had ever said such a thing to her. She believed deep in her heart that he had meant it; his words hadn't been just a line. It had taken two years for him to finally accept her place in his life.

"What are you thinking, Carmen?"

His voice was low, husky and unmistakably masculine. It was a voice that would not only get a woman's full attention but also send sensuous shivers through her body. Maybe she should tell him what she was thinking. Specifically, how happy she was that he'd come around. But the need that had been building inside her had reached its peak. They would talk about their future later.

"I was thinking that you're right, and we do have too many clothes on, Redford. How do you think we should remedy that?"

The smile that touched his lips sent even more shivers rushing through her. The man wasn't just sexuality on legs, he was that all over, especially in his smile. "Trust me. I have plenty of ideas."

Redford leaned down and took her mouth again in a very

demanding, deeply hungry kiss. He even gripped his fingers in her hair to hold her mouth in place while he plundered it.

Energy crackled in the air. Not from the storm outside but from the one raging inside. She placed her arms around his neck. His kiss was raw, inflamed and unapologetic. When he exerted even more provocative pressure on her mouth, she got weak in the knees.

His hands were at her back, hunting for the zipper to her dress. When he found it, he eased it down the length of her spine. Sliding his hands inside the opening, he gently stroked her back. The feel of his hands on her skin had desire lacerating her insides. Never before had she felt such primal want for a man. Now she fully understood why. He was meant to be hers like she was meant to be his.

Suddenly he broke off the kiss and she went to work on removing his shirt, trying not to pop any buttons in her haste. He must have felt her urgency because he began helping her. Easing the shirt from his shoulders, she ran her hands over his muscular upper torso, using her index finger to sign her name onto his skin.

Then she felt compelled to do something she'd never done before—she leaned in and kissed his chest. A chest she now thought of as hers. One kiss wouldn't do. She planted them nearly everywhere on his broad chest, determined not to miss a single spot.

Suddenly, he tipped her chin up to meet his gaze. The look in the dark depths of his eyes was filled with a degree of need that stunned her. "I think we should finish this in the bedroom. What do you think?" he asked.

At that moment, she couldn't think. All she could do was feel the need to be with him, to seal a commitment, to begin their relationship in the most elemental way. Later tonight they would talk about their future. The thought made her happy. Deliriously so. Smiling up at him, she said, "I think you are right."

Chapter Six

Redford swept Carmen into his arms, barely able to hold it together. It had to be the stormy weather sending them both over the edge. Also, for him it was her beauty and her scent. Just knowing that in mere minutes, he would take her sexy dress completely off had him quickly moving to the bedroom. The anticipation was killing him. He had one intent only and that was to make her his.

His...?

He nearly stumbled at that thought, but quickly recovered when he mentally clarified what he meant. She would be his only for tonight. One and done. That was the only thing he *could* mean because he considered no woman his.

The moment he reached her bed, he stood her beside it and quickly dispensed of her dress. His breath caught in his throat when he saw her. He had figured she wasn't wearing a bra, but the sheer, barely-there scrap of satin covering her femininity enticed more than it shielded.

His tongue felt thick in his mouth just imagining her taste. If it was anything like the deliciousness he'd discovered in her mouth then he was in deep trouble.

Lowering to his knees, he slowly slid the pair of thong panties down her gorgeous legs, while inhaling her arousing scent. When she stepped out of them, he tossed them aside and leaned back as his gaze trailed over her entire body, not missing anything.

"Now it's my turn to remove the rest of your clothes, Redford."

"Not yet."

She lifted a brow. "Not yet?"

"No. There's something I need to…"

"To what?" she asked when it was apparent that he'd lost his train of thought.

He needed to taste her as much as he needed to breathe.

"Redford?"

He met her gaze. The heat sizzling between them totally consumed him. Instead of answering her, he leaned forward, clutched her hips. Like a greedy man wholly ravenous for his next meal, he began kissing her all over her belly and lavishing licks around her navel. When she grabbed hold of his shoulders, the touch sent him spiraling over the edge.

His mouth inched downward from her belly to the juncture of her thighs. His target was the core of her femininity, and unadulterated desire ripped through him. Unable to hold back or keep himself in check any longer, he planted his mouth right at her center.

His tongue slid through the hot wetness of her feminine folds. Unable to help himself, he tightened his hold on her hips and drove his tongue deeper, stroking his tongue inside of her.

From the way her fingers dug into his shoulder blades and her deep moans, she was already there. But he wanted her totally consumed, like he was. With a greed he didn't know he possessed, his tongue delved even deeper. He stroked her clit faster. She was so hot he could taste her heat.

Driven by a need to make her even hotter, he began using circular motions with his tongue. This was only the beginning.

Carmen was convinced Redford was trying to kill her. She had lost the little control she'd had the moment he removed her dress and slid her panties down her legs. But nothing compared to the moment he'd slid his tongue inside her and began making love to her with his mouth.

She had read about it and heard about it, but to experience the real thing was sending her up in flames. First it was kisses and now this. She was convinced his tongue was a weapon of mass gratification. When torrid sensations ripped through her, she screamed, unable to hold back any longer. Her body exploded into what she knew was her very first orgasm.

It was everything she'd dreamed it would be with the man giving it to her. The intensity was so great she tried pushing him away one instant and then digging hard into his shoulders to keep his mouth latched to her the next. It was only when her screams ended, and her shivers subsided, that he got off his knees and swept her into his arms. She was glad because her knees were about to give out on her.

He placed her on the bed, and she gazed at him through glazed eyes, watching him unzip his pants and slide them down a pair of masculine thighs. His briefs followed and when he stood there naked her gaze automatically went to his middle.

The sight of his large, thick shaft nearly overwhelmed her, and she felt her satisfied body become needy again. What on earth was wrong with her? She needed to focus but the only thing her mind wanted to concentrate on was him. When he'd sheathed himself in a condom and moved toward the bed, she leaned up, ready for him.

He joined her and pulled her into his arms. The only thing that mattered was that the man she loved was about to make her his. When he positioned his body over hers, she gazed up at him, awed by the look in his eyes. Tonight would be the beginning of what she knew would be a wonderful relationship. She would heal whatever pain he'd endured, whatever had driven him to act the part of a heartbreaker. He would see that all women weren't the same.

When she felt him sliding his hard erection into her, she

adjusted her body as it became difficult for him to continue. She knew the moment he realized why. Before he could say anything, she wrapped her arms around his neck and brought his mouth down on hers.

She began kissing him the way he'd been kissing her. The tension she felt within him eased away under the onslaught of her mouth. He took over the kiss and their mouths mated with the frenzy of earlier. It wasn't long before he pushed through the barrier and began thrusting inside of her. Slowly at first but then her inner muscles began clenching him tight, harder and faster.

She felt no pain. The two years waiting for him had been worth it. Hopefully, he felt the same. Over the coming years she would show him that a soulmate was far better than a sex mate could ever be.

She stopped thinking when he began licking around her mouth, corner to corner, while he continued to thrust hard inside of her. "I can't get enough of you, Carmen."

That admission further thrilled her heart and then, simultaneously, their bodies exploded together. She screamed, and he threw his head back and hollered out her name. It was like an orgasmic volcano had erupted and they were caught up in the aftermath. She felt submerged in pleasure so profound that after her screams ended, she chanted his name over and over again.

Their bodies were still shuddering, and the magnitude triggered another orgasm, then another. Outside the cottage, Denver, Colorado, steadfastly felt the impact of the storm. Inside the cottage, Carmen experienced the impact of profound, unadulterated pleasure in Redford's arms.

Chapter Seven

It was no longer storming outside. The storm inside had ended as well. Redford glanced down at the woman sleeping peacefully beside him and, even now, heat spread low in his belly, indicating he was getting aroused all over again.

Carmen Golan was unlike any other woman he'd ever known, any other woman he'd made love to. Never in his life had he experienced multiple orgasms. Yet with Carmen, by the time one earth-shattering, apocalyptic climax had ended, another was right there, slamming into his body so powerfully he was still experiencing aftershocks.

When had he become such a greedy ass where a woman was concerned? Each orgasm had simmered in his balls, quivered in his stomach and thrilled at the base of his spine. Even now pleasure was washing over him, seeming to be absorbed in his skin along with her scent.

And she had been a virgin.

The reminder of that had him sitting straight up in bed. The movement so sudden, he'd nearly awakened Carmen, whose legs were entwined with his. Other than shifting in her sleep, she continued to doze peacefully.

The thought of her virginal state assaulted his senses. Never in his life had he made love to a virgin...other than Candy. At least Candy had claimed to be one. However, after her stunt with Sherman Sharpe, he'd been convinced he'd been played.

There was no doubt in his mind it had been the real deal with Carmen. He had felt the barrier, had pushed through it even when his mind warned him not to do so. He'd seen that flash of pain in her eyes before it was replaced by pleasure—a pleasure that kept coming and coming and nearly consumed them both.

He wanted to wake her up to make sure she was alright since it had been her first time. He was a womanizer, but he wasn't a thoughtless ass. At the end of their lovemaking, he'd gotten out of bed to run bath water to ease the soreness he was certain she would be feeling. However, when he returned to bed, she had fallen asleep and he'd decided not to wake her up. Feeling quite exhausted himself, he had gotten back in bed, taken her into his arms and joined her in sleep.

Even now he was tempted to snuggle her closer and doze off. Later, when they awakened, he would give her the hot bath he'd imagined last night. Then they would enjoy breakfast together before returning to the cottage to make love again…

What the hell!

Suddenly, he felt a panic attack coming on. Emotional overload. This was another first for him. He didn't cuddle with a woman after sex. They went their way, and he went his. And had he actually referred to what they'd done as lovemaking? Then there was the fact that he never, ever, repeated the process, regardless of how enjoyable it might have been. His number one rule was to never have sex with the same woman twice.

Trying to regain control of his senses, he slowly untangled their naked limbs and eased out of bed. He rubbed his hand down his face. He needed to get the hell out of there. He breathed in deeply then wished he hadn't when he inhaled Carmen's scent. His erection throbbed, an indication of just how badly he wanted her again.

Redford backed away from the bed. Picking up items of clothing off the floor, he quickly slipped into his briefs and pants. Glancing around for his shirt, he recalled she had taken it off him in the living room. He was about to leave the bedroom when he stopped and turned around.

He had a feeling that thoughts of this night would remain with him for the rest of the day, whereas with other women, memories were forgotten the moment he left.

Tonight, Carmen had given him something she'd obviously kept sacred for over thirty years. He hoped like hell she hadn't assumed doing so meant the start of a relationship between them because that was definitely not the case. Not understanding why he was doing so, he walked back to the bed and placed a kiss on her lips. A part of him wanted to believe there was a man out there who would make her happy. She deserved it.

Redford finally walked out of the room, retrieved his shirt and put it on. Glancing at his watch he saw that it was nearly four in the morning. There was no doubt in his mind—regardless of the weather, the Westmorelands, Outlaws and their friends had started a poker game at midnight and it was still going strong.

If he were to show up now, the guys would know why he was late. Hell, they might even suspect Carmen was the woman he'd been with, since he'd practically stayed by her side all night. He had even danced every dance with her. Sloan would definitely know what he'd been doing and with whom. Normally, Redford wouldn't give a damn if the name of his conquest was known, but for some reason he didn't want that for Carmen.

Fully dressed, he grabbed his jacket off the sofa and headed for the door, then something stopped him. It was a yearning that stirred deep within him. What was wrong with him? Why did the need to see Carmen again take over his senses? Unable to fight the craving, he headed toward where she slept.

Making sure the sound of his shoes was as noiseless as possible, he opened the door to the bedroom and looked at her still sleeping soundly. His breath caught at how beautiful she appeared. He wasn't sure how long he stood there before he closed the door.

Nothing about this made sense. Tonight he had intentionally ignored red flags, and there had been a lot of them. Allowing a woman to push him over the edge the way she had was not acceptable.

As Redford walked out of the cottage, locking the door behind him, he knew he needed to put as much distance between him and Carmen as possible. That meant changing his plans to remain in Westmoreland Country. He needed to leave now.

His company had a corporate jet, which was how he'd gotten here. He would call a private car to take him to the airport, spend the night at the hotel and then have his pilot return him to Anchorage first thing in the morning. He would leave a message for Sloan that he'd left because something had come up that needed his attention. That wasn't far from the truth.

What needed his attention was his common sense. For a short while tonight, he had lost it with Carmen.

Carmen came awake the next morning with a huge smile on her face. When she glanced around, it was apparent Redford had left. She was disappointed until she remembered the poker game. Evidently, he'd had the energy for other things after their lovemaking, but she had not. Multiple orgasms had worn her out completely. She'd heard about them but never in a million years had she thought her first experience would give her so much pleasure in rapid succession. Redford had definitely been worth the wait.

The last thing she remembered was drifting off to sleep in his arms. She couldn't wait to see him today, hopefully this morning. Even dedicated, card-playing men had to eat sometime.

Easing up in bed she grabbed the pillow where she knew

his head had lain the night before and squeezed it to her chest feeling over-the-top happy. By no means did she think last night would produce a marriage proposal, but at least they'd established a relationship.

A long-distance romance wouldn't be easy with him living in Alaska and she in DC, but together they could do anything. Wishing on a star for each other had been the first move and uniting their bodies had been the second.

Getting out of bed, she felt sore, but she couldn't expect not to feel that way since it had been her first time and it had been an explosive lovemaking session. Blushing profusely, she thought about her four orgasms with him. Five if you counted what he'd done to her while on his knees. Just thinking about it made even more color come into her cheeks.

She had showered and finished dressing when she heard a knock on the cottage door. She smiled as she quickly walked toward it, hoping it was Redford. More than anything she wanted a good morning kiss. The smile eased from her face when she opened the door and saw it was Leslie.

"Oh, it's you," Carmen said, taking a step back to let Leslie enter.

Leslie raised a brow. "Yes, it's me. Who did you think it was?"

Carmen found no reason not to tell her. Besides, she was bubbling with so much happiness it was about to spill out. "Redford."

"Redford?" Leslie stared at her curiously. "Why would you think it was Redford?"

Carmen couldn't help the huge smile that covered her face. "Because Redford and I have forged a relationship."

"What sort of relationship?"

"One where we agreed it was meant for us to be together."

Leslie didn't say anything. Instead, she stared at Carmen like she wasn't sure she had heard it right. "Are you saying

Redford committed himself to you?" Leslie asked in a disbelieving voice.

"Among other things," Carmen said, grinning widely. "And just so you know, he spent the night. That means I'm not a virgin anymore, Leslie. I feel great. He was great. It was the best night of my life. First, we had a picnic by Gemma Lake, and when it began raining, we came here to finish the wine and then—"

"Wait, hold up, you're going too fast and my head is spinning. Let's go back to when Redford committed himself to you. How did he do it?"

Carmen was trying not to let it annoy her that Leslie wasn't sharing her excitement. A part of her understood. Leslie honestly believed a man like Redford couldn't change.

"It was at the picnic. Everything about it was beautiful. The lake, the cheese and wine, and our conversation. The stars in the sky were beautiful, big and bright. It was like you could reach out and touch one. He suggested I make a wish upon a star. He did, too. Afterward, I asked what his wish was, and he said he had wished for me. He even said he wanted to make me his."

Leslie nodded and then said softly, "And of course, your wish was for him."

"Of course. And I told him I wanted to make him mine, too."

Leslie didn't say anything for a moment as she stared at her. "We need to talk, Carmen."

"What about?" she asked, allowing Leslie to lead her over to the sofa where they sat down.

"Just because Redford told you his wish was for you and that he wanted to make you his, that doesn't constitute a commitment."

Carmen rolled her eyes. "Of course, I know that, Leslie. However, for me it was his way of letting me know he's ready to settle down. Surely you think that as well."

When Leslie didn't say anything, Carmen patted her best friend's hand. "I understand why you're skeptical. You truly didn't think Redford was capable of changing and forging a solid relationship with a woman. I know it will be a process, and I'm fine with that. At least last night was a beginning."

Standing, she wrapped her arms around herself and twirled around the room. "I'm so happy this morning I can't stand it. A long-distance romance won't be easy but together we can make it work. We *will* make it work. I can't wait to meet his family and for him to meet mine. Be happy for me, Leslie."

She then checked her watch. "I can't wait to see Redford, hopefully at breakfast, so we can make plans. I told him I'd be leaving later today. After dinner."

Leslie stood. "You won't be seeing Redford at breakfast, Carmen."

Carmen lifted a brow. "Why? Did the guys decide to play cards through breakfast?"

"No, that's not the reason. Redford left Westmoreland Country to return to Alaska."

Shock appeared on Carmen's face. "He left?"

Leslie nodded. "Yes."

"But I don't understand. He'd planned to be here for a couple of days to participate in the card game. I figured that's why he wasn't here this morning when I woke up."

Leslie shook her head. "According to Sloan, Redford never made it to the card game. He sent Sloan a text around four this morning and said he was returning to Alaska."

Carmen was quiet before she asked, "Did he say why he left?"

Leslie nodded again. "Yes. He said something came up that needed his immediate attention in Anchorage."

A semblance of a smile touched Carmen's lips. "I'm sure whatever it was had to have been important, and the reason Redford didn't wake me up to say goodbye was because he figured I needed my rest. There's no doubt in my mind that I'll hear from him sometime today, and he'll explain everything."

Leslie just stared at her and said nothing. Seeing the doubt in her best friend's eyes, Carmen captured Leslie's hand in hers. "I know what you're thinking, but I refuse to believe I was a 'one and done' like all those other women. Last night was too special between us for me to think such a thing. Redford will contact me, Leslie. He will. You'll see."

Chapter Eight

A month later...

"**W**ill there by anything else, Mr. St. James?"

Redford glanced up at Maurice, the man who usually waited on him whenever he dined at Toni's, one of the most exclusive restaurants in downtown Anchorage. He'd been caught in deep thought, which was how things had been for the past month, and those thoughts were always on one person. Carmen Golan.

"No, Maurice, that will be all."

The man nodded and walked off. Redford figured Maurice noticed he wasn't his usual fun-loving self. Another thing the waiter probably noticed was that he'd been alone again. Usually whenever he dined here to enjoy a great meal and the live entertainment, he would do so with a woman. A woman he usually intended to sleep with before the night was over. Not this time, and not the other few times he'd come here since returning to Anchorage, and all because of Carmen.

How had one woman obliterated his desire for others? He hadn't known such a thing was possible. Especially for him. But four weeks later, he had to admit a night spent with Carmen had been a mind-blowing experience. What had knocked the hell out of him more than anything was discovering she'd been a virgin. That meant her experience level hadn't had a thing to do with her ability to infiltrate his mind and body the way she'd done. Other women with a lot more skill hadn't affected him this way. Even now, just thinking about her made sexual need curl in his stomach.

How could she still evoke such a strong sexual reaction from him a month later? What kind of passion had they shared that propelled him to break all his rules? Hell, he'd even slept through the night with her cradled in his arms. Something he'd never done with anyone else.

Dammit. What was even stranger was that he'd rushed back to Anchorage to reclaim his senses, but that hadn't helped one iota. Memories of their one night together were so strong they were damn unforgettable.

Never had a night with a woman left such a profound mark on him. He'd tried everything. Not even throwing himself into his work had helped. Her hold on him had him unsettled, agitated and downright troubled.

Why was he torturing himself this way? The sex with Carmen had been good. It had been great, off the charts, the best he ever had…but it was time to move on to the next conquest. So why couldn't he? He was certain whatever he was going through was just a phase he would eventually get over. Dammit, he had to.

After bidding Maurice goodnight, Redford walked to his car. It was windy tonight with a bit of chill in the air. That bite of cold reminded him that regardless of the fact it was July, he was in Alaska. Chilly summers were normal here. In the distance, he heard the sound of jazz music and knew an outdoor summer musical festival was happening somewhere beneath a late-night sunset.

When he'd arrived in Anchorage for college, he'd known he would make this city his home. Having the largest population of college students in the entire state of Alaska, there were always things to do, places to go and festivals to attend. Energy and adventure always seemed to flow in the air. He loved everything about Anchorage, and it was here that he'd built an empire he was proud of.

Less than an hour later, he arrived home with Carmen still on his mind. He had no regrets about that night. Even though he'd been tempted to break his own rule of not doing the same woman twice by calling Leslie for Carmen's phone number. At least that had been his thoughts before his conversation with Sloan a few days ago. Sloan had informed Redford that Leslie was royally pissed with him and had warned him not to call her about anything concerning Carmen.

From what Sloan had said, apparently Carmen had assumed that night had been a game-changer for them. A kickoff to what she thought would be their great love affair. Instead, she'd discovered she had been nothing more than a "one-and-done" like all the others.

He had racked his brain to recall what he might have said for her to make her think such a thing. Granted, he had told her he wanted to make her his...he'd meant just for that night.

Now more than ever he wished he would have clearly re-iterated just how things were between them. Especially after discovering she was a virgin. However, by then, he was too much of a goner. It had to have been the novelty of making out with a virgin that had gotten to him. And regardless of Candy's claims, he'd never had sex with a virgin before.

Redford tossed his keys on the table before heading to his bedroom. He would take a shower and go to sleep. Tonight, the memories would not siege his mind like they had all those other nights.

He hoped.

"You're in the hospital?"

Carmen heard alarm in her best friend's voice. She had waited until now to call Leslie for that very reason. "Yes, but I'm okay," she said in what she hoped was a reassuring voice.

"What happened?"

Carmen swallowed to fight back her tears and hoped Leslie didn't hear the sadness in her voice. "I've been sick for the past week and couldn't hold down any food. Things got worse and I got dehydrated. My doctor sent me straight from her office to the hospital."

"Was it food poisoning? A virus? Covid? An allergic reaction to something?"

"It wasn't any of those things, Leslie."

"Then what was it?"

Carmen paused and then said, "The doctor believes it might be a severe case of morning sickness that she's hoping won't turn into hyperemesis gravidarum."

"Morning sickness? Hyperemesis gravidarum?"

"Yes."

Of course, it didn't take long for Leslie to know what that meant. "You're pregnant?"

"You don't have to scream in my ear," Carmen said, holding the phone away from her face. "And to answer your question, yes, I'm pregnant. When I began suffering from bouts of nausea, I assumed it was a virus because I was throwing up all day and not just in the mornings. When I was late, I just assumed the virus had thrown my body off schedule. After my lab work, the doctor told me otherwise." Carmen paused again and then said, "I guess I don't have to tell you who's my baby's father."

It seemed to take a while for Leslie to recover. "Of course, you don't. When are you going to tell Redford?"

Carmen drew in a deep breath. "I'm not. At least not yet. Dr. Richardson has explained that at present my pregnancy is considered high risk," she said, still fighting back tears. "I'm at risk of losing the baby."

"Oh no, Carmen."

Wiping tears from her eyes that she was glad Leslie wasn't

there to see, Carmen added, "Taking care of myself and my baby is more important than telling a man who doesn't want kids that he's going to be a father."

"I hear you, Carmen, but regardless of whether Redford wants kids or not, he has a right to know about your condition."

"I'm not saying I won't tell him. I just won't tell him yet."

When Leslie didn't say anything, Carmen added, "And I prefer that you not mention anything to Sloan. He and Redford are thick as thieves, and Sloan might not feel comfortable keeping news of my pregnancy from him."

"You're right, he wouldn't feel comfortable keeping it from Redford. It's your decision as to when you tell him, so I won't say anything to Sloan."

"Thanks, Leslie."

"What does the doctor recommend, Carmen?"

"For now, six weeks of bed rest. I'll be on a strict diet geared to reducing nausea and dehydration. Unfortunately, the doctor won't release me to go home unless she knows someone will be there to assist me for the first week. After that she's arranged a nursing service to visit me twice a week to make sure I'm doing okay." Carmen paused and then said, "As you know, Chandra and her family are out of the country for the summer visiting the folks in Cape Town."

At first Carmen had planned to join them until she'd decided to begin writing her academic papers to be published next year. It would have taken her the entire summer to get started. Now it looked like she would be confined to bed rest most of the summer instead.

"I know this is a lot to ask, Leslie, but could you fly here so the doctor will release me from the hospital tomorrow? Then I can get one of my neighbors to check on me during the day for a week."

"Of course, I'll come there, and don't bother your neighbors, Carmen. I will fly out first thing in the morning and stay for a week. Longer if you need me. I'll need a reason to tell Sloan as to why I need to take an unexpected trip to DC for a while, but I'll think of something."

"I hate putting you in this predicament, Leslie. I know it's a lot asking you to keep anything from him."

"Let me worry about that. All I want is for you to take care of yourself and my future godchild."

Her future godchild… That made Carmen smile. "Thanks, Leslie. You're the best. And like I told you, I'll eventually tell Redford, but he's the least of my worries right now."

"I'm going to kill him," Leslie said, through what sounded like gritted teeth.

"You will do no such thing. Once I got over being angry and hurt, I was able to accept the fact that Redford never lied to me. The only lie was the one I told myself. I knew his type. Had known it from the very beginning. However, on that night I'd gotten it into my head that he had accepted his place in my life as my soulmate. It wasn't anything he'd said but what I had wanted to believe. For that reason, I lowered my guard, thinking he'd finally realized I was different from all those other women."

She paused a moment and then added, "I lost more than my virginity that night, Leslie. I lost my common sense to a man who was a master at seduction. A heartbreaker. A womanizer. In the end, he treated me just like he did the others. He slept with me with no intention of there being anything beyond that. I was wrong to think there would be more. That was my fault and not his. You tried to tell me. Now I wish I had listened."

Fighting back tears, she continued, "I now accept that Redford was never my soulmate and I was never his. There are no soulmates in my future. It was just an illusion I allowed my mind to concoct. For some people, true love does exist, but I've accepted that I'm not one of them."

"Carmen…"

"I'm fine, Leslie. I remember when one of my fellow professors came to school heartbroken because her boyfriend had lost interest in her. I can now top that. Redford didn't lose interest since there was never any interest on his part anyway. Just on mine."

Wiping away tears, she added, "Accepting my mistake about Redford is the least of my worries now. It's up to me to make sure I give my baby a fighting chance by doing what the doctor says needs to be done. Once the shock that I was pregnant wore off, and the doctor explained I could miscarry if I didn't take care of myself, I knew I wanted this baby even if Redford didn't."

"I believe Redford will want the baby, too, Carmen."

She shrugged. "I know what he told me, Leslie. That he didn't ever want kids. But it doesn't matter. Like you said, he has a right to know, and I will eventually tell him. But I don't plan to hold my breath that he will change his mind about fatherhood." She sighed deeply and then said in a soft voice, "I honestly don't know how this pregnancy happened when I know for certain he used protection. I saw him put it on. Of course, I wasn't using anything because I wasn't sexually active and hadn't planned to be. But it doesn't matter how I got pregnant, the fact is that I am."

"The most important thing right now is getting you released from the hospital and home to be taken care of," Leslie said. "I'll be there tomorrow. Don't worry about a thing, Carmen."

Chapter Nine

The buzzer on Redford's desk sounded. "Yes, Irene?"

"Mr. Sloan Outlaw is here to see you, Mr. St. James."

Redford raised a brow. The last time he'd talked to Sloan was when his friend had told him Leslie wasn't happy with him. That had been two weeks ago. He knew the last thing he should be contemplating was contacting Leslie for Carmen's contact information anyway.

He had awakened just that morning and decided enough was enough. It was going on another month, and he couldn't explain why the woman was still on his mind. No one could convince him such a thing was normal. There had to be a reason why thoughts of having sex with other women were a turnoff instead of a turn-on; and why thoughts of making love again to Carmen constantly dominated his mind.

If Leslie refused to give him Carmen's contact information, then he would hire a private investigator to get it. He had come up with a solution to this madness, one he believed would work. However, that meant seeing Carmen again.

"Mr. St. James?"

He'd forgotten his secretary had been waiting for his response. "Please send Mr. Outlaw in, Irene." He stood and came around his desk to sit on the edge of it. Obviously, Sloan had business in the city for him to be in Anchorage since he and Leslie had dual homes in Wasilla and Fairbanks.

Redford barely gave Sloan a chance to enter his office and close the door behind him before he said, "Funny you showed up here today. I had planned to call you later. I need Carmen Golan's contact information, Sloan. If you refuse to give it to me because of Leslie, then I'll hire a private investigator."

Sloan lifted a brow before dropping down into the chair across from Redford's desk. Frowning, he said, "You sound desperate. Didn't you seduce and drop her like you do all the others? So why do you want to contact her? Follow-ups aren't your thing, Redford. Besides, you claim it wasn't your fault if she assumed your night with her was the beginning of something more."

"Yes, but…"

"But what?"

Deciding to place all the BS aside and answer truthfully, Redford replied, "I honestly don't know what is happening to me, man. I refuse to believe I've been p-whipped, but I feel like I have. All I know is that I can't get Carmen Golan off my mind. I'm convinced her scent is embedded into my skin and the taste of her is a flavor I can't forget. I haven't thought about sleeping with another woman since spending that night with her, and I can't seem to desire anyone else."

"You're kidding, right?" Sloan asked in a disbelieving voice.

"I wish I was kidding, but I'm not. And it's mind-boggling as hell. I've never been in a state of sex deprivation before. I need to see Carmen again and bad."

Sloan frowned. "Why? So you can seduce her into sleeping with you again?"

Redford heard the disapproving hardness in Sloan's voice. Seducing Carmen again sounded pretty damn nice, considering his present sexually deprived state. However, he knew doing such a thing would only add to his troubles.

"No. I refuse to be that weak and break my rule of not having sex with the same woman twice. Besides, I've never bought into that asinine premise that in order to work a woman out of your system you need to sleep with her again. It's conjectural and unproven."

"So why do you want to see her again?"

"I did research on the matter," Redford said.

"Now why doesn't that surprise me?" Sloan responded, sarcastically.

Redford took Sloan's taunt in stride. During their days in college, not only was Redford known as the king of quickies, he was also regarded as an OCR. An obsessive-compulsive researcher. He loved gathering and analyzing data. Sometimes just to prove his point about something, and at other times just for the enthusiasm of acquiring knowledge.

"I'm going to ignore you, Sloan, since over the years a number of your companies have benefited from my skill at data crunching."

Sloan chuckled. "Touché. So why do you want to see her if not to seduce her again?"

Redford leaned closer to Sloan as if he was about to share some secret formula. "Some of the top relationship experts all suggest the same thing. It's all about the power of controlling your own body and mind, and not believing someone else has the ability to do so. That means I need to take Carmen out on a date."

"A date?"

"Yes. A date where we spend a nice evening together and where we won't end up in bed. I need to control my urges and desires and not let them control me. I have to prove my ability to do that with her."

"Do you honestly believe Carmen would go out on a date with you?"

"I don't see why not."

"Well, I do. Carmen slept with you that night believing

the two of you were soulmates. She was hurt to find out that wasn't the case."

"I don't believe there is such a thing as soulmates, Sloan."

"You've done research on the subject?"

"I didn't have to. I see a date with Carmen benefiting both of us. It will help me move on and it will also clear the air about a few things. Especially all her misconceptions of that soulmates thing. Over time, I hope we can become friends. After all, we're godparents to your daughter, so it's time we build a platonic relationship based on that, and for her to stop thinking there will ever be anything more between us."

Sloan didn't say anything for a long moment and then he said, "All that research you collected might have worked if there wasn't the issue of fatherhood."

Redford lifted a confused brow. "Fatherhood?"

"Yes, fatherhood. Carmen is pregnant."

Redford jumped to his feet. "Pregnant!"

"Yes, pregnant. So I can only assume you got sloppy that night, which is so unlike you, St. James."

"I used birth control." However, Redford could certainly see how a pregnancy could happen. A condom wasn't equipped to handle the overload from multiple orgasms. Why hadn't he thought about that? "Why didn't she tell me she was pregnant?"

"I understand Carmen isn't going to tell you anything about her pregnancy until she and the baby are out of danger."

Sloan's words broke into Redford's thoughts and he all but toppled over. "Danger? What kind of danger?" Suddenly, a panic he'd never felt before took control of him. Being told he was going to be a father one minute, and then being told he might not be the next, caused him to feel disoriented.

Reaching into his jacket pocket, Sloan retrieved a piece of paper. "She's experiencing a severe case of morning sickness that's putting the baby's and Carmen's health at risk. The doctor is requiring up to six weeks of bed rest."

"Six weeks?"

"Yes. There's even a chance her condition might lead to something more serious. I wrote down the name of the condition on this paper. I read up on it and suggest you do the same. It's pretty damn serious."

Redford glanced over at Sloan after reading the information on the paper he'd been given. "I should have been told, Sloan."

"It's my understanding that you mentioned to Carmen you didn't want kids. That probably has a lot to do with her not telling you right away. And again, she wanted to make sure she and the baby were out of danger."

He met Sloan's gaze. "Regardless of the relationship, or lack of one, I would never turn my back on my child, Sloan."

"I know you wouldn't, which is why I'm telling you. Leslie has no idea that I overheard her conversation with Carmen last night, and she won't be happy with me for telling you about it when Carmen swore her to secrecy. However, I know if the roles were reversed, you would do the same for me."

"Of course, I would."

Sloan nodded. "Leslie flew out this morning for DC. All she said was that Carmen's family is out of the country for the summer, and that Carmen caught something and isn't doing well. And she needed to go check on her. What Leslie didn't say, but what I overheard, was that Carmen was in the hospital and the doctors wouldn't release her to go home unless she had someone to be there with her for a few days."

Redford rubbed his hand down his face. "Thanks for telling me, Sloan, and I appreciate that you've included Carmen's address on this note as well."

"Don't mention it," Sloan said, standing. "Your research might have told you how to rid yourself of being p-whipped, but aren't you even curious as to how a staunch womanizer, a man who is dead set against a serious involvement with a woman, was able to get p-whipped in the first place?"

Redford didn't say anything because he honestly couldn't answer Sloan's question. "Maybe that's what you really need to research, Redford," Sloan said as he turned to leave. Before opening the door, Sloan added, "I'm in town until tomorrow, Redford. I'll call later to see if you're available to do dinner." And then he was gone.

Less than an hour later, Redford had read up on Carmen's condition. He'd even talked with the wife of a man on his executive team who had a gynecological practice. She'd explained that although severe nausea denoted a high-risk pregnancy, with the proper care the risks were lowered. Such care included bed rest, drinking plenty of liquids to stay hydrated, and avoiding foods that would aggravate the condition and make it worse. That's when the possibility of hyperemesis gravidarum would become a concern.

Redford paced his office. He would make sure Carmen got everything she needed. Even if it meant hiring a maid, butler and cook to be at her beck and call for six weeks. Yes, that's what he would do. He had reached for the phone to call someone who could arrange such services when suddenly he stopped and drew in a deep breath.

Carmen was having his baby. *His baby.* She was required to be off her feet for about six weeks while fighting for their child's life. At that moment something came alive inside of him. She was doing this for their child. He knew at that moment he didn't want anyone but him taking care of her and their baby.

Sloan was right. Control over mind and body might have been a fix, but it hadn't told him how and why he'd gotten in that position in the first place. Hopefully, spending time with Carmen would shed some light on it. Moving to his desk, he picked up his cell phone to call Sloan.

"Yes, Redford?"

"I'm flying out to DC in the morning. I want to be the one taking care of Carmen and our baby."

"Good luck with that. Leslie is there. Need I remind you that you aren't her favorite person right now? She won't let you in the door."

He knew Sloan was probably right. Leslie was a fierce protector of those she loved. "I'll just have to convince her I'm not there to cause Carmen stress, but to give her my support."

"Leslie still won't buy it, so I better go with you."

Redford wondered if the real reason Sloan wanted to tag along was because he was missing his wife already. "Fine."

After talking with Sloan, Redford called his company pilot to have the jet ready to fly out by noon tomorrow. Carmen's pregnancy was definitely a game changer.

"Are you sure you don't want anything else before settling in for the night, Carmen?"

Carmen glanced over at Leslie, who had arrived yesterday to discharge her from the hospital. The doctor had explained everything to Leslie, and she was taking her role of caretaker seriously.

"Honestly, Leslie, the only time I feel bad is when I can't keep anything down."

"Which seems to be all the time," Leslie responded with a worried expression on her face.

The last thing she needed was for Leslie to remind her how many times she'd thrown up already today. Following the doctor's instructions, she was to eat smaller amounts of food and get as much liquid into her system as she could to stay hydrated. She had been sleeping a lot today, which helped curb the nausea.

"You never did say what you told Sloan about being gone a few days."

Leslie glanced over at her as she adjusted the covers on her bed. "I told him your sister and her family were out of the country, and you weren't feeling well, and that I needed to come check on you. I gave him the impression you caught a virus or something. Thank God we have Nadine."

Nadine Boykins was Sloan and Leslie's live-in nanny. The fifty-something-year-old woman had been with them since Cassidy had been six months old, and Leslie had returned to work.

"I'm glad you have Nadine, too."

"Well, I'll let you get some rest now. I'll be downstairs in the living room watching a movie if you need anything," Leslie said, placing Carmen's cell phone within easy reach. "Just code me." They had established a special code on their phones if Carmen was in distress.

"Okay and thanks, Leslie, for being here."

"No need to thank me for anything, Carmen. That's what best friends are for. You would do the same for me."

Yes, she would have, but Leslie's pregnancy had been easy. She hadn't had a single day of morning sickness and had only gained baby weight. Not a pound more. She'd looked beautiful and radiant while carrying Cassidy.

Carmen switched her glance from Leslie to the view out the window. Night had settled, and she hoped the heat was departing. From what the weatherman had said, today had been one of those DC scorchers. She loved her townhouse. Especially, the side of the house where her bedroom was located. Since her bedroom window didn't face her neighbor's house, there were nights when she slept with the blinds open without worrying about anyone seeing inside.

Those were the nights she would stare up into the sky and see the stars. Now, whenever she looked at them, she was reminded of that night Redford had told her to make a wish upon a star. Nothing she had wished for had come true.

Feeling a thickness in her throat, she fought back a sob. It no longer mattered to her if she ever gained the love of her baby's father. She would have his baby. She gently caressed her stomach, amazed that a little human being was growing inside of her. A little boy or girl she would love and protect. Not being a part of his baby's life would be Redford's loss.

Another sob she couldn't hold back escaped. Suddenly, Leslie was there. Giving her the hug she needed. "Don't cry, Carmen. Everything will be alright."

Carmen wiped her eyes. "I didn't know you were still in the room. I thought you had left to go downstairs to watch a movie."

"No, I hadn't left yet. I'm not used to you being sad. You're usually the upbeat, happy-go-lucky, optimistic one. If you recall, it was your optimism that helped me get through some rough times when I broke up with Sloan. I want that Carmen back."

Carmen shrugged. "That Carmen doesn't exist anymore. She got knocked up by a man who doesn't want her or their baby."

"You don't know that, Carmen."

"Yes, I do. I know how he feels about a serious involvement with a woman, and I got it from his own mouth that he didn't want kids. So, there's no reason to think he'll want this one."

Pulling back, Carmen swiped what she was determined to be the last of her tears regarding Redford. "I'm fine now. Go on and watch your movie. I just needed to get the last of my crying out. Now I'm feeling sleepy. Before leaving, could you close the curtains for me?"

She no longer wanted to look out the window and see the stars.

Leslie heard a knock on the door. Using the remote to pause the movie, she quickly stood, not wanting the sound to wake

Carmen. It was close to ten at night. Who would be visiting at this hour?

Carmen had told her about Abigail Peters, her new neighbor who worked as a foreign service diplomat for the State Department. Carmen had said the woman would be traveling out of the country for the entire summer. Had those plans changed, and Abigail was letting Carmen know about it?

She moved to the door, leaned against it and asked, "Who is it?"

"It's me, baby. Sloan."

Sloan? What on earth was he doing here? He was to fly to LA today to take care of business with his film and production company. Had he gotten concerned about Carmen and come to check on her, too? If he stayed around for any length of time, there was no way he wouldn't figure out Carmen's condition. Maybe she could convince him to go hang out with his brother, Senator Jess Outlaw, who only lived a few miles away.

"Leslie?"

Sloan had to be wondering why she hadn't opened the door. "Just a minute."

After taking a deep breath, she undid the lock to open the door. She frowned. Not only was her husband standing there, but of all people, so was Redford St. James.

Chapter Ten

Redford saw how the look of surprise on Leslie's face quickly turned to a frown. "What are you guys doing here?" she asked, crossing her arms over her chest and not moving from the doorway.

He could tell by the harshness in her voice that she wasn't happy to see him. "I'm here to see Carmen," Redford said.

Leslie's eyes narrowed at him. "Why?"

It was Sloan who answered. "I told him about Carmen's condition. I felt he had a right to know."

Leslie turned sharp eyes on her husband. "And just how did you know about it?"

"I overheard your conversation. You thought I was still in the shower and your voice carried."

She glared at him. "It was a private conversation, and you had no right to tell Redford anything."

"I disagree. I had every right. That's how Redford and I roll. You of all people know that. Need I remind you that if it hadn't been for him telling me about that asshole Martin Longshire trying to take away your company, I would not have been able to help you keep it?"

Sloan's reminder worked somewhat. Leslie dropped her arms to her side, and she took a step back to let them in. The moment Redford walked inside, he took note that the two-story townhouse had a spiral staircase off the living room. He liked the design of the modern furnishings and the bright colors of several large throw rugs on the polished wood floors. Several art pieces hung on the wall and bestowed a cheerful and sophisticated air to the room.

Redford thought the decor suited Carmen. He then wondered why he would think that when he didn't know her that well. He was basing his assumption on what he did know. Whenever he saw her, she was prone to wear bright colors that blended well with her cocoa-colored skin. He would even say the colors also blended well with her cheerful disposition.

"In the kitchen, guys. We need to talk."

From the curtness in Leslie's voice, maybe the reminder of how he'd helped her hadn't worked to the extent that Sloan and Redford had hoped. However, he would let Sloan handle his wife since his best friend didn't seem the least bit bothered by her tone and glare.

They followed her through the dining room into a spacious kitchen that appeared just as modern as the rest of the house. Shiny stainless steel appliances and granite countertops. They all sat down at the table.

"So what do you want to talk to us about, sweetheart?" Sloan asked, leaning back in his chair and giving his wife a charming smile.

Her frown deepened and so did her glare. "I will deal with you later, Sloan. Right now, my issue is with Redford."

She then gave Redford her full attention. "As far as I'm concerned, you've done enough. You've turned one of the most cheerful and optimistic people I know into someone who now believes she's been living a lie all her life. That she doesn't deserve her happily-ever-after. That she will never have a soulmate. You did that to her, Redford."

Redford took offense to what she'd said. "How? By being me? I've never pretended to want anything from a woman other than sex, Leslie. I am a one-and-done guy, a womanizer to the third degree and a man who never intends to get married. You of all people know that."

"You're also a heartbreaker, Redford," she retorted. "You broke Carmen's heart."

He frowned. "That's not fair. I would never deliberately break someone's heart because I know how it feels. I've been there myself. That's the main reason I make sure any woman I sleep with knows the score. Carmen knew. There's no way I'll believe you didn't warn her about me."

Leslie lifted her chin. "I did warn her."

"Then it's not my fault or yours that she didn't heed the warnings. She took it upon herself to believe anything different about me." Redford rubbed his hands down his face. "But now there's a bigger concern than what Carmen assumed. She's having my baby, and I understand that she isn't well. I want to be the one to take care of her and our baby."

Leslie glared across the table at him. "There's no way Carmen will let you do such a thing."

"Why? Is she angry about that night?"

Leslie shook her head. "No. She knows it's not your fault she assumed you had accepted her as your soulmate."

Redford didn't say anything for a minute, then he asked, "In that case, why wouldn't she let me stay here and take care of her and our baby?"

"Mainly because she doesn't think you want the baby. She heard it directly from you that you never wanted kids."

Yes, he had told her that. "I might have felt like that before, but I don't now." He then shared with her the reason he'd never wanted children. From her expression, he knew Sloan had never told her about Candy, but he wasn't surprised. He, Sloan and Tyler had a bond; what they shared was between them.

Leslie met his gaze for a long moment; her glare was gone. "I regret what that Candy woman did to you all those years ago, Redford, which led to you not wanting anything permanent in your life such as marriage and kids. But even if you shared that same reason with Carmen, you're still going to have a hard time convincing her you feel differently about her pregnancy."

"There's no way I can leave without trying, Leslie."

Her glare was back. "Then what? What happens if you convince Carmen you want the baby? What about her?" Leslie asked.

Redford released a deep sigh. He should have been expecting that question from Leslie since he'd been asked the same thing by Sloan on the flight here. He met her gaze and provided the same response he'd given Sloan. "I honestly can't answer that. For me, it will be one day at a time with Carmen. I had planned to come here to see her again even before I found out she was pregnant."

Leslie's glare deepened. "Why? Did you expect her to sleep with you again after treating her like other women? And when did you begin sleeping with the same woman twice?"

"The reason I wanted to see Carmen again was to prove to myself that I could control the chemistry between us, that we wouldn't sleep together again."

He could tell from the look on Leslie's face she was confused, so he tried to explain. "I was attracted to Carmen the first time I saw her at your wedding rehearsal. But I dismissed it as nothing more than an intense sexual attraction. Then after hearing about her outlandish claim that we would one day marry, I decided to keep my distance and that's when I deliberately began avoiding her. I will now even admit I did so because deep down I knew she could do something no other woman had ever done."

"What?" Leslie asked.

"Get under my skin. I knew the warning signs, yet two years later, I slept with her anyway."

"And?"

In deference to Leslie's delicate ears, he changed the terminology from what he'd told Sloan and said, "And I became bewitched. Since spending that night with Carmen, I haven't been able to get her off my mind. Nor have I desired any other woman."

Leslie blinked. "You're kidding, right?"

There was no doubt in his mind why Leslie was surprised by what he'd said. She knew him, and she knew his mode of operation with women. "No, I'm not kidding. That's the reason I wanted to call you for Carmen's contact information."

"I would not have given it to you."

"Then I would have hired a PI. I did research and figured all I had to do to cure myself of her bewitchment was take her out on a nonsexual date where I could prove I had control over my mind and body."

"And then Sloan told you she was pregnant."

"Yes. And the moment he told me, Carmen became an exception because one of my rules was to never get a woman pregnant."

"And now?"

He released a deep breath. "And now the most important thing is her well-being and that of our child. More than anything, I want to take care of both of them."

Just like every morning upon waking, Carmen immediately felt nauseated. Quickly easing out of bed she went into the bathroom. Leslie had placed everything there within reach. The washcloths, her toothbrush and toothpaste, mouthwash, bottles of water that were kept on ice and a jar of her favorite candy—peppermints. She'd even placed a cushy mat in front of the commode for those times Carmen had to be on her knees over it.

One of the first things Leslie had done once she'd gotten Carmen home from the hospital and settled in her bedroom was wash and then braid Carmen's hair. All her strands had been pulled back from her face and a huge single braid hung down her back.

"I'm going to have a lot to tell you one day, my little bun," Carmen said a short while later as she dampened her face with a cool washcloth. After brushing her teeth and rinsing out her mouth, she decided to take a shower and change into a new gown while her stomach was somewhat settled.

She had insisted that Leslie not be at her beck and call. Carmen had accepted she was in this for the long haul. For as long as it took her body to adjust to her pregnancy. She would do whatever it took because, more than anything, she wanted her baby.

After her shower she felt refreshed. Just because she felt sick most of the time, she refused to look sick. When she'd come home from the hospital yesterday and glanced in the mirror, she had almost scared herself. Her hair had looked a mess and bags were forming beneath her eyes.

She was determined to be PWP, "pretty while pregnant," to boost her morale. She was happy about her pregnancy even if Redford wouldn't be. After her shower she walked out of the bathroom to find Leslie sitting in the chair her best friend had placed next to the bed, a tray of food on the nightstand.

"Aren't you looking pretty and refreshed. How do you feel?" Leslie asked, smiling.

"Thanks. My little bun is still kicking my butt as usual. I stayed over the commode longer than usual this morning, but I feel better now," she said, sitting on the side of the bed.

Leslie placed a tray of food in Carmen's lap. After she had eaten a piece of cinnamon toast and a boiled egg, Leslie handed her the prenatal vitamins and medication the doctor had prescribed, along with a huge glass of water.

Carmen watched Leslie walk over to the window and look out. She'd known her best friend long enough to know when something was bothering her. Before she could ask what was wrong, Leslie turned and said, "There is something I need to talk to you about, Carmen."

Carmen heard the strain in Leslie's voice. "Okay, but I already have an idea what it's about."

Leslie came back over to sit in the chair. "You do?"

"Yes, and I owe you an apology."

Leslie lifted a brow. "What for?"

"I asked something of you that I should not have."

"And what was that?"

"I asked you not to tell Sloan why you're here with me. I had no right to do that. He's your husband and you lied to him for me. Now I feel responsible for your deceit. Married couples shouldn't keep secrets."

Leslie leaned across the bed and captured Carmen's hand in hers. "I didn't consider it keeping a secret, Carmen. I considered it keeping my word to my best friend. Besides, it doesn't matter now because Sloan knows the real reason I'm here. That's what I want to talk to you about. He overheard our conversation when I thought he was in the shower."

"Well, you were talking loud that night," Carmen said, smiling. "If you want to tell me that he'll tell Redford, that's fine. I know how Redford feels about kids, so he won't contact me. When my sickness passes, I will contact him and assure him I don't expect anything from him. In fact, I don't plan for his name to be on my child's birth certificate."

Surprise shown on Leslie's features. "Why?"

"Because as long as I don't recognize Redford as my baby's father, he doesn't have to worry about having legal obligations. The last thing I want is for him to assume me or my child will stake claim to his wealth. I am giving him an out."

"You're serious, aren't you?"

"Yes, and I've made up my mind about it, Leslie. I want this baby, and Redford doesn't. So my decision to omit his name from my little bun's birth certificate makes perfect sense to me."

"And what if Redford has changed his mind about being a father?"

Carmen rolled her eyes. "Why do you keep suggesting such a thing when we both know he won't? I know what he told me."

"People can change their minds about things, Carmen."

"Yes, but I doubt he will."

"But what if he does?"

Carmen rolled her eyes again. "In that case, he'll have a hard time convincing me, Leslie. Even then I'll think his reason for changing his mind is suspect."

"Suspect how?"

She shrugged. "Like there's an ulterior motive. Namely, that he feels obligated, and that's the last thing I want or will accept. I have a good job and can take care of my baby on my own. And once I tell my family about my pregnancy, they will be overjoyed and will give my baby all the love my little bun will ever need."

Leslie didn't say anything for a while. Then, "Sloan did tell Redford, Carmen, so be prepared."

"Prepared for what? Redford doesn't want to be a father and I accept that."

"Okay," Leslie said, standing and taking the tray now that she'd finished eating.

Carmen knew by the way Leslie said "okay" that she didn't necessarily agree. When Leslie didn't add anything else, Carmen knew that meant Leslie was putting off the subject of Redford for later. Honestly, she preferred that his name didn't come up at all.

"Get some rest, Carmen. I'll be back later," Leslie said, taking the tray away.

"Okay."

An hour later, Carmen was coming out of the bathroom

after dealing with another bout of morning sickness when there was a knock on her bedroom door. She wondered why Leslie was knocking. "Come on in, Leslie."

She had made it to the bed and was sitting on the side of it when a husky male voice pounded through her ears. It was a voice she recognized immediately. "It's not Leslie, Carmen."

She jerked her head around to stare into a pair of dark, penetrating eyes. She was too shocked to do anything but stare back. Then somehow, she found her voice to ask, "Redford, what are you doing here?"

Crossing the room to stand in front of her, Redford said, "Good morning, Carmen. What's this I hear about you not putting my name on our baby's birth certificate?"

Chapter Eleven

The moment Redford's gaze met Carmen's something fired to life inside of him. Had it been a month? How could she look so damn beautiful while ill? Granted he could see the circles under her eyes, but her skin looked radiant, her eyes bright and those lips he had kissed so many times looked ready to be kissed again.

He knew at that moment it would not have been as easy as he'd assumed to take her out on a date and have the willpower to not make love to her again. Even now, intense desire flowed through his veins, making him aware of everything about her. Even that cute baby-doll gown she had on.

"What are you doing here, Redford?" she asked again, quickly placing the bed covers across her thighs, which had been exposed by her short nightgown. Evidently, she'd noticed his gaze.

"I arrived last night after finding out you were pregnant and having a difficult time."

"And this affects you how?"

He couldn't believe she had the audacity to ask him that. "If you're pregnant, the baby is mine."

"You're sure of that? You used a condom."

He knew her words, spoken sharply, were meant to get a rise out of him. They didn't. "Yes, I used a condom, but I'm also aware that we shared multiple orgasms that night. A condom can only hold so much, Carmen."

The blush on her cheeks was priceless. She recovered quickly and lifted her chin even higher. "I admit your sperm might have contributed, but my baby isn't yours nor is it ours. It's mine. I got it from your own lips that you don't want kids."

"Yes, but that's a moot point now since you are pregnant. I'm not the type of man to walk away from fatherhood."

"Tell that to the next woman you impregnate. At the time we slept together you didn't want kids, so there's no reason for me to think you'd want mine."

"I'm telling you I do."

"Well, I don't believe you."

He crossed his arms over his chest. She was being difficult. Leslie had warned him that she would be. "Then I guess I need to prove it to you."

"You can't prove it to me."

"I believe that I can."

"You can certainly try."

She'd said just the words he had wanted her to. "Thanks for allowing me the opportunity to do so, Carmen. I will make sure you don't regret it."

He saw the confused look on her face. "What are you talking about, Redford?"

"You've just told me I can prove to you that I want our child."

"And?"

"And I intend to do so."

He thought she looked cute rolling her eyes when she replied, "Whatever."

"Don't you want to know how I intend to do so?" he asked.

"No, because such a thing can't be done."

"We'll see. Now I'll let you rest." When he reached the door, he turned and asked, "Is there anything you need before I go?"

"Not a thing."

Redford gave her a smile before leaving. He doubted she knew just what she had agreed to. However, she would find out soon enough.

* * *

Carmen watched Redford leave, confused as all heck. Where had he come from? When had he gotten here? More importantly, why on earth would he claim to want her baby when he'd told her he didn't want kids? And what was that nonsense about him proving something to her?

She was about to pick up her phone to summon Leslie when her bedroom door opened, and Leslie walked in. "I was just about to call you," Carmen said. "When did Redford get here?"

"Last night with Sloan. I told you Sloan had told him about your pregnancy. I didn't tell you about him being here because we got sidetracked when you said his name wouldn't go on your baby's birth certificate. I knew that wouldn't fly with Redford and felt he was the one who should tell you that. I gather he did."

"Yes, but like I told you, I don't believe him."

"But I understand you agreed to let him prove otherwise."

"Yes, but he will be wasting his time."

"I guess he feels he can prove it while he's here taking care of you."

A dumbfounded look appeared on Carmen's face. "What are you talking about? Redford will not be taking care of me."

"Did you not tell him he had to prove he wants the baby?"

"Yes, but I didn't say anything about him staying here to take care of me."

"You told him to prove he wants the baby and staying here to take care of you is his way of doing so."

"That's utter nonsense."

Leslie crossed her arms over her chest. "Redford said he asked you if you wanted to know how he intended to go about proving it and you said that you didn't want to know."

Yes, she had said that. "But I had no idea what he was planning."

"Well, he did offer to tell you."

Carmen frowned. "Whose side are you on, Leslie?"

"I will tell you what you would tell me if our roles were reversed. I am on the side of what's fair. You would take any opportunity to right a wrong, Carmen. You and I both know it. We also know you don't go back on your word and you all but gave Redford your word that he could prove he wanted the baby the two of you made together."

Carmen's frown deepened. "We might have made it together, but this is my baby and my baby alone."

"Redford thinks otherwise."

Carmen didn't say anything for a moment, and then asked, "Where is he?"

"He left to go to the hotel to gather his stuff to move in here."

"That won't be happening. When he returns, let him know that I want to see him immediately."

"Okay, I will do that. But I want to give you something to think about."

"What?"

"There are some men who would run away from their responsibility, whether they wanted to be a father or not. You should appreciate a man who wants your baby and is willing to prove that he does."

Carmen was quiet and then she said softly, "That's something I did notice during my conversation with Redford."

"What?"

"He never referred to my baby as mine, although I always do. During our discussion, he always referred to it as *ours*."

"I think that's a good mindset for Redford to have. No matter what kind of relationship you and he might share, the bottom line is that the two of you created a life together. Now... are you ready for lunch?"

She saw how easily Leslie changed the subject and knew her best friend well enough to know the move had been intentional. She'd wanted to leave her with something to think about. "Yes. I'm hoping I keep it down."

When Leslie left her alone, her thoughts shifted back to Redford and just what she would say to him when she saw him. One thing was for certain, he would not be staying here to take care of her and that was final.

Redford tapped lightly on the door before entering to find Carmen sleeping. Leslie had told him Carmen wanted to see him as soon as he returned. He figured she now knew his plan of action and wasn't happy with it. Too bad. He refused to let her renege on her word that he could prove her wrong.

Glancing around the room, he saw the colors in here were even brighter than those in her living room. The bright yellow walls were almost blinding. However, the mint green curtains managed to tone the effect down a bit. Huge throw pillows, a good half dozen or so, were lined against one wall and he figured they would have a place on her bed when it was empty.

Laying on top of the bed covers was the most beautiful woman he'd ever seen. She was slumped with her back against a pillow while sleeping in what he assumed was a comfortable position. Her hair was combed back in a single braid situated across her shoulder. He had noticed the hair style earlier; it looked rather cute on her. Sleeping made her long lashes more pronounced and her lips appeared even more kissable than he remembered.

He slid into the chair across from the bed with his gaze still trained on her. She wore a robe over her short gown, and his gaze lingered on her tummy. It was hard to imagine a child growing inside her at this moment and giving its mother a hard time while doing so.

He recalled his mother telling him how sick she'd been in the early months of her pregnancy with him. His father had told him one time, or two, maybe three, what a difficult pregnancy she'd had. He had been tempted to call his mother and ask her about it, but then she would question his inquiry.

Right now, he was reluctant to let anyone know. Especially Lorelei St. James. She would catch the next plane out of Skagway—although she hated flying—to help take care of the woman who would be giving birth to her first grandchild.

His parents would demand he do the right thing, and to them that meant a wedding. Redford would have to reiterate to his parents how he felt about marrying any woman, baby or no baby. Although he could accept becoming a father, there was no way he could accept the role of husband to anyone. Ever.

More than once, his father had questioned why he hadn't gotten over what Candy had done and moved on after all this time. It was hard to explain to a man who'd married the woman he loved at twenty and who'd been faithful to her through high school and a nearly forty-year marriage that a deceitful Candy had broken his heart in a way that could never be repaired.

Carmen shifted in bed and so did his gaze on her. It moved from her stomach to her face. She still had that peaceful look, and he was glad for that. When he'd returned with his luggage, Leslie told him Carmen had thrown up for the third time that day. He could tell Leslie was concerned. According to Leslie, the doctor had warned Carmen that things might get worse before they got better. More than anything, he wanted her to know he would be here for her and their child. No matter how long it took, he would remain right here.

Last night from his hotel room, confident of his executive team's ability to handle things in his absence, he had told them he would be taking an official leave of absence for the next six weeks, possibly longer. Although he was certain they were curious as to the reason, he hadn't told them any more than that.

Redford moved the chair sideways, closer to the bed. Then, leaning back, he stretched out his legs in front of him. He might as well grab some sleep. He had a feeling when she woke up and he laid out his plans for the next few weeks, she would not be happy about them. That meant he needed to come up with a counter-plan.

Not only was he an obsessive researcher, but he had the art of persuasion and negotiation down pat. He intended to use those skills because he refused to leave her. She was having his baby, and he was determined to take care of them both.

Carmen's eyes felt heavy, but she lifted them open when she picked up the scent of a man. Not just any man but that of Redford St. James. There was no way she could not recognize his cologne when the fragrance had been entrenched in her skin after they'd made love. Was that the reason she had dreamed about him practically every night since? Replaying in her mind everything they'd done? Their actions in the cottage were what had gotten her in this condition. But still, she couldn't wipe from her mind all those images of a naked Redford, his dark eyes heated with desire and a certain body part fully erect.

Now he was here, clothed, with his head tilted back, sleeping. And she couldn't take her eyes off him. For now, she wouldn't question why. Her gaze moved over his gorgeous facial features. She couldn't help wondering which of them he would pass on to her son or daughter. Maybe the shape of his nose, or maybe the hypnotic curve of his lips, or possibly his noble yet angular jaw. She was certain her child would be beautiful because of him. Carmen shifted her gaze back to his eyes.

She was certain she hadn't made a sound, but suddenly his eyes opened and she fought back a gasp when his intense gaze held hers. She felt a tingling sensation that began in her breasts and slowly moved down her body to stop right there in the apex of her thighs.

Surely this wasn't supposed to be happening to her when

she was a sick woman. A woman who couldn't keep anything in her stomach. Evidently, that had nothing to do with desire. Well, it should. Did she need to remind herself again that desiring Redford St. James was the reason she was in this condition?

"You're awake."

His voice was deep, husky and too sexy for this time of day. "Did you expect me to sleep the entire day?"

"It wouldn't be uncommon for a pregnant woman."

She wondered how he would know such a thing and decided to ask him.

"Research. You wouldn't believe all the information I've read on pregnancy since finding out about yours."

She'd heard about his obsession with research. More than once she'd heard Sloan call him Einstein. "We need to talk, Redford," she said, deciding not to put it off any longer.

"Okay," he said, straightening up in his chair and looking at her intently with a sensual smile on his face.

Carmen refused to let his smile get to her. There was no way she would let him stay here to take care of her, no matter what he wanted to prove. She was about to tell him that when nauseousness swept over her, and she recognized what it was. Ignoring the dizziness, she quickly got out of bed to rush into the bathroom. Before her feet could touch the floor, she was swept into strong arms—arms whose strength she remembered—as he quickly carried her to the bathroom.

Chapter Twelve

The moment Redford had placed Carmen on her feet, she dropped to her knees in front of the commode. He stood there feeling useless because there was nothing he could do. Then he felt a degree of guilt because he had brought this on her by getting her pregnant. He wasn't an amateur when it came to having sex with a woman and he had taken precautions. However, he hadn't known being inside her body would drive him over the edge four times.

He hadn't expected it and definitely hadn't prepared for it. When it had happened, all he could do was let things rip. He'd been too gripped in the throes of ecstasy to do anything other than maintain a frantic rhythm while thrusting deeper inside of her.

The sound of her throwing up caught his attention and he dropped down on the floor beside her to gently rub her back, while wishing there was more he could do. At that moment she and the baby were the center of his thoughts, and the sound of her emptying her stomach like this tore at his heart.

He wasn't sure just how long the two of them remained on that floor, but he'd known she'd finished when he felt her back flinch beneath his hand. That's when she must have realized he was down there with her. He hadn't been around a pregnant woman who'd had a difficult pregnancy before. Leslie had had an easy pregnancy, and according to Tyler, Keosha had

had morning sickness but had only thrown up a few times. He could definitely see why Leslie was worried about Carmen.

"Thanks for bringing me in here. Not sure I would have made it in time."

When she stood and flushed the toilet, he stood as well. His hand moving from her back to gently stroke her braid. "You don't have to thank me, Carmen. I'm glad I was here."

She didn't say anything as she moved to the vanity. He watched as she uncapped a bottle of water on ice to drench a face cloth before using it to pat her face. Then she brushed her teeth and thoroughly rinsed out her mouth with mouthwash. She met his gaze in the mirror.

"You look beautiful, Carmen."

"Thanks."

"You're welcome."

"We still need to talk, Redford."

"Right now, I need to get you back in bed. Do you need to change your gown?"

She shook her head. "No, but I'll need another robe. Could you have Leslie come in here, please? She'll know where they are."

"Leslie isn't here."

He saw the surprised look on her face. "She's not here? Where is she?"

"Since Sloan is leaving in the morning, she went with him to visit his brother and his wife."

"Oh. I'd forgotten Jess and Paige live here in DC, too."

"Leslie told me to let you know she'd only be gone for a few hours. Tell me where a fresh robe is and I'll get it for you."

She hesitated and then said, "There's one in my closet, hanging up on the left side."

He nodded and went to get it. He wasn't surprised to see how neat and orderly her closet was compared to his. It was also a lot smaller, although she definitely had a lot more clothes. One of the first dresses he saw was the shimmering blue one she'd been wearing at Jaxon and Nadia's wedding. The one he had taken off her. He pulled a robe off the hanger while potent memories flooded him.

He made his way back to the bathroom and handed her the robe. "Thanks," she said, taking it from his hand and then looking at him expectantly.

When he didn't move, she said, "You can leave now. I need to change."

He lifted a brow. She was just changing robes, not gowns. Even if she had been changing gowns, he had seen her naked before.

Instead of reminding her of that, he said, "I'll be outside the door if you need me."

She frowned. "I'm not incapable, Redford."

Leslie had warned him she would say that. She didn't want anyone to do for her what she could still do for herself, and he admired her for that. He studied her for a moment before gently caressing her cheek. "I know you're not, Carmen. I just want you to know I'm here if needed."

He smiled before turning to leave, closing the door behind him.

Carmen released a deep whoosh of air from her lungs. Why had he given her one of his notorious smiles before walking out the door? And why did he have to play the part of the gallant hero by sweeping her into his arms and carrying her into the bathroom, where she'd performed the most unromantic act? She recalled the exact moment she'd felt his hand stroking her back and realized he was down on the floor beside her. His care had sent shivers of desire racing through her.

Desire?

Desire should be the last thing on her mind, especially with Redford St. James, she thought, removing her robe to put on another. Just knowing he was outside the door unnerved her because whether she wanted to admit it or not, she still desired him.

And then he'd told her she was beautiful. *Beautiful?* He had to be kidding. However, her parents had raised her to accept a compliment, even if it was an outright lie. Anyone looking at her could see she was a mess. Like she'd been rung through a wringer a few times.

Why was he being so nice? And why did he want to claim her child? Doing so had to benefit him somehow. What other reason could there be? And because she was convinced he had some kind of ulterior motive, she wasn't having any part of it.

There was a soft knock on the bathroom door. "Yes?"

"Are you okay?"

She frowned. What had Redford thought? She'd drowned in the commode? She bit back the retort and instead said, "Yes, I'm fine. I'll be out in a minute."

After tying the sash around her waist, she opened the door and he was right there. Before she could say anything, he swept her into his arms. "I can walk, Redford," she snapped.

"I know that. Just humor me."

She didn't want to humor him. She honestly didn't want him there. Instead of placing her in the bed like she thought he would do, he sat down on the love seat with her in his lap.

"What are you doing?"

"Holding you so we can talk."

Yes, they definitely needed to talk, but did she have to be in his lap to do so? "We could have talked while I was in the bed."

"I prefer this way. You're closer to me. I need to hold you and feel the connection to our baby."

Now why would he say something like that? The last thing she wanted was her thoughts to soften where he was concerned. "Okay, let's talk. I want to know—what's your hidden agenda?"

He honestly looked confused. "My hidden agenda?"

"Yes. There has to be a reason why a man who's always said he never wanted kids suddenly wants them. I figure there has to be a hidden agenda. What is it?"

"You honestly believe that?"

"Why shouldn't I?"

He stared at her for a long moment. "I see what I told you about not wanting kids has put you into a super protective mode where our child is concerned."

She nodded. "Of course I'm protective when it comes to *my* child."

He nodded. "I think I should tell you why I said I never wanted children, Carmen."

She wished she could ignore the fact that his voice was not only soft and husky, it was also intimate. It was as if there was more between them than a baby that she wanted but he didn't.

She studied him and saw the intense look in his penetrating gaze. "Yes, maybe you should."

He didn't say anything for several moments and then he began. "Years ago, at the age of seventeen, I met this girl. She moved to town when her father's job with the railroad transferred him to Skagway. We saw a lot of each other over the summer and at some point in our senior year of high school we decided to make a go at things. I had planned to attend college in Anchorage and her plan was to attend school in Juneau."

"What was her name?"

"Candy. Candy Porter. She and I talked about marriage after college and things seemed great. We also talked about the children we would have together one day. We wanted four."

A knot formed in Carmen's chest. She could hear the pain in his words, which made her ask, "Did she die? Is that why you can't envision yourself falling for someone else and sharing a child with them?"

His chuckle was derisive enough to send a shiver through

her. She immediately knew her assumption was wrong. "Yes, in a manner of speaking, she did die, but not the way you think. She died in my heart."

Carmen swallowed deeply and didn't say anything. Instead, she waited for him to explain. "At the end of our senior year of high school, I felt something was off-kilter but didn't know what. I figured we were busy trying to make good grades and get into the colleges of our choice. I never guessed that she was sneaking around behind my back with another guy."

"What! She was cheating on you with a guy who attended your school?"

"No, he was an older guy who'd graduated two years earlier and worked on the docks."

Carmen nodded. "How did you find out about them?"

"They kept their affair secret until prom night. I took her there and found her in the parking lot, in the back seat of the guy's car, making out. From the sounds of her orgasmic screams, she seemed to be enjoying herself. Unfortunately, others were with me and saw what happened. By the next day, the entire town knew what she'd done and with whom. I felt betrayed and humiliated. She had taken advantage of my love and my entire life was left in shambles. I knew then that I could never fall in love with anyone again. As for kids, I'd always connected any kids of mine as hers. I honestly believed I would never want to be any woman's husband or any kid's father."

He held her gaze as if what he was about to say was important, something he needed her to hear and understand. "Nothing has changed about me never falling in love again, Carmen. Candy Porter's betrayal destroyed my heart, as well as my desire for marriage and a family. However, the moment Sloan told me you were pregnant, something happened I hadn't expected."

"What?"

"A father's love. I hadn't known such a thing could exist until then. But the more I thought about it, the more it makes sense. There's no reason I wouldn't make a good father since I had a great role model. My dad was the best. And my two closest friends are great dads. I am a responsible person, and don't mind taking on commitments. The only reason I had decided against kids was because I knew I would never get married."

Carmen didn't respond for a moment and then she said, "Thanks for sharing that with me, Redford."

"The reason I told you, Carmen, is for you to know why I've felt that way over the years. And why it's important to me to be here with you during this difficult time. This baby isn't just yours, it's ours. We're not married, and I can't see myself marrying someone I don't love just for the sake of a child. However, there are some things I hold sacred. Fatherhood is one of them. I have moral and ethical standards. Marriage or no marriage, I will always be there for our child and for you as the mother of our child. There is no hidden agenda for wanting to claim my child. And it's important to me to be here to take care of you."

"What about your job?"

"I'm taking a leave of absence. I have a good executive team in place. If an emergency comes up that needs my attention, they know how to reach me."

She didn't say anything at first, and then, "You've given me a lot to think about, Redford. I'm not sure, even after what you've told me, that my thoughts will change. Earlier you said I'm in a super protective mode when it comes to my child, and I am. I'm not sure you're there."

"I wouldn't be here wanting to take care of the two of you if I wasn't there, Carmen."

"Is Candy still living in Skagway?"

"No. The guy she betrayed me with dumped her. Then she

left for college and met and married a military guy. I understand they have two kids."

She wondered how he knew that. Did he keep up with her? As if he'd known her thoughts, he said, "Her parents still live in Skagway, and she often comes to visit them. At some point, she apologized to my parents. The whole thing was one hell of a scandal, and for years her reputation was in shambles."

"Did she ever apologize to you?" Carmen asked.

"No, but not for lack of trying. I refused to accept her calls and letters, and I made sure our paths didn't cross whenever I returned to Skagway."

Deciding to change the subject, she asked, "I'm feeling a little hungry. Did Leslie leave the soup out for dinner?"

"Yes. I'll prepare you a bowl," he said, standing with her in his arms and then placing her on the sofa. "Do you prefer getting back in bed?"

"No, sitting here is fine."

He nodded. "It won't take me long to warm up the soup. I hope you'll be able to keep it down."

"I hope so, too."

She watched him leave, thinking about what he'd shared with her. Candy had broken his heart and that was the reason he would never love anyone else. It was sad that after all this time Candy hadn't died in his heart like he thought, but that she still had a hold on it.

Chapter Thirteen

Redford noted the lifting of Carmen's brow the moment she tasted the soup. Before returning to her home, he had gone to the grocery store and purchased ingredients for a soup he'd wanted to make for her. He'd also made a stop at a retail store to purchase one of those over-the-bed eating tables versatile enough to be used when she was out of bed and sitting on the loveseat like she was doing now. He sat in the chair across from her bed and was surprised she hadn't asked him to leave so she could eat in private.

She glanced over at him. "This isn't the soup I had yesterday."

"No, it isn't. It's a recipe I discovered that's rich in nutrients. I thought it would be good for you and our baby."

"And you discovered this how?"

He smiled at her. "During my research."

She must have been amused by what he said because she returned his smile and began eating again. He had wanted to make her a sandwich to go along with the soup, but before leaving Leslie had warned him the only solid foods she could consume were the ones on the list the doctor had given them. He had studied the list and already his mind had conjured up several recipes he could put together for her. That is, if she decided to let him stay.

Although he had wanted to use his powers of persuasion and negotiation, after she had accused him of having an ulterior motive for wanting to claim their child, he knew the only thing that would work would be the truth.

It had been hard reliving that part of his life, which he'd done twice now in the past twenty-four hours. First to Leslie and then to Carmen. He hoped that would be the last time he'd have to bring it up to anyone. He had moved on. It was in his past and he wanted it kept there.

"This is really delicious, Redford."

"Thanks. I recall telling you that I liked to cook but not bake."

"Yes, that was one of the things you did tell me."

Had her comment been meant to remind him of what he'd said about not wanting kids? Leslie had warned him that even after telling her about Candy, it might not matter. A part of him wanted to believe that it would.

"Tell me about your childhood, Redford."

Her request caught him off guard. He glanced over at her. "Any particular part you want to know?"

"Yes, your younger years, like before you started school."

"Whoa. Not sure if I remember that far back. I would say I was a good child; however, my parents might beg to differ."

She nodded. "They only wanted one child?"

"Nope. I understand they wanted a house full but didn't get that. It wasn't for lack of trying. However, pregnancy doesn't always come easy. They'd been married close to eight years when Mom finally got pregnant with me. They declared if she got pregnant again that would be great. If not, then I would be their only little blessing. Their words, not mine."

He hadn't told that to anyone else before. But then no one had ever asked him about his early childhood. "Any reason you wanted to know?"

She stopped eating and looked at him. "I was just wondering what I'd be in for...if my child's temperament mirrors yours."

Did that mean she was no longer considering their child as just hers? "What kind of child were you growing up?" he decided to ask.

A smile touched her lips. "I'm told I let it be known very early on that since I was the baby in the family, I wanted all the attention. And they all gave it to me. My sister Chandra was just as bad as my parents. There is a five-year difference in our ages, and she claims the only reason she helped them spoil me rotten was because she was tired of playing with her dolls alone. She had warned my parents that if they had a boy, she would order that he be sent back."

Redford couldn't help but find that amusing. "I don't think that's the way it works."

"You couldn't convince Chandra of that, so I'm glad I was born a girl. Mom and Dad tried having another child. She got pregnant but lost it. It was a boy." She stopped eating again and met his gaze. "I've been thinking about that a lot. Comparing my pregnancy with hers. But she lost the baby due to a car accident that almost killed her. A man ran the traffic light."

"Wow, that's sad. How far along was she?"

"Six months. I remember Dad sneaking me and Chandra into the hospital to see her. I was five at the time and didn't fully know what was going on. All I knew was that my mom was inside that big building in a little bed with all those big machines connected to her, instead of being home with us and sleeping in her own bed. She stayed in the hospital for almost a month."

She paused. "Dad took care of Mom, refusing to accept assistance from his mother or Mom's. He said he wanted to be the one to take care of her, and that they needed that time together to heal after losing their child."

He nodded and wondered if she saw the similarities. In case she didn't, he said, "I understand your father's position. I want to be the one to take care of you. Although we might not love each other, I honestly believe we need time together to bond, Carmen."

"To bond?" she asked, looking at him curiously. He also noted the cautious look in her eyes.

"Yes, for the sake of our child. You, as the baby's mother and me, as their father. We'll need that bond for the rest of our child's life. It will be unbreakable. Regardless of the fact that we won't be getting married, we need our child to know that above all else, we put them first and always will."

An unbreakable bond...

Could such a thing exist between them? Carmen wondered, shifting in bed. She had been thinking about Redford's words most of the night when she should have been sleeping. It didn't help matters that when Leslie returned and came in to check on her last night, she had forgotten to ask her to close the blinds. That meant whenever Carmen woke during the night, she saw the stars, forcing her to remember a night when she and Redford had gazed up at them together.

Carmen had told Leslie just how good Redford's soup had been and that she hadn't thrown up after eating it. She had taken a nap and had slept until Leslie returned to check on her. She hadn't seen Redford anymore that night.

"Good morning."

She glanced over at Leslie and raised up in bed. "Good morning."

She should be glad it wasn't Redford greeting her, but for some reason she wasn't. Had he changed his mind about the bonding thing because he thought she was being too difficult, too wishy-washy? Or had he thought about it overnight, and after seeing her empty her stomach yesterday, decided taking care of her was too much?

"Did Sloan get off okay, Leslie?"

"Yes. Since he flew here in Redford's jet, Maverick volunteered to fly in and pick him up."

Maverick was Sloan's youngest brother. Leslie had once told her that due to Alaska's very limited road system, one of the most common ways of getting around was by aircraft. It seemed that more Alaskans owned personal planes than cars. "That was nice of him."

Leslie smiled. "The one thing I discovered upon meeting Sloan's siblings years ago was that they were close. Although they give each other a hard time once in a while, they look out for each other." A concerned look etched into her features. "Did you sleep well, Carmen?"

"Not really." There was no need to say more.

Leslie gave her one of those looks. "What bothered you enough to interfere with your rest? Rest that you need?"

She didn't say anything for a minute and then she said, "Redford and I had a deep discussion yesterday. He told me why he'd never wanted kids."

"And how do you feel about that?"

"After what that girl did, I can only imagine his pain and heartbreak at seventeen."

"Yes, but he's thirty-six now. Shouldn't he have moved on?"

Those had been her feelings yesterday, too. However, she had thought about it during the night and now she kind of understood Redford's position. "Moving on isn't always easy for people, Leslie. You of all people should know that. Need I remind you what you went through when you thought Sloan had wronged you?"

"No, you don't have to remind me so withdraw the claws," Leslie said, chuckling. "I thought I'd play devil's advocate and remind you."

Carmen frowned. "Why did you feel the need to do that?"

"Because I recall, during that time when I thought Sloan had betrayed me, you were very insistent that I be fair with him.

Just like you wanted me to be fair to Sloan and give him the benefit of doubt, I think you should do the same for Redford."

Carmen didn't say anything as she considered Leslie's words. "He wants to develop a bond between us for our child's sake."

"I think you should. Remember when you taught public school before getting into the college system? One of your pet peeves was the absence of fathers in their kids' lives. You felt they should be there, whether they were married to the mother or not."

"Yes, I recall that."

"That's all Redford is asking for, Carmen. He not only wants to claim your child as his, he wants to be a part of his or her life. But the bigger question is how do you feel about that, knowing the three of you will never be a real family? How do you feel knowing that although he wants to be a father to your child, he doesn't want to be a husband to you?"

Carmen released a deep sigh. "Redford has made it very clear that although he wants us to bond for our child, he has no plans to give up his single status, and I'm fine with that. I won't marry a man who does not love me, and Redford doesn't love me. I was wrong to assume he did. Nor is he my soulmate. Redford and I are alike in one way now. He never intends to fall in love again and neither do I."

"I think you and Redford are both making a mistake by giving up on love, Carmen. Especially you. I also remember something else you would constantly preach to me when I was going through my troubles with Sloan."

"What?"

"To see the good in everyone and not the bad. I would think that even includes Redford."

"I tried doing that, Leslie. That's the reason I fell in love with him in the first place. Although I admit I had false assumptions about that night we spent together, it doesn't negate the fact that he broke my heart."

"Then tame the heartbreaker. Specifically, tame your heartbreaker."

Carmen rolled her eyes. "I recall you once warning me that Redford couldn't be tamed."

"I might have been wrong. He never wanted fatherhood, yet because of you he is embracing it now. All I'm saying is that Redford feels he has no reason to trust his heart to another woman. He might see things differently after spending time here with you. God knows you are the most positive person I know."

Carmen shook her head. "I used to be. I can't risk getting my heart broken again, Leslie."

"Then maybe this time you should approach things differently than just announcing to the world that you intend to marry Redford, like he didn't have a say in the matter. Let him get to know you, Carmen. Now is the perfect time."

"Honestly? While I'm in this condition? Sick most of the time while fighting to give our child a chance at life?"

"Yes, because both of you are fighting for the same thing. Already I can see where the two of you have made some progress."

Carmen lifted a brow. "What kind of progress?"

"Redford wants to prove your child's the most important thing in his life, and it seems he's already proved it."

"What makes you think that?"

"Because you referred to the baby as 'our baby' and not 'my baby.' That's a good start, Carmen."

Carmen was about to say the jury was still out as to whether it was a good start or not when she quickly got out of bed to rush to the bathroom.

"Come in."

Redford entered Carmen's room to find her sitting on the love seat. The same place she'd been sitting when he'd last seen her yesterday.

"Good morning, Carmen."

The moment their gazes connected, a shiver shook him. He was getting used to her beauty overwhelming him, but now their baby was growing inside her. And the sexual vibes between them were just as strong as always.

"I understand you had a rough morning," he said, taking the chair across from her.

She shrugged. "No more than usual." After downing the last of her apple juice, she glanced over at him. "I have another question for you."

"Regarding what?" he asked, extending his legs out in front of him. He rather enjoyed his conversations with her.

"Your family."

He lifted a brow. "What about my family?"

"I want to know their history."

Did she think there was something in his family's history she should be concerned about? "Why?"

"So I can one day share it with…our child."

He could see the emotional struggle in her gaze. She had referred to the baby as *theirs*. Did she not think he would be around to share that history with their child?

Pushing such thoughts from his mind, since he knew there was no way he would not be around, he asked, "How far back do you want me to go?"

"I understand your family are Native Alaskans. Did they come from Russia?"

He shook his head. "No. My father's ancestors are part of the Tlingits tribe. They were known as the Southeast Coastal Indians, and began inhabiting Alaska over ten thousand years before Russia sold it to the United States. They, along with several other Native Alaskan tribes, were living on the land together peacefully."

"How did they get there if not through Russia?" she asked,

tucking back a loose tendril of hair. Why did seeing her do something so insignificant increase his desire for her?

"In school we were taught our history, which I've always been proud of," he said. "It is believed all the Native Alaskan tribes came to North America by way of the Bering Strait Land Bridge."

Over the next hour, while she nibbled on dry cereal, he told her of his heritage. The legacy that would be their child's. She seemed to enjoy listening and he definitely enjoyed telling it. It was history not only told to him in school, but relayed to him by his parents and grandparents. He told her how even after the sale of Alaskan land to the United States, very little changed. Any Russians living in Alaska at the time of the sale vacated the land, leaving it completely to the Alaska Natives. It was only close to thirty years later that the land became more inhabited due to the Klondike Gold Rush. During that period, over one hundred thousand prospectors migrated to Yukon in search of gold.

He could tell by the drooping of her eyes that she was getting sleepy. When he got tired of seeing her fight back sleep, he stood. Crossing the room, he swept her into his arms.

"What are you doing?" she asked. He figured she was exhausted since she wasn't putting up much of a fight.

"I'm putting you in the bed. Time for your nap."

She cuddled her face in his chest. "You smell good."

He chuckled. "Thanks."

When he reached the bed, he placed her on it and watched as her body automatically shifted into what he perceived as her favorite sleeping position. He drew in a deep breath that held her tantalizing scent and fought like hell to ignore the tightening in his groin as he watched her. For the first time since arriving on her doorstep, he wondered if he was making a mistake by being here. How would he give her the proper care she needed when her beauty and desirability were playing havoc on his senses?

She hadn't demanded that he leave. But she also hadn't said if she would agree to put his name on their child's birth certificate. They had a lot to work out.

Yet even while she slept, Carmen had a calming effect on him. Redford had to believe everything would work out between them in the end. He had to believe that.

Chapter Fourteen

Carmen opened her eyes to the sound of music. She slowly eased up in bed and wondered how long she'd slept. It was daylight outside her window so hopefully it hadn't been long. A glance at the clock on the nightstand showed she'd slept for several hours.

Where was the music, a classical number by Mozart, coming from? She then saw the cell phone in the chair beside her bed and knew Redford had left it there. Had he been sitting there while she slept?

When she suddenly felt nausea coming on, she quickly got out of bed to rush into the bathroom. It was a full half hour later before she came out and almost collided with the hard figure standing there. "Are you okay, Carmen?"

Where had he come from? Had he been outside the bathroom the entire time? Now she was glad she'd closed the bathroom door. She was about to answer and say she was fine when he traced his fingertips across her cheek. She went still beneath his touch. The look on his face displayed both tenderness and concern.

"Carmen?"

He was looking at her with intense dark eyes—eyes a woman could drown in. "Yes?"

"Are you okay?"

Quickly reclaiming her common sense, she said, "I'm fine.

Just the regular. I'm going to have a lot to tell my little bun one day."

He stroked her braid. "Your little bun?"

"Yes," she said, using that opportunity to scoot around him and sit on the edge of the bed. Each time he touched her, she wanted more of the same. And that wasn't good. "My little bun."

He nodded. "Is that your pet name for our baby?"

"Yes, for now. I might change it when the doctor tells me the sex."

He nodded. "Would you want to know the sex of the baby before it's born?"

"Don't know. Sloan and Leslie couldn't wait to find out."

"You and I both know, as well as a thousand others, why they wanted a girl. However, I'm sure they would have welcomed a son if Leslie had had a boy."

Carmen nodded, knowing that was true. Sloan had been obsessed with having the first Outlaw granddaughter, and he had. "Do you have a preference?" she asked him.

"No. Just a healthy baby, which means I need to make sure there's a healthy mom. That leads me to ask, are you ready for dinner?"

Carmen couldn't help but grin. The man was as smooth as he was handsome. "I guess I slept through lunch."

"Yes, you did. For a minute I thought you would sleep through dinner, too, but then I heard the pitter-patter of feet above my head."

That meant he'd been in the guest bedroom downstairs. The thought that he was sleeping in the bed directly beneath her sent sensuous chills through her body. "Are you cold?"

He must have seen her tremble. "No, I'm fine, and yes, I'm ready for dinner."

He smiled. "I made you another soup. This one has bits of chicken in it. That way you'll be getting some protein."

She didn't have a problem eating anything, even protein, the problem was keeping it in. "Sounds good, but before you go, we need to talk."

"Okay."

He sat in the chair and looked at her expectantly. After taking a deep breath, she said, "First, I want to say I liked the music. It was soothing and nice to wake up to."

He smiled and her tummy tingled. "I'm glad you liked it. I researched what type of music might relieve nauseousness. I guess it didn't work because you threw up anyway."

She couldn't help the smile that touched her lips. "I think it's going to take more than music to help me with that, Redford. However, I appreciate the effort. When the baby grows up and becomes a teenager, I will tell them what I went through to bring them into this world." She paused. "I want you to know, Redford, that I've decided to put your name as the father on our baby's birth certificate."

She could tell by his smile that he was happy about it. "Thanks, Carmen."

She nodded. "Since you don't have to prove anything to me about wanting the baby, you can leave."

"Leave?"

"Yes."

"Isn't Leslie leaving at the end of the week?" he asked.

"Sooner if I can convince her. Although I'm still having bouts of nausea throughout the day, I know what to expect now and I can take care of myself."

"Who will cook meals for you?"

"I can hire someone to bring food to me, Redford."

"Leslie said you have a doctor's appointment next week."

"Yes, but it will be virtual, and the doctor has arranged

for a nurse to start coming here to check on me at least twice a week."

He leaned forward in his chair. "Regardless, that's not going to work, Carmen."

She lifted a brow. "What isn't going to work?"

"You taking care of yourself."

"It will work, Redford." Now that she had agreed to legally acknowledge him as the baby's father, did he assume that meant he could boss her around or have a say in her affairs? She was about to ask him that when his next words stopped her.

"I think I should stay here with you."

She tilted her head to look at him. "Why?"

"Because of that other issue you and I discussed."

Carmen arched a brow. "What issue is that?"

"Our bonding of friendship for our child. Have you forgotten about that?"

Yes, she had. "We can do that after the baby is born."

"I prefer starting the process now." He captured her hand in his, pausing as if he was trying to collect his thoughts. "It's important for me to see you through this period of your pregnancy, Carmen."

"Why?" she asked, trying to ignore the sensations flooding her being while he held her hand.

He looked down at their joined hands before glancing back up at her. "Just like you said, there are things about your pregnancy you intend to tell our baby when he or she gets older. There are things I'd want to tell them as well. More than anything, I want him or her to know I was here with you during that rough time. I want them to know I'm a father who cared and loved them from the very beginning. Since we won't be getting married, that's important to me. Will you give me the chance to do that, Carmen?"

* * *

Redford stared at her, taking in the way she nibbled on her bottom lip as she thought about his request. Although she was the one who'd suggested they talk, he figured she hadn't counted on the turn their discussion would take. More than likely she'd assumed that the moment he was told he could leave, he would do so and that would be the end of it. He could tell by the look in her eyes that she'd been surprised he wanted to stay. There was no way he could leave her like this.

He had stood outside the bathroom door and heard her. She might be getting used to all that throwing up, but he wasn't. He had done his research and knew if it continued or worsened, her condition could escalate into hyperemesis gravidarum. He didn't want that and figured she didn't either.

While waiting for an answer, he knew the one thing he should do was stop looking at her mouth. Otherwise, he would recall how it had tasted each time he'd kissed her that night, and the shape of her lips beneath his and how they were a perfect fit.

Redford forced his gaze to the bright yellow gown she was wearing. It was sleeveless and showed a pair of beautiful shoulders. He also noted the way the tops of her breasts were visible beneath the V-neckline. That's one thing he'd taken notice of since being here, her sexy gowns. Although they weren't anything too revealing, they looked sexy on her nonetheless.

Thinking it was best to tame the lust he felt humming through his veins, he lowered his gaze to her hand, which he was still holding. He suddenly noticed how it felt—smooth yet tense. He sensed vulnerability and had a feeling he was responsible for it. That night they'd spent together had been nothing but a one-night stand for him, but it had meant a lot more than that for her.

He raised his gaze from their hands to look into her eyes.

That's when he saw a multitude of emotions in their depths. He saw the vulnerability he had suspected, as well as uncertainty and fear. *Fear?* What was she afraid of? He stared deeper and saw what she was trying to hide. Desire.

He now understood her apprehension. She was concerned that if he hung around, she would let her guard down and something would develop between them. He had to assure her that wouldn't be happening. He broke the silence between them by saying, "Just so you know, Carmen, I made a decision to come here to see you even before I knew about the baby."

"Why?" Her voice conveyed her surprise.

"Because after that night I spent with you, I wasn't myself."

Her forehead bunched. "You weren't yourself how?"

He could feel the tension slowly easing from her hand. Satisfied with that, he released it to stand up. He paced, gathering his thoughts. It was important that she understood why the last thing she should do is fear him. If anything, he should fear her.

He stopped pacing and stood in front of her. "A lot happened between us that night that I hadn't counted on."

"I bet my pregnancy was one of them," she said.

He knew her statement was meant to shake off the awkwardness between them, to lighten the mood. "You're right. Your pregnancy was one of them because I honestly thought we'd used sufficient birth control."

He didn't say anything for a minute and then spoke again. "What I hadn't counted on, Carmen, was still thinking about you days and weeks later. Reliving that night in my mind and thinking it was the most perfect night I'd ever shared with a woman. So perfect that…"

She lifted a brow when he paused. "That what?"

"I haven't desired another woman since then."

Carmen stared at him. "You're kidding, right?"

He frowned upon hearing amusement in her voice and seeing her smile. He stared at her, his expression serious. She stared back and then the smile vanished. "You aren't kidding."

"No, I'm not kidding, and I don't appreciate it worth a damn." There was no reason to tell her he had dissected every second, minute, hour of their time together in order to determine what the hell had happened to him. Making love to her had literally blown his mind. He could truly say sex had never been that good with any other woman. On a scale of one to ten, with ten being totally great, he would give it a damn twenty for being undeniably exceptional. In the end, he figured it had to have been those multiple orgasms. He refused to believe such a thing was common. Okay…maybe doubles, but quadruples had to be outside the norm.

"Are you saying you haven't slept with another woman since me, Redford? And that you haven't desired one?" Although there was a blush tinting her cheeks, he didn't miss the sly smile around the corners of her lips that she was trying to keep from showing. Did knowing she was the last woman whose bed he had been in please her for some reason?

"That's exactly what I'm saying. However, I did research on the matter and discovered a way to cure my problem."

"Research?"

"Yes."

"And just what were the findings of your research?"

He was glad she asked. "Some of the top relationship experts all suggest we have the power of controlling our body and mind. I have to believe no one else has that control. That would be giving in to a weakness. Being strong and not vulnerable is the key. In order to accomplish that, I would have needed to take you out on a date."

"A date?"

"Yes. A date where we would have spent a nice evening together without ending up in bed again. I would have used my willpower to control my body's urges and not let them control me. I believe I could have done that."

She didn't say anything for a minute. "There's no way I would have gone out on a date with you, Redford."

Sloan and Leslie had said the same thing.

"Not even if you were the last man on earth," she added. "In fact, it had been my fondest desire to never see you again."

They'd said that, too. He shoved his hands into the pockets of his jeans. "The reason I told you all that, Carmen, is to clear the air between us. There's still a strong physical attraction between us, and we both know it. However, I want to assure you that you don't have to worry about me acting on it because I will never again let lust control me. I now have power over it."

She didn't say anything, and Redford hoped he'd reassured her. He wouldn't seduce her no matter how hot things got between them. What she might not realize was that even while she was under the weather, she was still sexy as hell and beautiful as sin. Lust was a powerful thing, but he intended to prove that his control was even more so.

"Okay."

He lifted a brow and stared at her. "Okay?"

"Yes, okay. Because when it comes to you, you don't have to worry about me acting on anything either. I've regained control of all my senses since that night, and I didn't have to research anything to come to a certain conclusion."

"What?" he asked.

"I was wrong. We were never soulmates and it was never meant for us to be together. I accept that." She was quiet and then when she spoke again, she said, "I understand you wanting our child to know you were a part of its life in the early stages, Redford, and I appreciate you for wanting that. Some men wouldn't. As long as you believe you'll be able to control your lust, like I know I will control mine, then I have no problem letting you stay. However, I don't think we should think about anything long term. I suggest we take it a week at a time to see how things work out."

He intended to be around long term, but he'd go along with her suggestion. "I'll agree to that," he said, pulling his hands from his pockets. "Now, I'll get your dinner."

"Alright, and please let Leslie know I'd like to see her. I need to tell her of my decision."

He headed for the door. Before reaching it, he turned around and said, "Thanks, Carmen. You won't regret it."

When the door closed behind Redford, Carmen stared at it for a long moment. Although she might not have any regrets, there was a chance he might. For her, this connection between them had never been about lust but love. She shook her head at his assumption that he could research almost every single thing. Did he not know there were some things that couldn't be analyzed?

Then for him to admit that he hadn't had the desire to sleep with another woman was hard to believe, but she had seen the look in his eyes and knew he had been telling the truth. He hadn't seemed happy about it either.

And he was right that the sexual attraction between them was still hot, even in her less than attractive condition. That was proven wrong when he'd been holding her hand. And when their gazes had met, she had seen it. Intense desire. She had felt it. A longing she shouldn't be feeling.

A longing like the one they'd shared that night at the cottage in Westmoreland Country. The night that had produced the baby she was carrying.

Knowing Redford would be returning soon with dinner, she moved to sit on the love seat where the mobile table was still in place. She couldn't help but be amazed at all the stuff Redford had said, and couldn't wait to see if all his research would pay off.

She had accepted that she was not his soulmate. Yet, frustration was building inside of her because there was a part of her that refused to move on. Namely, her heart. As much as she wished otherwise, she was still very much in love with Redford St. James. However, he would be the last person to know that.

Maybe it was time she did her own research. Specifically, on how to stop loving a man who would never love her back.

Chapter Fifteen

Redford knocked on Carmen's bedroom door and then took a deep breath before slowly exhaling.

"Come in."

He entered and his gaze immediately went to her. Instead of being in bed, she was sitting on the love seat with her laptop and studying whatever was on the screen. She didn't even glance up at him.

The brightness from the light in the ceiling seemed to highlight her radiant features. He could imagine having a daughter who looked just like her.

She was wearing a different gown from the one she'd had on earlier. This one had a matching robe. He recalled she had mentioned when he'd brought her dinner that she would shower and go to bed early. Obviously, she had changed her mind about sleep and was on her laptop.

"I just wanted to see if you need anything else before I retire for the night."

She glanced over at him and smiled. "No, but you might want to key your phone number into my phone. That's how Leslie and I communicated with each other. It's over there on the nightstand. The passcode is my birthday."

He looked at her when he picked up the cell phone. "When is your birthday?"

"August the twenty-first."

"That's next month."

"Yes, and I'm hoping my health improves since Chandra and her family will be back from South Africa by then."

"Have you told your sister or parents that you're pregnant?" he asked, glancing over at her while adding his phone number to her contacts.

"No. My parents will be happy to have another grandchild, and my sister would love a niece or nephew."

He nodded. "Any reason you've put off telling them?" He happened to notice on her phone, when the call list popped up, that she talked to them daily.

She crinkled her nose and her brow furrowed before she said, "Yes, there is definitely a reason. There's no way I could tell them about my pregnancy without mentioning how sick I am. Chandra would shorten her trip and come home immediately if she knew. And my parents would come, too. The last thing I need is to have all of them here making me feel helpless. I'm hoping by the time I tell them I'll be back to my old self. Have you told your parents?" she asked him.

He placed her phone back down on the nightstand and eased into the chair beside her bed. He saw she had closed her laptop so he figured she was finished with it for tonight. "No, I haven't told them for basically the same reason you haven't told yours. This will be their first grandchild. A grandchild they never thought they would have."

He shook his head and chuckled. "It would not have mattered if your pregnancy had been smooth sailing the entire nine months. My mother would have shown up on your doorstep anyway. Just to get to know you, the future mother of her grandchild. Trust me, you would never have gotten rid of Lorelei St. James."

He watched her smile spread and couldn't help thinking for the umpteenth time just how kissable her lips looked. "What about your father?"

He chuckled again. "Dad would have waited for an official invitation. But not Mom."

"I have a feeling I'm really going to like her."

He had a feeling his mother would like Carmen as well. Already he knew there would be problems. He didn't know about her parents but he knew his would expect them to marry, which wouldn't be happening. "How will your parents handle the fact that we won't be getting married, Carmen?"

"They will handle it just fine. They stopped meddling in my and Chandra's lives when we left home for college. That's the one thing I've always appreciated about them. Besides, I will assure them I will be married when I have my second child."

Why was tension suddenly building in his body? There was no way he could be jealous of the thought of her marrying one day. Any man would appreciate a woman like her. Even him, if he was the marrying kind. But he wasn't. He figured the tension was the result of thinking that the man she would marry might assume that his child would be more important in their family dynamics than hers and Redford's.

All it took was for him to recall David Lattimer, a guy who went to college with him, Sloan and Tyler. David lived across the hall in their dorm and when they noticed he never went home during the holidays or school breaks, they'd inquired why. That's when he'd told them all the horror stories of the torment he'd endured with a stepfather while growing up.

Redford refused to let his child go through such a thing. He would demand custody of him or her before anything like that happened. There was no need to get Carmen upset by telling her that now. Besides, for all he knew, the guy she eventually married might be swell. If Redford thought that, then why was even more tension building inside of him?

"Can I get you anything before I leave, Carmen?"

Hadn't he asked her that already? Why was he asking again? And why had he suddenly become aware of her outfit when she stood? Because she'd been sitting down, he hadn't realized just how short the nightgown and robe were. The hem fell halfway down her thighs. The yellow silk robe seemed to hug every curve on her body and the color seemed to make her skin glow.

He wanted to call himself all kinds of names when lust invaded his thoughts. His gaze roamed all over her, and it took every ounce of willpower he could muster to hold back the desire permeating his body. Why did her legs look so sleek? The fit of the top of the gown did a good job exposing the shape of her breasts. She definitely looked too sexy for his peace of mind.

"No, there's nothing else I need," she said, padding over to the bed. He watched as she threw back the covers, and then, ignoring his presence, untied her robe and shrugged it off her shoulders to place at the foot of her bed. Then she eased into the bed. It suddenly occurred to him that this was the first time he'd seen a woman get into a bed without him.

When she was beneath the covers, she shifted to what he knew was her favorite position. Then she raised her head from the pillow to glance over at him. "Is something wrong?"

"What makes you think that?"

She gave him one of those "duh" looks before saying, "You're just standing there staring at me."

"Oh, sorry. I guess I was thinking that you don't look pregnant." That hadn't been what he'd been thinking; however, at the moment, that was the best answer he could come up with.

A smile touched her lips. She wouldn't smile so often if she knew what it did to him. "It's early yet. The baby is still small. No larger than a lemon at this point."

He chuckled. "Hard to believe something that small could cause so much trouble."

She chuckled as well. "Like I told you, I'm going to have a lot to tell our child when he or she gets older."

He nodded. "I'll let you get some rest now. Good night, Carmen."

He was headed toward the door when she called out to him. "Redford?"

He turned around. "Yes?"

"Could you close the curtains? I prefer not looking at the stars."

He paused to consider what she'd just said. He couldn't help but recall the night she'd not only looked at the stars but had also made a wish upon them. So had he. He also remembered her telling him how much she enjoyed staring at them while in bed. Was what happened the night they spent together the reason she preferred not looking at the stars now?

"Why not? It's a beautiful night," he decided to say.

She glanced out the window and then looked back at him. That's when he saw the pain in her eyes thanks to the moonlight peeking through that same window. Her voice was almost a whisper, "Like I said, I prefer not looking at them."

In a way, he had his answer. Crossing the room, he closed the curtains, bringing the room into total darkness. He moved to leave the room again as she said, "Thanks."

He didn't deserve her thanks because he now knew that, although not intentionally, he had hurt her. Both Sloan and Leslie had told him he had. Now he saw it for himself and his heart ached.

"Honestly, Leslie, you've only been gone two days and you're not giving me a moment's rest," Carmen said with a chuckle in her voice.

Yesterday her best friend had called around five times and from the look of it, she would beat that number today. "If you keep it up, Redford will assume you don't trust him to take care of me."

"Is he taking care of you?"

She paused in nibbling on the dry cereal she liked eating as a snack during the day. For some reason, it was a good feeling knowing she was being cared for by the father of her child. He might not love her, but he was doing his best to take care of them.

He prepared a delicious breakfast for her every morning, fixed a tasty sandwich for her at lunch, and then at dinner he always surprised her with some nutritious meal. She still loved his soups the best, but he'd even taken a shot at baking and prepared brownies for her last night when she'd said she had a sweet tooth.

She knew letting him stay here could result in emotional pain, but she liked knowing he was sleeping in the guest room beneath hers. Last night, he'd listened to her complain that she would be missing her pedicure appointment, so he'd seen her vain side. However, he hadn't seemed to mind. While she ate dinner, he'd been on his laptop. She figured he was researching something but hadn't bothered to ask what.

"Carmen, if you have to think about an answer, then that concerns me."

She had not intended to stay quiet for so long. A concerned Leslie could become a worrywart, and that's the last thing she wanted. "No reason for concern, Leslie. Yes, Redford is taking good care of me and our little bun."

However, what she wouldn't tell Leslie was that sickness or no sickness, her hormones were kicking whenever he was around, which was all the time. The only reason he wasn't in the room with her now was because he'd wanted to give her and Leslie privacy.

He had come in after her lunch and nap to make sure she was on schedule with her medication. Then he had remained to watch a movie with her. Not once had he complained that it was a chick flick.

She thrown up three times today and no longer felt embarrassed that he saw her in such a way, and afterward he was always ready to assist her. The last time, she had finished brushing her teeth while standing at the vanity and happened to glance at the mirror while rinsing out her mouth. He'd been watching her. His brow had been furrowed in deep concentration and worry. When their gazes connected, she had felt hot all over. She'd broken eye contact with him to soak a face cloth in cool water for her face. He had come to her, covered her hand with his and said in a husky voice, "Here, let me do that."

She should not have been surprised at how painstakingly gentle he was. And when he had pulled her tenderly against him, she sighed into his chest while he held her close, telling her everything would be alright. Then, as if it had been the most natural thing for him to do, he had kissed her on the forehead. She was convinced she could still feel the warmth of that kiss on her skin.

"Well, if you're sure you are in good hands, Carmen..."

She of all people knew just how good Redford's hands were. "I'm sure," she said, bringing her thoughts back to the present. "Letting him stay here with me was a good decision. He's been telling me a lot about his family's history. That's good to know so I can pass it on to our child."

She and Leslie talked a little while longer before they ended their call. Whatever Redford was cooking smelled good. The aroma seeped into her bedroom without upsetting her stomach. She was glad of that. The visiting nurse had assured her that although she still threw up a lot, her condition hadn't gotten worse.

Carmen eased up in bed when she heard the knock on the door. "Come in."

The bedroom door opened and there he stood. Handsome as ever. Bigger than life. Sexier than any man should be. And then her heart pounded when the corners of Redford's mouth lifted in a smile. If she wasn't careful, that same smile would be her undoing.

"How do you feel, Carmen?"

There was something about how he said her name. He had an accent, sort of Midwestern. However, there was a noticeable difference whenever he or any of the Outlaws spoke. She thought their speech articulation was rather unique and she loved the sound of it.

"I feel fine."

He came into the room and slid into the chair by her bed. "Do you think that maybe your appointment with the doctor should be at her office instead of one of those laptop visits?"

She heard the concern in his voice and knew why. Yesterday hadn't been a good day for her. She'd been sick so many times. "I'll tell her about yesterday. If she wants to see me then I'll go in."

"And I'll take you."

"Thanks." She appreciated his offer. "The nurse said I'm holding my weight. I haven't lost any, thank goodness. In fact, I've gained a couple of pounds."

"I can't tell. Your stomach is still flat."

She wondered how he figured that. When had he seen her stomach? She then remembered that while throwing up profusely yesterday, he'd been on the bathroom floor beside her not only stroking her back but also gently rubbing her stomach.

"Whatever you're cooking smells good."

"It's a lemon pasta dish I came across."

"In your research," she asked, unable to fight back a smile.

He chuckled. "Yes, in my research. Are you ready for dinner?"

"Yes, I'm ready."

"I'll be back in a minute."

When he left, she released a deep sigh, wishing there was some way to avoid such a potent attraction to him whenever they were in the same room.

Easing out of bed, she moved to the love seat and the table. Although she had researched it, there wasn't much advice on how to stop loving a man who didn't love you. At this point she didn't care. She loved Redford, and maybe one day he would realize she was a woman who could heal his broken heart.

Chapter Sixteen

"You've gained weight and that's good, but after telling me about what happened earlier in the week, I want to see you. How about on Tuesday?"

Redford saw the worried look on Carmen's features. She must have felt his gaze because she looked at him with a forced smile before turning back to the doctor's face on her laptop screen. "Yes. What time do you want to see me?"

"I'd like to review your lab reports first. That means I'll need you to go to the lab before I see you here. They are in the same building as my office. I will make the appointment there for around eleven and will see you around one."

"Alright."

"And don't eat anything that morning," the doctor instructed.

Redford and Carmen sat side by side on the loveseat. When the virtual doctor visit ended, he tightened his arms around her. He could feel her tension. What stood out more than anything was the doctor saying she was concerned about the number of times Carmen had thrown up recently. Honestly, so was he, although he tried hard not to show it.

Things hadn't gone well for Carmen that morning. He had awakened to the sound of her feet rushing to the bathroom. By the time he had slipped into his pajama bottoms and rushed up the stairs, she'd been in her usual spot on the floor over the commode.

There she had stayed, longer than she had ever before. He

had been so concerned at one point that he'd thought about calling 9-1-1. When she'd finally finished, he had picked her up in his arms to help her over to the vanity, certain she was too weak to walk. He had wiped her face with a cool cloth before handing her a toothbrush and cup of mouthwash.

He had then carried her over to the love seat and eased down to sit with her in his lap. Once cuddled in his arms, she had drifted off to sleep. After a while, so had he. The sound of the phone ringing had awakened them. It had been Leslie checking to see how she was doing. Following Carmen's request, he hadn't mentioned anything to Leslie about her severe episode of morning sickness earlier.

"How do you feel now?" he asked.

"Okay, after such a rough morning. It's not even noon yet."

He nodded. "Hungry?"

She smiled. "Yes, a little."

As far as he was concerned, that was a good sign. The doctor had reiterated she should eat light meals but more of them. "What do you have a taste for?"

Her smiled widened a little and she said, "I might pay greatly for it later, but I have a taste for ice cream."

"What flavor?"

"My favorite is vanilla."

He chuckled. "So is mine."

Several minutes passed in silence while he cradled her in his arms, then he said, "Everything is going to be okay, Carmen. I know I have a lot of nerve saying such a thing when I'm not the one throwing up their guts every day, but I believe it."

She pulled slightly away to look at him. "She didn't deserve you, you know."

He lifted a brow. "Who?"

"Candy."

He wondered what had made her say that. As if she read his thoughts, she said, "You're such a nice guy."

"Thanks." He then asked, "You still want ice cream?"

"Sure," she said, snuggling back into his body. "But right now, I just want you to hold me, Redford. Whenever you do, I don't feel afraid about the baby. You help me believe it will be alright. That I will be alright."

"You both will. I'm going to make sure of it, Carmen."

"I believe you."

He doubted she knew how much her words meant. He'd never been a sound sleeper so even the littlest movement in her bedroom would get his attention. He knew whenever she got up to use the bathroom or was restless. Those nights when he knew she was getting a good night's sleep were the ones when his own mind would be calm. That's when he would lie in bed and remember his one night with her. Even now he could still say, without a doubt, it was the best lovemaking of his life, and he was still in awe as to what they had shared. The memories made his body simmer inside. Like what was happening now.

Without thinking about what he was doing, merely acting on instinct, he took her face in his hands to study it. Even while under the weather, she was beautiful. "I want a daughter who looks just like you, Carmen."

He could tell by the look in her eyes that his words had surprised her. Redford searched her eyes. Obviously, what he'd said had meant something to her, and he was glad. He couldn't lose track of the fact that she'd been through a lot, not only today but other days as well. Just for their baby.

"Thank you."

He was about to tell her she didn't have to thank him when something welled up inside of him. It was a longing he'd been fighting since seeing her again. A longing he'd convinced himself he had power to deny. However, he didn't want to deny it now. He wanted to act on it.

Unable to control his emotions any longer, he lowered his mouth to hers.

* * *

The moment Carmen felt the taste of Redford's tongue, memories consumed her and broke down every defense she had against him. Not only was she moaning, but she was returning his kiss with a greed that astounded her. The way he devoured her mouth bordered on scandalous, and she was right there with him.

Carmen recalled how, after their night together, she would have endless dreams about him. She still did, and in those dreams, he would always kiss her this way. With a greed and hunger that set every cell in her body on fire. Finally, he released her mouth and they both drew in a deep breath as he rested his forehead against hers.

He murmured against her lips. "I should not have done that, Carmen."

She didn't hesitate in responding. "I'm glad you did, Redford."

He seemed surprised by her response. "Why?"

She knew what he was asking. There was no reason not to be honest. "Because I enjoyed it, and after feeling lousy over the past weeks it was nice to engage in something I enjoy."

"And you enjoy kissing me?"

"Just as much as you enjoy kissing me." There was no point in him denying he enjoyed the kiss they'd just shared. She could tell he had.

He smiled at her. "You're right, Carmen, I enjoy kissing you. Probably, too much."

"I guess everyone has a weakness, Redford."

There was no doubt in her mind he would furiously deny he had a weakness of any kind, especially one pertaining to a woman. However, instead of denying it, he swiftly changed the subject. "Are you ready to see the doctor next week?"

His question forced her to think about what the visit meant. "Yes and no. Yes, because I'm hoping she will tell me that everything with the baby is fine. And no, because the vain side of me wishes I was more presentable."

His brow lifted as if taken aback by what she'd said. "More presentable how?"

She couldn't help but roll her eyes. "Look at me, Redford."

For a minute she wished she hadn't asked him to do that. The heat of his gaze seemed to touch every inch of her body. He then met her eyes. "I don't see anything that makes you not presentable."

Carmen figured she should take his words as a compliment but couldn't. Holding her hands in front of her, she said, "Although my nails are passable, my toes are a different matter. I missed my last two pedicure appointments."

"Oh, I see."

She figured he did see since she remembered having mentioned the issue before. He probably figured she was vain. Now it was her turn to change the subject. "Tell me about the resort you're thinking about building in Skagway." He had mentioned something about it yesterday, saying the city had finally decided to sell him all the land he needed.

"Now that the land deal is finalized, it will be full steam ahead."

They discussed the resort plans for a long while. Then, it wasn't long before she began feeling sleepy. Obviously, Redford had detected it. He stood with her in his arms, walked over to the bed and placed her in it. "Will you be alright for a while? I need to run out."

She felt herself nodding and then he leaned in and placed a kiss across her lips. "Be good while I'm gone."

Before sleep took over her mind, Carmen mumbled, "I will be good. But our baby might misbehave."

She dozed off with pleasant memories of Redford's kiss floating through her mind.

Chapter Seventeen

A few hours later Redford returned and knocked on Carmen's bedroom door.

"Come in."

Opening the door, he saw she was sitting up in bed wearing a gown he'd never seen before. That meant she'd had another bout of nausea while he was away. "Are you okay?"

She nodded and smiled. "I am now."

He couldn't help but smile back. "Does that mean our child acted up while I was gone?"

She chuckled. "Afraid so."

"Well, hopefully, this will cheer you up," he said, producing the bag he'd been holding behind his back. He handed it to her.

When she glanced in the bag and back at him, her face lit up. "Ice cream!"

He grinned at the excitement in her voice. "Yes, and your favorite flavor."

She eyed him suspiciously. "Does that mean we have to share?"

He laughed. "Not at all. Besides, I'll be busy while you're eating the ice cream."

"Busy doing what?" she asked, not wasting any time digging the spoon out of the bag along with the pint of ice cream.

"I will be performing my first pedicure."

"Pedicure? Are you serious?"

"Yes." He saw the concern on her face and smiled. "Relax. I did some research. I'll be back with everything."

He left and returned within a few minutes with a box labeled "At Home Pedicure." She had gotten out of bed and was sitting on the love seat. He went into her bathroom to get a towel and a few cotton balls he'd seen in a container on her vanity.

In no time at all, he had removed everything from the box and filled the basin with water. He then added everything needed, including the oil Leslie had shared was Carmen's favorite fragrance. Kneeling in front of her, he lifted her feet and placed them in the water. The sweet scent of the oil wafted between them and filled him with a sense of pride that he was doing this for her. It was the first pedicure he'd ever done for a woman. But then, Carmen was becoming his first for a number of things.

Redford thought she had pretty feet; and honestly, he didn't see anything wrong with her toes. However, if she thought there was, he wasn't about to argue. He wanted to take care of her.

And he did.

Taking his time, he went through the process, step-by-step, as outlined in his research. He appreciated that Carmen trusted him to do this. She calmly ate her ice cream while listening to the music he had turned on: Beethoven. He grinned when he noticed her toes moving to the music.

An hour or so later, he leaned back on his haunches pleased with what he'd done. The polish matched her nails; again, thanks to Leslie who knew her favorite color.

He looked at her. She had finished her ice cream. "So, what do you think, Carmen Golan?"

Carmen glanced down at her toes, and a huge smile curved her lips. She seemed happy. He knew, at that moment, that if given the chance, he would keep that smile on her face forever.

"You did a great job, Redford. I'm beginning to think you might be in the wrong line of work."

He chuckled. "Thanks, but I'd rather stick to resort development." He stood. "There's a casserole dish that's ready for the oven." He glanced back down at her feet. "Let your toes dry before moving around."

"Alright and thanks."

"You're welcome."

Redford was halfway down the stairs when his cell phone rang. Recognizing the ring tone, he pulled it out of his back pocket. "Yes, Sloan?"

"What's this I hear about you giving a woman a pedicure?"

He grinned as he thought about the past hour or so. But he hadn't given just any woman a pedicure. He'd given one to the woman who would be the mother of his child. He'd felt like pampering her, and he had. She deserved it, and he intended to see that she had plenty more pampering while he was here.

"What of it?"

"Nothing, I guess."

Upon reaching the living room, he leaned against the bookcase. "Out with it, Sloan."

"Out with what?"

"The reason you called. I'm sure Leslie told you."

"Yes, she told me of your plans. Doing something like that just doesn't sound like you."

Redford rubbed his hand down his face. "In case you've missed it, a number of things I've been doing lately that involve Carmen don't sound like me. The main one is getting her pregnant."

"Mistakes happen to the best of us."

The last thing he wanted to tell Sloan was that he honestly didn't think Carmen getting pregnant was a mistake. Although it certainly hadn't been intentional, why was he beginning to think it was meant to happen? Like fate, which was something he normally didn't believe in. Therefore, he decided not to respond.

Wisely, he chose to change the subject. "How's my god-daughter?" He smiled knowing that question would work each and every time. Sloan loved giving Cassidy updates.

As Sloan went on about his daughter's latest escapades, Redford's mind drifted back to Carmen's smile. Since she wasn't someone who could easily mask her feelings, he knew she was genuinely appreciative of the pedicure and pleased with what he'd done.

Sloan's voice trailed off and Redford knew it was time to end the call before his best friend chimed back in on the pedicure. "Time for me to prepare dinner, Sloan. I'll talk with you later."

Redford clicked off the phone and headed into the kitchen.

Carmen couldn't help staring down at her toes yet again. Just the thought of Redford giving her a pedicure still had her in awe, and he'd done a good job. His hands on her legs had kept sensual sensations flowing within her. She was certain he'd been aware of them, which was probably why he'd spent such a long time massaging her legs.

Each time he'd touched her feet, ankles or legs, her heart beat wildly. One time, even her breathing became erratic. When that happened, he'd looked up at her and their gazes locked, and she could see the heat, need and hunger reflected in his eyes.

Using her hands, she fanned herself. Honestly? How could her body even think of sex while in this condition? Easily, when she had a drop-dead gorgeous man living under her roof. A man who had no problem touching her and kissing her.

Carmen dragged in a deep breath. The last thing she needed were reckless impulses.

Less than an hour later, Redford was back with dinner that

he shared with her while they watched a movie. They ended up watching two. It was during the second movie that she felt nauseated again, but the moment quickly passed. She hoped that was a good sign and shared those hopes with Redford.

"I hope so, too. I can't wait to hear what your doctor says next week," he said.

Carmen was nervous about the doctor's visit but refused to share those anxieties with him. She had to believe everything would be alright, especially since the morning sickness seemed less severe than it had been even a few days before.

Yet that seemed to pose another sort of challenge. With less bouts of nausea, she noticed Redford more and more. Not only did she notice him, but she also desired him. And when he did all those nice things for her, she fell deeper in love.

Later that night, after telling her goodnight, Redford brushed a kiss across her lips. A short while later, she was tossing and turning, unable to sleep. She slid out of bed, went to the window and pushed back the curtains to look at the stars. She didn't want to remember the night she'd made a wish upon them, but she did.

She turned when she heard a knock at her door. "Come in."

Redford strode in with his pj's riding low on his hips and concern etched on his face. "Are you okay, Carmen? I heard you moving around."

She recalled him saying how sleeping below her bedroom meant he could hear all the sounds above him. "I'm fine. I just couldn't sleep."

"Feeling nauseated again?"

"No. Just restless."

"Oh."

He came to stand beside her at the window. Her attention was no longer on the stars but on him. He was shirtless, and she recalled another time when she'd seen him wearing nothing at all.

That had been the first time she'd seen a man strip off his clothes. She'd watched him from the bed, wide-eyed, as he removed every single stitch. When she'd seen his naked body, she couldn't get over just how well-endowed he was. There hadn't been an inch she hadn't found impressive. Why was she remembering that now, and why could she feel heat radiating from his body to hers?

"The stars are pretty tonight, aren't they?"

Stars were the last thing she wanted to discuss. That's how that night had started. Her believing in the stars. "Yes, they're pretty."

She made a move to turn from the window when he touched her arm. The connection was so hot, she almost jerked away.

"I was restless tonight too," he said.

"You were? Why?"

"I was thinking about you and the kiss we shared earlier."

There was no way she would admit the reason she'd been restless was because she had been thinking not only of him and that kiss, but that night when their child had been conceived. "What about me and the kiss?"

"I was thinking how good it was and how delicious you tasted."

She nibbled on her bottom lip. Did he have to be so direct with his answers? His words stimulated her hormones. Something she didn't need. "Why would you be thinking about that at this hour?"

He smiled at her. "I will admit that since our night together, I think of you at all hours of the night."

This was the first time they had talked about that night. They had only discussed the results, namely her pregnancy. He'd even told her how that night had left him unable to desire another woman. But as of yet, they hadn't talked about how making love with her had done that to him. Something so unprecedented. She doubted he would bring it up, so maybe she should force him to do so.

"Tell me about that night, Redford."

He didn't respond immediately, and she thought maybe he hadn't heard her request. He proved her wrong when he asked, "What do you want to know about that night?"

"Everything. I'm sure you're aware that was my first time with a man."

He looked out at the stars and then back at her. "I know. At least it didn't take me long to find out. You're in your thirties. What had you been waiting on?"

Deciding to be honest, she said, "I thought I was waiting on you."

"Sorry I disappointed you."

"You didn't. As far as the lovemaking went, you were worth the wait." She allowed a shy smile to touch her lips when she added, "It was definitely better than anything I'd read in my romance novels."

"Is that a fact?" he asked. She didn't miss the arrogant smile that quirked the corners of his lips. Typical man.

At the risk of stroking his ego anymore, she said, "Yes, that's a fact. But then there was nothing I had to compare it to other than those novels. For all I know, multiple orgasms might be common."

He wrapped his arms around her shoulders and looked at the stars again before saying, "They aren't."

"Oh."

He didn't say anything for a minute. "There was a lot I could have compared it to, Carmen, considering my reputation with women. However, I must say, you rocked my world that night. I hadn't expected..."

When he didn't finish, she refused to let him stop now. "You hadn't expected what?"

He turned slightly and stared down at her. "So much passion from someone so inexperienced."

She honestly didn't know what to say to that, so she said nothing. Instead, her body reacted to the way he was looking at her. It was as if he wanted to deliberately stir that passion he was talking about. It didn't help matters that he had what she thought was a beautiful chest.

He lowered his head toward her, and she lifted hers to him. When their lips touched, like before, heat flared into flame. And when he captured her tongue with his, she didn't think it was possible for more passion to be generated than before. Yet it was, when he deepened the kiss and sucked on her tongue.

That prompted salacious thoughts to enter her mind. She loved all the feelings his tongue invoked. His warm chest against her robe offered no barrier to the heat, and when she felt the hardness of him pressed against her middle, it took everything she had to keep her knees from buckling. He must have sensed it; he swooped her up into his arms and carried her over to the bed.

She was tempted to ask him to join her there but couldn't. If they ever made love again, he had to be willing. When and if that day came, she would be willing, as well. There was no way she could not be with all the love flowing in her heart for him.

After placing her on the middle of the bed, he leaned down and brushed a kiss across her lips again before whispering, "Good night, Carmen."

"Good night, Redford."

She then watched him leave her bedroom.

Chapter Eighteen

"**I**'m ready, Redford."

He turned at the sound of Carmen's voice. "Wow," he mumbled, studying her. He'd only seen her in nightgowns lately and now seeing her dressed in a pair of slacks and a fashionable blouse made him even more aware of why he'd been attracted to her from the first.

Redford fought back the urge to cross the room and take her into his arms. Instead, he stood there and allowed the scent and beauty of her to ram through his senses. He noticed her braid was gone. In its place were thick brown tresses flowing around her shoulders.

"Well, how do I look?" she asked, probably because of the way he was staring at her.

"Beautiful." And he meant it. Finally crossing the room to her, he leaned in and lightly brushed his lips against hers. Their kisses were one area where he fought to maintain control. He enjoyed kissing her, and from her own admission she enjoyed kissing him. However, he knew kissing could lead to other things if they weren't careful.

She smiled. "And I think you look handsome."

He chuckled. "Thanks."

He'd decided to wear a pair of dark slacks and a light blue button-down shirt. He'd never accompanied a woman to a doctor's appointment before and didn't know what to expect.

However, what he did know was that he wanted to be there for Carmen and their baby. Like he'd told her a number of times over the past few days, her pregnancy was something he wanted them to share together.

Moments later, he ushered her out to the private car he'd ordered. Once they got into the backseat and the driver closed the door, Redford placed his arm around Carmen's shoulder. "All things considered, this is a nice town."

She smiled. "I take it you don't visit here often."

"No. The only other times I've been here were with Sloan whenever he visited Jess."

It didn't take long to reach the medical complex where both the lab and doctor's office were located. The staff was friendly and efficient, and he appreciated they didn't wait long to be seen. In trying to keep Carmen relaxed, he fought hard to keep himself calm as well. He refused to think something wasn't right with the baby; it was normal procedure for her doctor to order lab work before seeing her.

His anxiety grew, though, when the doctor was an hour late. Of course, he didn't voice his concerns to Carmen. Had the doctor found something wrong with her lab work? He was glad when a medical assistant finally entered the examination room and said the doctor had gotten delayed because she'd been called away to deliver a baby.

When the doctor finally arrived, she went straight to discussing Carmen's lab reports. Redford was relieved to find there was nothing concerning in the labs, and he could tell Carmen was relieved too. It seemed that even with the nausea, everything was in the expected range. She stressed that Carmen wasn't out of the woods yet, but that her condition was definitely improving. Hopefully, over the next few weeks the nausea would be less severe. That was good news to hear.

"In the meantime," the doctor said, closing Carmen's chart, "I want you out of the house more, even if you have to carry a barf bag around with you. I suggest you take walks in the morning and afternoon, breathe in some fresh air. You can even go bicycling. The only thing I would not suggest yet is horseback riding." The doctor then gave them a cheeky grin when she added, "And in case you had stopped engaging in sexual activities, there's no harm in resuming them now."

Redford refused to look at Carmen but figured she was blushing. So was he. When had the subject of sex ever made him blush? Obviously, the doctor assumed that because they were here together they were in a solid relationship. Neither he nor Carmen corrected her assumption.

The doctor then told them something Redford hadn't been prepared for. "I want to listen to the baby's heartbeat."

While listening, he held tight to Carmen's hand and wiped tears from her eyes. He knew this moment was just as special to her as it was to him. He would never forget the experience. The gentle, steady, strong beats made him realize the significance of the life he and Carmen had created. He was convinced he had fallen in love with their child the moment he'd learned of her pregnancy. But listening to the heartbeats made him fall in love with their baby even more. It was a moment he'd honestly thought he would never share with a woman. Together they would one day tell their little bun about it.

"It's too early for me to reveal the sex of the baby today, but I'll be able to do so during your next visit if either of you are interested," the doctor said, smiling.

Redford met Carmen's eyes, and as if he could read her thoughts, he said, "We'd rather it be a surprise."

The doctor nodded and entered their request into her records. Moments later, after Carmen had dressed, she wrapped her arms around him and they held each other. A profound feeling of happiness washed over him, and he touched his lips to her forehead. She snuggled closer to him. When she buried her face in his chest, he knew she was crying. He felt his composure slipping.

Leaning in, he whispered words he hoped comforted her. He told her that he knew she would be a great mother to their child, and he couldn't think of any other woman he would want to share parenthood with.

She raised her tear-stained face and thanked him and then she leaned up on tiptoes to place a kiss on his lips. Everything about that moment felt right. She was the center of his thoughts and his feelings as he deepened the kiss. When he finally released her mouth, he continued to hold her close. He needed to share this moment with her.

He needed her.

When had he ever needed a woman other than sexually? Emotions he'd never felt before seeped into him, and he wasn't sure how to handle them.

He decided right then that he *wouldn't* handle them. He would just let things take their course. The most important thing was that he had heard his child's heartbeat. For a moment, the sound had seemed perfectly in sync with his own.

Carmen leaned back to look up at him and gave him a bright smile. He doubted she had any idea what that smile did to him. How it made him feel. "Ready to go, Dad-to-be?" she asked.

A huge grin spread across his face. He liked the sound of that. "Yes, Mom-to-be. I'm ready."

He took her hand in his and they left the examination room.

"Wow! You actually heard the baby's heartbeat. That's wonderful, Carmen," Leslie said in an excited voice.

"Redford and I thought so, too." She then told Leslie everything else the doctor had said, including the part about encouraging her to engage in more outside activities. "I'm glad I'm able to do more than be confined to a bed now. I'm more than ready to start going on those walks."

"Just don't overdo it."

She chuckled. "I won't. I doubt Redford will let me. Even now, he's downstairs in the kitchen trying out another new recipe for dinner."

"You like having him there, don't you?"

Carmen thought hard about Leslie's question before answering. "Yes. I really didn't think I would. I appreciate that at no time does he try to exert dominance. He lets me handle things, and when I can't, I know he's here for me and the baby. That's a good feeling."

"I know it can be. Sloan and I are surprised at how he's stepped into his role as your caretaker. Never in a thousand years would we have pictured him giving a woman a pedicure."

"And he did an awesome job."

"I know. I got the photos you sent over. Redford might be in the wrong business."

Carmen chuckled. "That's what I told him." She then got serious for a second as she told Leslie of the doctor's other suggestion. The one about them resuming sexual activities. "I wonder why she would think we would be in that kind of relationship."

"Honestly, Carmen, why wouldn't she think it? Redford was there with you today, and I'm sure the doctor noted how attentive he was to you. And I bet the two of you were transmitting strong sexual vibes. I doubt you and Redford realize how easy it is for others to pick up on it."

"You think that was it?"

"I'm sure it was." Leslie paused and then asked, "So are you and Redford going to take the doctor's advice and resume things?"

Carmen rolled her eyes. "We only slept together that one time, Leslie. There's nothing to resume."

"Are those your thoughts or Redford's?"

"They're both of ours."

"Does that mean you and Redford aren't sharing any more hot kisses? Like the ones you've been telling me about?"

Leslie's question made Carmen recall the scorcher of a kiss they had shared at the doctor's office. "I wouldn't say that."

"Then I wouldn't say making love is off the table. Kisses are known to lead to other things, so be prepared if they do."

"That's not possible. Redford won't let things get out of hand."

"He's a man. And according to him, he hasn't desired a woman since making love to you. He's probably all but climbing the walls about now."

Carmen arched a brow. "You think so?"

"Yes, and there's a way to find out for certain, if you're interested."

Was she? She sighed deeply when curiosity got the best of her. "Okay, tell me."

"It's simple. Seduce him."

Chapter Nineteen

Redford felt himself slipping into the deep throes of ecstasy. He was about to make love to Carmen, and he refused to accept that this was only a dream, one he staunchly refused to wake from. He eased into position above her, ready to slide in, anticipating…

Suddenly, he was awakened by movement in the room above his. Carmen was awake and pacing. Why? Was she restless again tonight? Was something medically wrong? The thought had him bolting out of bed, rushing from the guest room and up the stairs. Forcing his overstretched nerves under control, he knocked on her bedroom door.

"Come in."

He opened the door then stopped short. She stood in the middle of the room and, unlike last night, she wasn't wearing a robe. She wore a nightgown that looked even shorter than the one from last night.

He swallowed the deep lump in his throat before asking, "What's wrong, Carmen?"

She lifted a brow. "What makes you think something is wrong?"

He frowned. "I heard you moving around. Why aren't you in bed asleep? Are you restless again tonight?"

She shook her head. "No, I'm not restless."

He nodded and came farther into the room. The way the light from the hallway shone into her bedroom highlighted not only how short her gown was, but also the lack of undergarments beneath it. Why were there so many tempting curves on her body? Her hair flowed loosely around her shoulders. He recalled that when he'd left her tonight she had bound it back in a ponytail. The wild mass gave her an even sexier look. He'd offered to help her wash it and re-braid it tomorrow.

"If you're not restless tonight, then what's wrong?" he asked, coming to a stop in front of her. Was he imagining things or was she emitting heat? Why? Was she running a fever? Instinctively, he checked her forehead.

"What are you doing?" she asked.

"Checking your temperature. You feel a little hot."

"I'm not running a fever, Redford. At least not exactly."

He dropped his hands from her face to his side. Her words confused him. "Then what exactly?"

She began nibbling on her bottom lip, and he detected she was nervous. "What's wrong, Carmen? What's bothering you at this hour? You can tell me anything. Remember, we're in this together."

He watched her draw in a deep breath, and then as if she'd made up her mind about something, she said, "I've never been into game-playing and want to be completely honest with you about something."

This sounded serious. "Okay. What?"

She paused. "I knew if you heard me moving around up here that you would come check on me. I apologize for that."

"You don't have to apologize."

She looked at him with a very serious expression in those beautiful, almond-shaped, light brown eyes. "But I do."

He tilted his head to look at her. "Why do you feel that way?"

Instead of answering, she nibbled on her bottom lip again. He doubted she knew how much of a turn-on that was. Reaching out, he took her hand and brought it to his lips to kiss her palm. He tried convincing himself he'd done it to calm her nervousness more than to placate his raging testosterone.

"Tell me, Carmen, why you feel that way," he said, releasing her hand.

He watched her draw in another deep breath before saying in a low voice, "I wanted you to come up here so I could seduce you."

He blinked, thinking he'd heard her wrong. "Seduce me?"

Now she was nervously wringing her hands together. "Yes."

Desire surged through him at the thought that she'd wanted to seduce him. "Why?"

She looked up at him. "Why what?"

"Why do you want to seduce me?"

She released what sounded to him like a disgusted sigh. "The doctor planted the seed in my head by thinking we're intimate."

He nodded. "A logical conclusion since you're having my baby."

She shrugged. "That's what Leslie said when I gave her a recap of my doctor's visit."

"I gather you changed your mind about this plan of seduction, then?" he asked, and thought his voice sounded husky, even to him.

"Pretty much. I can't be that manipulating, especially since I know how you feel."

He took her hand in his. She seemed to be a mass of nervous energy, flustered and apprehensive. "And how do I feel?" he asked.

"You said that we would never be intimate again. That you needed the willpower to make sure such a thing didn't happen. Knowing that, it wouldn't be right for me to try to seduce you."

He was convinced Carmen was way too honest for her own good. She had more integrity in her little pedicured toe than some people had in their entire body. In a way, he had known from the beginning that she was different, but initially, he had refused to let that mean anything. Like all the others, he had put up his "do-them-before-they-do-you" defense.

"So, you can go back to bed, Redford. I'm sorry to have disturbed you," she said, breaking into his thoughts.

Was she actually dismissing him now? Did she think he could walk away after everything she'd told him? He released her hand and tenderly caressed her cheek, loving the feel of her soft skin. And the degree of desire he saw in her eyes was something she couldn't hide, and he was so glad that she couldn't.

"What if I told you that I have no problem with you seducing me, Carmen?"

"Why? Because you know that I can't?"

"No, because I know that you can. And as far as my willpower, I've discovered over the past week, it's a lost cause where you are concerned."

Her eyes widened like saucers. "Why?"

"Because of the magnitude of what we shared that night. A night I still have strong memories of. Now I understand why our lovemaking made such a lasting impression on me."

"You do?" At his nod, she asked, "Why?"

"Because something that wonderful and magnificent was never meant to be a one and done."

Without giving her a chance to say anything, he leaned in and brushed a kiss across her lips and whispered, "So go ahead, Carmen. I give you permission to seduce the hell out of me."

A lump formed in Carmen's throat when she repeated Redford's words in her mind. Staring deeply into his eyes, she saw a longing in their dark depths and couldn't ignore the sense of satisfaction that fueled her own desire. When a smile spread across his lips, she felt emboldened to seduce him, although she'd never done any such thing before in her life.

"I wouldn't know where to start," she admitted.

"Start anywhere you like and do anything you want," was his response. The deep sound of his voice did things to her. Made her feel things that only he could make her feel. Suddenly, she felt very warm. The sliver of the moon through an opening in the curtain highlighted his features. His very handsome features.

His words floated back through her mind once again. They motivated her, made her want to do just what he'd suggested, to start anywhere and do anything. Just the thought sent a sensuous tremor through her.

So what was she waiting for?

Leaning up on tiptoes, she pressed her mouth to his. He returned the kiss but in no way did he try to dominate it, even though he was holding her solidly against him. Yet this kiss stirred something deep within her. Although he let her control every aspect of it, at the same time, in his own way, he assured her that he was all in.

In no time at all, the kiss ignited a craving within her, one she'd tried to contain since his arrival a week ago. There was a greediness unleashed within her that made every part of her ache with an urgency that was overtaking her senses.

If someone had told her after her last encounter with Redford that she would be allowing such a thing to occur again, she would have laughed. But here she was, back in his arms again and anticipating what she knew would happen next.

Nothing she and Redford shared had anything to do with love. At least not on his part. The chemistry between them was strong, unrelenting and nearly burning out of control.

She broke off the kiss to take a deep breath, filling her nostrils with his masculine scent and her eyes with all that was him. The last time they'd been together, he had undressed her. Tonight, she wanted to experience how it would be to undress him. He was already shirtless and his jeans hung low on his hips with the fastener unsnapped. Evidently, he had slipped into them quickly when he'd heard her move around up here.

"Need my help with anything?"

She met his gaze and saw the heat of desire in his eyes. Knowing he wanted this as much as she did had her melting inside. "No, I got this."

To prove her point, she took a step closer and immediately felt the hard throb of his erection against her middle. She tried not to react to it but couldn't help doing so. There was no way he didn't see genuine female appreciation in her eyes.

Reaching down, she began easing down his zipper. Then kneeling down in front of him, she tugged on his jeans. After a few tries, she finally eased them down his legs. Since he wasn't wearing any briefs, she could only assume he slept in the nude. The thought of such a thing was a total turn-on for her.

When he kicked the jeans aside, she stood back up to let her gaze roam over his naked body. She thought the same thing now that she had their one night together. He was a perfect specimen of a man. She couldn't help leaning in to brush a kiss across his lips and whispering, "We're halfway there."

As she took a step back, his dark eyes stared at her as she eased the nightgown from her shoulders to drop at her feet. Now it was his gaze roaming over her nakedness.

There was something hot about his look that made her move toward him. She reached up to wrap her arms around his neck and recaptured his mouth with hers. Kissing him in ways she'd spent several nights dreaming about.

Evidently, she was doing something right, she thought, when she felt his hands stroke her back. In no time at all she became lost in the sensuality that was the epitome of Redford St. James. Although he let her dominate the kiss, there was something about the way he was doing so that had her senses reeling. Not only was she trying to light his fire, he was also lighting hers.

She pulled away from the kiss and unwrapped her hands from around his neck. Then she began doing something she'd wanted to do the last time but hadn't been bold enough to try. Mainly to touch him. All over.

Her hands trailed over his chest and shoulders before moving lower to his hips and thighs. Feeling bolder still, she cupped that ultra-male, large part of him in her hand, amazed at the hardness of it. Just thinking how this particular part had been instrumental in making a baby with her elicited a sensual moan from deep within her throat.

His voice was husky, his breathing choppy and erratic, when he murmured, "I love the feel of you touching me, Carmen."

Carmen had news for him. She found this part of him fascinating and loved touching him, too. The more she did so, the more she wanted him. From the sounds he was making, he wanted her, too.

"Not sure how much more I can handle of you doing that," he said in a throaty voice while framing her face in his palms. She had no choice but to look at him instead of looking down at what her hands were doing.

He released her face when her fingertips began making circular motions around the tip of his manhood. She looked into his eyes when he inhaled sharply, as if his breath had been snatched from him. "What's wrong?" she asked, concerned, but not enough to stop what she was doing to him with her hands. The eyes staring back at her were so filled with heat, they nearly snatched her own breath away.

"You have no idea what you're doing to me, Carmen," he said through gritted teeth.

He was right, she didn't know, but she had a good idea. Feeling naughty, she leaned in and licked the side of his face and whispered, "What I want to know is whether I've seduced the hell out of you yet, Redford."

Reaching down, he gently cradled her face in his hand. "Yes, sweetheart. You have done that and more. Now it's my turn to seduce you, Carmen."

He swept her off her feet and into his arms.

Chapter Twenty

Redford placed Carmen on the bed. The air around him seemed inflamed with the scent of her. Why did she have to smell so good and taste so delicious?

He stared at the naked woman who'd seduced the hell out of him, like he'd suggested. He was a pro at seducing women and never had one seduce him. Until tonight he hadn't thought such a thing was possible. In the past, he'd not only called the shots but was also the one who decided when and where his game of seduction would be played out. However, tonight Carmen had taken that decision out of his hands and placed it into hers. Literally.

He tried fighting back his body's demands. If just her touch could do that to him, he didn't want to remember what being inside her body would do. He tried breaking eye contact with her but couldn't. Now he recalled his earlier assertion to Sloan that she had p-whipped him. However, he was beginning to think it was more than that. What? He wasn't sure.

Every muscle in his body desired her to the point where emotions he'd never had to deal with before crowded in on him, taking over his mind the same way they'd taken over his body. Could nearly three months of forced celibacy do that to him? Or…had he finally met his match? He didn't want to think that such a thing was possible, but at that moment his mind was too messed up, and he was filled with so much need for her that he couldn't think straight.

"Are you sure you're up to this?" he asked her, indicating his huge erection.

She gave a somewhat shy smile and said, "Just as long as I know it's *up* for me."

He couldn't help but grin at her play on words. "Trust me. It is. Only for you." Even more desire surged through him, yet in consideration of her health, he had to make sure he wasn't being an insensitive ass. "And you're sure you're okay, healthwise?"

She eased up on her haunches and his gaze followed the movement. "I am, so don't try to back out now, Redford."

"The only thing that can stop me at this point is you telling me to do so."

"And I won't do that. I want you too much."

Her words slipped him into the sensual world that was Carmen Golan. A world he had been part of once and hadn't been the same since. More than anything, he wanted to see if all those orgasms were a fluke or common for them.

He moved toward the bed and she leaned in to meet him. Drawing her against him, he captured her mouth with a need he felt not only in his erection but in his entire body. His hands began stroking her all over, her bare skin felt hot beneath his fingertips. He specifically liked tracing a path over the smoothness of her shoulders. From the sounds she made, he knew she was enjoying his touch…just like he'd enjoyed hers earlier.

His tongue greedily explored her mouth. When he finally got a mind to end the kiss, he pressed her back against the pillows. She stretched out her arms to him and that was an invitation he intended to accept. Before moving to her, his gaze roamed over every inch of her delectable curves, a pair of beautiful breasts with hardened nipples and a flat stomach. She'd told him the other day that she could detect a little protruding stomach, but as of yet, he could not. Then his gaze lowered still to the very essence of her—namely, her feminine folds. Just the sight of her made his erection throb and her scent made his tongue thicken in his mouth.

"What's taking you so long, Redford?" she asked in a voice filled with need. He switched his gaze to her face and smiled. A thick mass of hair was fanned out against the pillow.

"I just want to savor the moment. You are very beautiful, Carmen," he said, truthfully. "And, lying here like that makes you look delicious, too."

"Delicious?"

His smile widened. "Yes, delicious. Let me prove what I mean."

Moving closer, he pulled her forward and let his hands rest on a pair of firm breasts. Cupping them, he used the pads of his thumbs to gently finger the hardened nipples.

She moaned deeply in her throat. "You're driving me to madness, Redford."

"You haven't experienced anything yet, sweetheart." Then he leaned in and began devouring her breasts.

Seeing them and touching them had done something to him. He believed it had to do with knowing that one day these twin globes would be the source of his child's nourishment. Whatever the reason, at that moment he couldn't help but greedily feast on them himself. The more he tasted of her, the more he wanted.

Knowing he couldn't make love to her breasts forever, no matter how good they tasted, he finally pulled his mouth away and then lowered her to the pillows. He was a man who appreciated beauty, and he was convinced his gaze was taking in the most beautiful creature ever created.

"Now to taste another part of you," he said, reaching down to stroke her inner thigh. From her expression, he knew the same sensations stirring within him were also stirring within her. When his fingers slowly stroked her feminine folds, the skin there felt soft. He glanced up and saw heat lodged in her eyes and understood. She had confessed to having her dreams like he'd had his.

Knowing he couldn't delay tasting her any longer, he lifted her legs over his shoulders and put his mouth on her center. His tongue eased inside and found her hot and wet, like he'd remembered. Just the way he liked. First using the tip of his tongue to lap her up and then easing his tongue farther inside, he delved deeper, then retreated to capture her clit. He actually heard himself moan at the same exact time that she did.

Then he locked his mouth down and held tight to her thighs. He had almost three months to make up for, and he intended to do just that. His tongue thrust deeper and he felt the slight pain when her fingers grabbed hold of his shoulders, then the side of his face as if to keep him in place right there. She definitely didn't have to worry about him going anywhere. He was enjoying the delicious taste of her way too much.

He knew the exact moment her body was about to explode, and he was more than ready for the decadent appetizer he knew awaited him.

Carmen screamed as a multitude of spasms rushed through her body. She was convinced that never had an orgasm been as needed as this one. Her world spun out of control as every nerve ending inside her came alive and shattered her to a million pieces.

Through dazed eyes she saw the moment Redford pulled his mouth from her and lowered her legs from his shoulders. He then eased back to stare down at her while licking his lips. "You taste good, baby. Simply incredible."

He then leaned in and captured her lips. He kissed her with the same intensity he'd used just moments ago between her legs. Within seconds he had stirred her hunger again to the point where she felt hot blood racing through her veins.

Obviously, the chemistry flowing between them hadn't lessened any. If anything, it had heightened. The very thought of them making love again caused sensual stirrings to erupt in the pit of her stomach. As if he felt it, too, he moved in place over her.

He continued to stare down at her and she was captured by the beauty, as well as the heat, she saw in the depths of his dark eyes. Moments later, while he still held her gaze, she felt him ease inside of her and fill her completely. Was she imagining things or was his erection actually getting bigger, longer and harder inside of her?

Before she could dwell on that possibility, he began moving. Going in deep and then pulling out. Advancing and then retreating, over and over again, deliberately establishing a sensuous rhythm that had her groaning and moaning. He'd started out slowly, and then, as if he was seized by an overabundance of desire, he began thrusting harder and faster.

She released a series of moans, and he placed his mouth over hers. That's when their mouths picked up the same mating rhythm as the lower parts of their bodies. She gripped his shoulders as their tongues moved in a frenzy that had them moaning even more.

Regardless of what this was for him, for her it was displaying what she felt for him in a physical way because she would never speak it aloud. This wasn't just sex for her, it was love.

At the first sign of her orgasm, he pulled his mouth away and she released a scream. She hoped her neighbors couldn't hear her but a part of her didn't care if they did. When she opened her eyes to stare up at Redford, his gaze was both hot and predatory. That's when another orgasm hit and she saw it had hit him as well. Then another, and she sensed a need within them both that was taking over their bodies.

She widened her legs for him, wanting it all, and watched in hot fascination as he threw his head back and the cords in his neck tightened while the solid hardness of him continued to stretch her. The thought of him embedded so deeply within her had her moaning. She felt him all the way to the hilt.

When she screamed his name again, he screamed hers, detonating a barrage of passion that spread through them, seeming to ignite every cell in their bodies. When one orgasm ended and before one scream stopped, another orgasm was beginning to capture them in its clutches.

She could recognize his orgasm from the way he would slow his thrusts, only to start up again in a fast pace, then groaning her name. They kept coming, nearly nonstop. Then finally, as if he refused to collapse on top of her, he quickly shifted his body off her for them to face each other.

He kissed her with a tenderness she felt all through her body while cuddling her in his arms. Before dozing off, she recalled each and every time she felt the essence of him explode inside of her. The hot, molten liquid felt right. Like it belonged only to her, and from what he'd told her, she was the only woman with whom he'd shared himself to that degree. The last time hadn't been intentional. Tonight, it was as if he hadn't cared. Probably because she was already pregnant.

Regardless of the reason, it made her smile knowing she had again shared something with him no other woman had. Considering his history with women, that said a lot. But then that wasn't all. His baby was growing inside of her. Their baby. She cuddled closer to Redford and breathed her happiness into his chest.

She might not have his love, but she would always have a part of him they would share forever.

The sound of Carmen in the bathroom brought Redford awake. He was lying flat on his back in her bed. And it was morning. Memories of their night together rushed through him, lighting his body with a fire that only Carmen could ignite. That had been proven over and over during the night.

He'd been concerned about exhausting her in her delicate condition, but she dismissed his worry and proceeded to show him that the depth of her need for him was just as great as his had been for her. After pleasuring each other time and time again, they had finally succumbed to a peaceful sleep.

He glanced at the clock and saw it was a little past seven in the morning. The sound of her in the bathroom immediately caught his attention again. That's when he realized she was enduring a bout of morning sickness.

Rushing from the bed, he opened the bathroom door and immediately found her on the floor in front of the commode. Crouching down beside her, he pulled her hair back from her face and then began gently stroking her back, whispering calming and what he hoped were comforting words to her. When she finished, he lifted her to stand in front of the vanity while she brushed her teeth, rinsed her mouth and wiped her face with a cool cloth.

"I didn't want to wake you," she said, turning to ease into his arms.

"You should have," he said, softly, placing a kiss across her lips. "We're in this together, remember."

She nodded. "I need to take a shower."

"Okay."

Moving away from her, he started the water. She removed her robe to reveal her nakedness, and he was glad she wasn't showing any signs of morning-after shyness or regret. Before stepping into the shower, she glanced over her shoulder, smiled and asked, "Would you like to join me, Redford?"

It was early, yet it seemed the desire in her gaze was just as potent as what she probably saw in his. "Most definitely, sweetheart."

Typically, he didn't use terms of endearment with women. However, he'd used a number of them with her last night. For some reason, doing so had come naturally for him. "Besides, I promised to wash your hair today," he added.

They showered together, tenderly washing each other's bodies before he began washing her hair. Then they made love in the shower, a novelty for both of them.

After their shower ended, he and Carmen toweled each other dry before he re-braided her hair the way he'd watched Leslie do for her one day and thought he'd done a decent job. He then suggested they go for a walk after breakfast. It was a beautiful day. Instead of walking the neighborhood again, he ordered a car to take them to the National Harbor. They walked at a steady pace along the Potomac River and even visited several shops along the way. Afterward, they returned to her home in time for him to prepare lunch.

Carmen got sick later that day. Considering that was a reduction in the number of times, he thought it was a good sign. She thought so, too. Instead of going upstairs and taking a nap when they returned, she hung out down in the kitchen and kept him company while he prepared dinner. He enjoyed hearing about the classes she taught and how the current bill in the senate was vital for the country's economy.

Neither said anything about the night before. However, the sharing of smiles, less than innocent touches and stolen kisses whenever they felt like it, spoke of a heightened level of intimacy between them.

Nothing was said about sleeping arrangements but that night they took another shower together. When he joined her in bed, it seemed like the most natural place to be. All he'd intended to do was hold her in his arms; however, she had other ideas.

"What do you think you're doing?" he asked when she slid from his arms and placed her body over his.

She smiled down at him. "Feeling naughty."

He chuckled. "Weren't you naughty enough last night?"

"No."

And after that single word, she lowered her mouth to his. He didn't hesitate returning her kiss.

Chapter Twenty-One

The following weeks seemed to fly by. Carmen's morning sickness wasn't as severe as it had been. During her most recent doctor's visit, she was told her body was showing increased signs of improvement and there was a chance the nausea would be gone altogether in another week or two.

It was.

Carmen knew that meant it was only a matter of time until Redford would be leaving. Her next appointment with the doctor was on Friday, and she saw no reason why the doctor would not give her a clean bill of health and tell them her pregnancy was no longer at risk.

She figured Redford thought the same thing. Just that morning she had overheard him communicating with his management team that chances were, he would be returning to the office within a week. She wanted to believe he hadn't sounded all that excited about leaving, but a part of her knew she'd probably just imagined it.

They still shared a bed every night and woke up in each other's arms every morning. She'd tried not to get used to having him there, but he had become a monumental part of her life. There was no doubt in her mind she would miss him something fierce when he was gone. The time she had spent with Redford, and the way he had taken such good care of her, was something she would forever appreciate and something she would never forget.

She had gotten to know him as someone other than the father of her baby. He was a person she could talk to about anything, and he was someone who was full of information on any given topic. For those topics he wasn't sure about, he wasted no time in doing the research. In addition to enjoying their conversations, she looked forward to the times they lay cuddled up together watching movies.

Over the past month they had formed a special relationship, and the thought that it would soon end made her heart ache. She knew the only way to prepare for his departure was to start withdrawing. That way the pain of him leaving wouldn't cut so deep.

That resolution was on her mind later that night while she lay in his arms after they'd made love. Having him in bed with her whenever the sexual need struck definitely had its benefits. There was never a time he didn't pleasure her immensely. He'd been her first, and she was certain he had ruined her for any other man. In a way, that wasn't good.

But still, she couldn't regret the time they had spent together. Her only regret was in knowing their days together were numbered and it was time to start protecting her heart. Redford didn't love her; he would never love her. That was a reality it was time for her to accept, no matter how good things were between them now.

Redford awoke with a start. Glancing over at Carmen, he saw she was still sleeping snugly in his arms with their limbs entwined. Recently, he'd begun noticing changes in her, and it was more than the little pudge he saw in her stomach or how her nipples had gotten darker. He'd also noticed she had begun withdrawing from him.

He had detected it a few nights ago. Although they still made love with abandon, with a yearning and intensity that took his breath away, he could tell their relationship was changing. He couldn't help wondering if now that she felt better that meant she was ready for him to leave.

Honestly, there wasn't a reason to hang around any longer since her doctor had stated during her last visit that she was out of danger. From here on out, all signs indicated she should have a rather normal pregnancy. Of course, they'd been glad to hear that, but he'd gotten used to taking care of her, of being here with her.

He'd contacted his office one morning to tell them he would be back in a week and before that day had ended he'd called them back and told them to disregard his earlier call. He wasn't sure exactly when he'd be back, mainly because he wasn't ready to leave.

If anyone had told him weeks ago that he would have this frame of mind, he would not have believed them. The past weeks with Carmen had meant everything to him, and thanks to her he'd been able to face a lot about himself. He now realized that episode with Candy had affected him more than he'd known.

It had taken Carmen to show him that there were women who could be trusted completely. Women who didn't have any deceitful bones in their bodies. Women worth risking his heart for.

So many had tried convincing him of that—Sloan, Tyler, his parents and others—but he had refused to believe them. It had taken Carmen's pregnancy to show him another side of a relationship, other than a purely sexual one.

He now knew he had fallen in love with her. Although he wasn't sure exactly when it happened, it had happened. However, thanks to his earlier actions of treating her like all those other women he'd been involved with, she would never love him again. He felt a painful ache in the pit of his stomach in accepting that.

At least he had his memories of the days they would wake

up together, shower together, go walking together, prepare meals together and go to bed together. The one thing they hadn't talked about was raising their child together as a unified family. Where they lived in the same house in a loving and committed relationship. Namely, marriage.

Maybe it was time they talked about that possibility, because he knew without a shadow of a doubt that he adored her. Every part of her that she had shared with him over the past month or so. He had fallen in love with her and had fallen hard.

She had been right from the beginning. They were soulmates, and it had taken her getting pregnant for him to accept that. He couldn't imagine any other woman in his life. Carmen was the one woman he refused to live without. However, the big challenge would be convincing her of that.

He would make his first attempt to do so tonight when they made love.

Carmen glanced up when Redford entered her bedroom. Tonight, he had surprised her with a candlelight dinner. It had been beautiful and romantic; however, she would have appreciated his efforts a lot more if she hadn't known it was his way of letting her know he was leaving. She could barely enjoy the delicious dinner he had prepared because she was waiting for him to tell her he was going back to Alaska. But he hadn't told her at dinner, so she could only assume he had decided to tell her later...which was now.

She watched him lean against the closed door staring at her. Her heart began pounding when he pulled off his shirt and tossed it in the chair and then proceeded to slip out of his jeans and briefs.

Carmen wondered if he intended to make love to her first before breaking the news he was leaving. There was no reason to think he would not return every once in a while to check on her and the baby, but still. She had gotten used to the time they'd spent together and had hoped...

What? That a man who'd stated more times than she could count that he would never fall in love with a woman would miraculously change his mind and do so? Why had she been kidding herself when she had vowed not to? Her only excuse was that things had been so good between them lately, and he'd honestly seemed to enjoy being here. But then, in the end, she had to face the fact that it had only been about the baby and the sex.

He strolled across the room to her. "I don't know why you bothered to put this on," he said, clasping the hem of her short night gown, removing it and tossing it across the room to join his clothes in the chair.

She no longer wore her hair braided and he glided his hands through it. "You're beautiful, do you know that?"

Forcing a smile to her lips, she said, "Only because you tell me." And he did so, often.

He smiled and then captured her mouth with his. She wanted this kiss; she needed this kiss. She would add it to all the other memories stored in her brain of the kisses and love-making they'd shared.

When he began walking her toward the bed, she decided to be the one in control tonight. When he tried easing her down on the bed, she shifted her body and eased him down on his back instead. His features showed his surprise seconds before she positioned her body over his. Widening her legs, she lowered her body to his erection, moaning when he assisted by lifting his hips off the bed for deeper penetration.

He was so powerfully male, and the feel of him embedded deep inside made her body begin to shiver. He gripped her hips when she began moving up and down, while he lifted his body to make each thrust even deeper.

"More, Carmen. More."

His guttural plea got to her, made her give him just what he wanted. More. Clutching his sides with her knees, she began riding him the way she'd learned to ride a horse years ago. She established a rhythm and he fell right in sync.

Over and over, she thrust down and he thrust up, and when she began flexing her inner muscles as if to drain everything out of him, he pulled her mouth down to his and took it with a hunger that made her moan again. Breaking off the kiss, she threw her head back as she continued to ride him to her heart's content. Making memories she would need when he left.

Suddenly, everything inside her exploded, seeming to rip her in two, and she noticed the same thing happening to him. They always came together and never knew when to stop.

"Carmen!"

"Redford!"

They screamed each other's names as orgasms ripped through them. Seemingly nonstop. And she knew that no matter what tomorrow brought for them, she would always have memories of tonight.

Chapter Twenty-Two

A short while later, Carmen was slumped down on Redford, unable to move after what he knew had been one hell of a love-making session. Somehow, he managed to raise his hand to stroke her back. He knew at that moment just what she meant to him.

"Carmen?"

She slowly raised her head to look down at him. "Yes?"

"There's something I need to tell you."

"There's something I need to tell you, too, Redford."

Deciding to let her go first, he asked, "What is it?"

"Since I'm doing better, there's no need for you to hang around here any longer."

Redford tried not to flinch at her words. "There's not?"

"No. I'm sure you want to get back to work, and I need to start writing that book. I got an extension on the deadline and figured if I get started on it right away, I'll be finished with it by the end of the year."

She shifted her body to lay beside him and added, "Besides, Chandra will be returning in a couple of weeks, and since she hasn't seen me most of the summer, I have a feeling she'll be paying me a visit."

He nodded. "Do you think she suspects something?"

"I doubt it. My family assumes I've been busy working on my book, which is why they haven't been calling a lot lately."

"I see." He really did. She wanted him gone before her family arrived. Why did the thought of that bother him?

"What did you have to tell me, Redford?"

There was no way he would say what he'd intended to say. Especially now that she'd made it clear she wanted him gone. In that case, he had no reason to stay any longer. "I was basically going to say the same thing," he lied. "Since you're doing a lot better now, my services are no longer needed here. It's time I go back to work. I've got that resort in Skagway to build, and you have that book to write."

"Right."

"I'll make arrangements with my pilot to come tomorrow."

"Okay." She leaned over and placed a kiss on his lips. "Thanks for everything, Redford. You were a big help, and I appreciate it."

"Don't mention it."

"At least we accomplished what we set out to do," she said, looking at him.

"What's that?"

"Bond. Although we don't love each other, we used the time together to bond for our baby's sake. That's what we wanted, right?"

He stared into her eyes, thinking yes, that's what they wanted, but in the end, he'd also gotten something he hadn't thought he wanted. A woman he would love for the rest of his life. "Yes, that's what we wanted."

"Time to go to sleep now," she suggested, resting her head in the cradle of his shoulder. He had gotten used to her sleeping that way beside him and knew in the coming nights he would miss it. He would miss her.

Redford was still awake, long after he'd detected from Carmen's even breathing that she had fallen asleep. Sleep might have come easy for her tonight, but it hadn't for him. He had a feeling during the coming nights, after he returned to Anchorage, he would lie awake and think of her. However, he'd never been a man who stayed where he wasn't wanted. Nor would he remain with a woman who didn't want him, no matter how much he might want her. Or love her.

He exhaled a long breath knowing that he'd taken a chance on love for the second time in his life. This time he had truly learned his lesson.

"I think I got everything, but if you find something I'm leaving behind, let me know," Redford said.

"I will."

Carmen thought he wasn't wasting any time leaving. He had called for his jet that morning, prepared breakfast for her one last time and talked her into going for a walk around the neighborhood. When they'd returned, it hadn't taken him long to pack after receiving word a private car would be picking him up at one o'clock.

"Will it be okay if I call and check on you and our baby sometimes?"

"Yes, of course."

"Good."

Taking a step closer to her, he brushed her chin with the pad of his thumb. "Take care of yourself, Carmen, and our son or daughter," he said in that throaty voice. The one that could turn her on in an instant.

She forced a smile, fighting back the urge to tell him she didn't want him to go. "I will."

He leaned in and feathered kisses along her jaw. "I'm going to miss you."

Would he really? Didn't he understand she had to send him away? She couldn't go through life loving a man who would never love her. The longer he was here, the more she was bound to get attached to him, and she would be setting herself up for heartbreak of the worst kind. But still, she couldn't stop herself from saying, "I'm going to miss you, too."

Suddenly, he kissed her fully on the mouth, capturing her tongue in his as he stroked a need within her she didn't want to deny but knew that she must. It would be for the best. When their paths crossed again, hopefully by then she would be better equipped to deal with the only kind of relationship she and Redford would share.

Pulling her mouth away, she said, "If you don't get going your driver will wonder what the holdup is in here." She knew her words sounded unemotional, but she couldn't wane on her resolution. Nodding, he took a step back before turning and walking out the door.

Carmen moved to the window and fought tears as she watched Redford get into the private car. Not once did he look back, and that made the pain in her heart worse. Knowing she needed to leave, get out of the house for a while, she decided to go walking around the neighborhood.

She needed time to think and come to terms with what she'd done to protect her heart. She had sent away the man she loved.

"I just got word from air traffic control that takeoff is being delayed for about thirty minutes due to foreign dignitaries arriving in this air space, Mr. St. James," the pilot said over the intercom.

"Thanks, Todd." Unfastening his seatbelt, Redford stood and stretched his body before heading for the minibar. His phone rang and the special ringtone indicated it was Sloan.

He clicked it on. "Yes, Sloan?"

"I heard that you're returning to Alaska."

Redford selected a bottle of bourbon from the rack. "Any reason I shouldn't? Carmen is better now."

"Unless you lied to me yesterday when you admitted to being in love with her, I can think of a number of reasons why you shouldn't be leaving. Did you tell her how you felt about her?"

A part of him wished he hadn't confessed his feelings about Carmen to Sloan. "No, I didn't tell her. She didn't give me the chance. She said there was no reason for me to stay, and she asked me to leave."

"I still think you should have let her know how you feel, Redford."

"Evidently, you didn't hear what I said, Sloan. She all but asked me to leave."

"Did she ask you to leave or suggest that you leave?"

Redford rolled his eyes. "What difference does it makes?"

"A big difference since the two are not the same. Do I need to remind you that Carmen thought she was your soulmate and you broke her heart when she discovered that she wasn't? I suspect she's trying to protect herself from further heartbreak since you haven't told her that you have fallen in love with her. All I'm saying is that miscommunication can destroy a relationship. Trust me, I know. You remember what happened to me and Leslie for those ten years."

Yes, Redford thought. He remembered. He and Tyler had tried a number of times to get Sloan to go to Leslie and straighten things out, but he had refused to do so. "I don't think confessing how I feel to her is a good thing now."

"Would it ever have been a good time for you?"

Redford frowned. "What does that mean?"

"You've been protecting your heart for years. Maybe it's time to let go."

Redford released a deep breath. "I had let go. In fact, I had intended to tell Carmen last night. But she suggested I leave before I had a chance to do so."

"You should have done so anyway. I think you're making a mistake by not sharing your true feelings with her. And knowing Carmen like I do, I suspect she's doing something else, too."

"Something else like what?" he asked.

"Giving you an out. Maybe the reason she said you should leave was so you wouldn't feel bad about leaving her when you did so."

Redford hadn't thought of that possibility. "I hadn't given Carmen any reason to think I was leaving or that I wanted to leave." Had he?

"Well, I still think you're making a mistake. Safe travels back to Alaska, Redford."

"Thanks."

After disconnecting the call, he again racked his brain. Had he given Carmen any reason to think he had wanted to leave? He then recalled the phone conversation with his vice president yesterday morning while Carmen had been in the shower. Had she overheard it and assumed those were his plans? He'd discovered showers had ears. Leslie had assumed Sloan had been in the shower when he'd overheard her conversation with Carmen about her pregnancy.

"Mr. St. James, I just got notification from the tower," his pilot broke into his thoughts to say. "We'll be ready to take-off in ten minutes."

Redford placed down the bottle of bourbon he was about to pour into a glass. He pushed the button to the intercom on the wall. "I've changed my mind about leaving, Todd."

Carmen adjusted the earbuds while walking and talking to her sister. "We miss having you spend the summer here with us, Carmen. I hope you got a lot of writing done."

Releasing a deep breath, she wanted to let her sister know she had something to tell her, but she decided to wait until Chandra returned to the States. Instead of responding to what her sister had said, she asked, "Will Mom and Dad be coming back with you guys for a short visit?"

"Yes. They plan to take a cruise out of Florida before returning to Cape Town in September. We should be back in Atlanta in two weeks."

"I plan to come visit. I miss you guys."

"And we miss you, too. It wasn't the same without you."

Carmen rounded the corner to where her townhouse was located and slowed her pace when she saw Redford getting out of the same private car he'd left in a few hours ago. "Chandra, I'll call you back later," she said quickly, clicking off the phone.

She increased her steps when she saw him heading toward her front door. He no longer had a key since he'd returned it before leaving. "Redford?" she called out to him. "What happened? Did you forget something?" she asked, joining him on the porch and then opening the door.

"Yes, I forgot something."

"Oh." She figured it must have been important for him to come back for it when she'd agreed to send him anything he had left behind.

When they entered her townhouse, he closed the door behind him. "You went walking. That's good," he said.

She nodded. "Trying to follow doctor's orders." She glanced around, not wanting to stare at him. "So what did you forget?"

He slowly moved away from the door to walk over to where she was standing. "It's nothing I forgot per se, Carmen. I didn't do something that I should have done before I left."

She lifted her head to look up at him. "Oh. And what didn't you do?"

He shoved his hands into the pockets of his slacks. "Tell you how I feel about you. That I have fallen in love with you and that I want you and our baby as a permanent part of my life."

She knew her features showed her shock. "But you said

you would never fall in love again. That you weren't capable of loving anyone."

"And I meant it when I said it. However, that was before I spent time with you here. Quality time. Meaningful time. You showed me that you aren't like Candy. You're different. You're unique. You're you. And you are who I fell in love with, Carmen. I was going to tell you last night after we made love, but before I could, you asked me to leave."

"You were planning to leave anyway. I overheard you giving your employees notice that you were returning."

"I only did that because I noticed you withdrawing from me over the past few days."

Yes, she had been. "I was withdrawing because I was trying to spare my heart, Redford. I had fallen in love with you before and erroneously assumed you had fallen in love with me, too. I'd learned my lesson and didn't want to make the same mistake again."

He took a step closer. "I love you, Carmen, and you were right all along. You truly are my soulmate. I never knew such a thing was possible, but you've proved me wrong." He wrapped his arms around her waist. "My question to you is, do you still love me?"

That was an easy answer to give. "Yes."

"Then will you marry me? Not for the baby's sake but for my sake? I realize how much I need and want you in my life. The thought of me, you and the baby as a family is what I want more than anything."

"Oh, Redford," she said, burying her face in his chest, loving his scent as usual. "Yes, I will marry you."

Lowering his mouth to hers, he captured it and then swept her off her feet. When he carried her over to the sofa, he broke off the kiss and sat down with her in his lap. "I know you hate cold weather so we can live here if you like."

"I want our baby to grow up loving his or her father's homeland. I'm willing to try Alaska for a while. I've gotten used to the weather somewhat whenever I visit Leslie and Sloan."

He gathered her close. "Tomorrow, we go looking for your engagement ring. I want to make it official before we bring our families into the thick of things."

"Good idea," she said, looking forward to meeting his family and him meeting hers.

She wrapped her arms around his neck, knowing for them the best was yet to come. They loved each other and they loved their baby. Life was good and they would be sharing it together.

"And now to celebrate our engagement." Redford stood with her in his arms and headed for the guest bedroom. "It's closer and we've never shared that particular bed."

He placed her on the bed and then joined her. "And just so you know, Carmen," he whispered close to her ear in that throaty voice she loved. "You and I never had sex. From the first, our experience was different. I didn't understand why. Now I do. Every time we shared a bed, we made love. I love you."

"I'm inclined to agree with you. And I love you, too, Redford."

Then he kissed her with all the longing and hunger she was happy to return to him. They had a wedding to plan, but first things first.

Epilogue

Redford glanced into Carmen's eyes as he slid the ring on her finger. Moments earlier in the presence of their families and wedding guests, he had vowed to love her, cherish her and honor her, forever, and he'd meant everything he said.

They had decided on a small wedding in DC with family and close friends. Sloan and Tyler were his two best men, and Leslie and Chandra were Carmen's matrons of honor.

He would never forget the happiness he felt watching Carmen walk down the aisle to him on her father's arm. The degree of love he saw shining in her eyes matched his own. Today, he was marrying the woman who'd truly captured his heart.

After the reception they would fly to spend two weeks in Bora Bora for their honeymoon. He was happy with the decision they'd made to set up residence in Skagway since he would be spending a lot of time there during the construction of the resort. And his parents were close by whenever he needed to travel.

Just like he'd known they would, his parents fell in love with Carmen and were excited to learn they would be grandparents in six months. The same thing with Carmen's family. They were happy about the baby, and he got along great with them.

"I now present Redford and Carmen St. James," the minister said, breaking into his thoughts. "You may kiss your bride, Redford."

Smiling down at Carmen, he kissed his wife with all the love he felt and knew that he'd been well and truly tamed.

* * * * *

HUSBAND MATERIAL

Chapter One

Carmen Akins made her way around the huge white tent, smiling at those she recognized as neighbors, knowing most had heard about the demise of her marriage. And to make matters worse, she figured the article in last week's tabloid had probably fueled their curiosity about the man rumored to be her current lover.

They would definitely be disappointed to know her alleged affair with Bruno Cascy was nothing more than a publicity stunt cooked up by their agents. Her divorce from renowned Hollywood producer and director Matthew Birmingham had made headlines, especially since they had been thought of as one of Hollywood's happiest couples. Many had followed their storybook courtship, wedding and subsequent marriage, and all had been convinced it was the perfect romance. It had come as a shock when it had all ended after three years.

Carmen had hoped she and Matthew could separate both peacefully and quietly, but thanks to the media that had not been the case. Rumors began flying, many put into bold print in various tabloids: Oscar-winning Actress Leaves Husband for Another Man, which was followed by Renowned Producer Dumps Oscar-winning Wife for His Mistress.

Those had been two of the most widespread, although neither was true. Yes, she had been the one who'd filed for a divorce but there was no "other man" involved. And the only mistress her ex-husband had ever had while they'd been married was his work.

The first year of their marriage was everything she'd ever dreamed about. They were madly in love and couldn't stand to spend a single minute away from each other. But that second year, things began to change. Matthew's career took precedence over their relationship. She had tried talking to him but had no luck. And to keep their marriage solid, she had even turned down a couple of major movies to spend time with him. But it was no use.

The breaking point had come after she'd shot the movie *Honor*. Although Matthew had flown to France a few times to see her while she was filming, she'd wanted more private time with him without being interrupted by others on the set.

After filming had ended, she had arranged their schedules so they could spend time together in Barcelona at a secluded villa. It was there that she had planned to share with him the news that he was to become a father. She had been so happy about it—she couldn't wait for him to arrive.

But he never did.

Instead he'd called to let her know something had come up, something of vital importance, and suggested that she arrange another excursion for them at a later date. That same night, she began having severe stomach pains and heavy bleeding, and she lost their baby, a baby who, to this day, Matthew knew nothing about. Nor did he know about the time she had spent at the villa under the care of a private doctor and nurse. It was a blessing none of it had gotten to the media. The only thing Matthew knew about was the divorce papers he'd gotten a few weeks later.

She glanced around as she kept moving, not bothering to stop and strike up a conversation with anyone. There was a crowd but luckily the media was being kept off the grounds so as not to harass any celebrities in attendance. She appreciated that. It was certainly comforting since a slew of cameras had been following her around lately, especially after the rumor about Bruno had been leaked.

Her plans were to spend the entire summer in the Hamptons, watching the Bridgehampton Club polo matches at the Seven Oaks Farm. She needed some unwind time. However, she had to be careful—there were gossips everywhere and the Hamptons were no exception, especially since Ardella Rowe had purchased a home in the area. The woman was considered Joan Rivers's twin when it came to having loose lips. The secrets of more than a few celebrities who owned summer homes here had made it to the media thanks to Ardella.

"Carmen, darling."

Carmen inwardly cringed. It was as if her thoughts had conjured up the woman. She considered not answering, but several had heard Ardella call out to her and it would be rude not to respond. And while Ardella was someone you wouldn't want as a friend, you definitely wouldn't want her as an enemy, either.

Taking a deep breath, she pasted a smile on her face and turned around. The woman was right there, as if she had no intention of letting Carmen get away. Evidently she figured Carmen had some juicy news to share.

"Ardella, you're looking well," Carmen said.

"Carmen, darling, forget about me. How are *you*?" Ardella asked with fake concern, leaning over and giving her a quick kiss on her cheek. "I heard about all those horrid things Matthew Birmingham is doing to you."

Carmen lifted a brow. She could only imagine the lies being spread now. The truth of the matter was that her ex-husband wasn't doing anything to her. In fact, as far as Matthew was concerned, it was as if she had never existed. She hadn't heard from him since the day their divorce had become final a year ago. However, she had seen him in March at the Academy

Awards. Like her, he'd come alone, but that had just fueled the media frenzy as they walked down the red carpet separately.

When she'd accepted her best-supporting-actress Oscar for the blockbuster hit *Honor,* it had been natural to thank him for the support and encouragement he'd given her during shooting. The media had had a field day with her speech, sparking rumors of a reconciliation between them. He had refused to comment and so had she—there was no point when both of them knew there would not be a reconciliation of any kind. Their marriage was over and they were trying to move on, namely in different directions.

Moving on had taken her a little longer than Matthew. He hadn't wasted time after their divorce was final. Seeing those photos with him and his flavor of the month had hurt, but she hadn't gotten involved with anyone to get back at him. Instead, she'd concentrated on keeping her career on top.

With a practiced smile, she said, "Why, Ardella, sweetie, you must be mistaken. Matthew isn't doing anything to me. In fact, regardless of what you've heard, we've decided to remain friends," she proclaimed, lying through her teeth.

Matthew couldn't stand the ground she walked on. She'd heard from mutual friends that he'd said he would never forgive her for leaving him. Well, she had news for him. She would never forgive him for not being there when she'd needed him most.

"So you can't believe everything you read in those tabloids," Carmen added.

The woman gave her a shrewd look while sipping her wine. "What is this I'm hearing about you and Bruno? And I understand Matthew is seeing that lingerie model, Candy Sumlar."

Blood rushed to Carmen's head at the mention of the woman's name, but she managed to keep her cool. "Like I said, you can't believe everything you hear or read."

Ardella sharpened her gaze. "And what about what I've

seen with my own eyes, Carmen? I was in L.A. a few weeks ago and I saw Matthew at a party with Candy. How do you explain that?"

Carmen gave a dignified laugh. "I don't have to explain it. Matthew and I have been divorced now for a year. He has his life and I have mine."

"But the two of you have remained friends?"

If they weren't friends this woman would be the last to know, Carmen thought, remembering the column that had appeared about her a few years back, claiming the only reason Matthew had cast her in one of his movies when she'd first started out was because they'd slept together. Sources had revealed Ardella as the person who'd spread that lie.

Thinking that one lie deserved another, Carmen acknowledged, "Yes, Matthew and I are friends. It will take more than a divorce to make us enemies." She hoped the woman never got the chance to question Matthew regarding his feelings on the matter.

Ardella gazed over Carmen's shoulder and smiled. Carmen could only hope the woman had spotted her next victim. "Well, look who's here," Ardella said, glancing back at her with a full grin on her face.

The hair on the back of Carmen's neck stood up as the tent went silent. Everyone was staring at her. Her body had begun tingling. That could only mean…

She pulled in a deep breath, hoping she was wrong but knowing from the smirk on Ardella's face that she wasn't. Matthew had entered the tent. Ardella confirmed her guess when she commented, "Looks like your ex just showed up. Imagine that. Both of you here in the Hamptons. But then, you did say the two of you *are* friends."

Carmen could tell from Ardella's tone that she was mocking Carmen's earlier claim. And from the way the tent had gotten quiet, it was clear that the spectators who'd come to see the polo game were finding the drama unfolding under the tent more interesting than what was on the field.

"He's spotted you and is headed this way. I think this is where I say farewell and skedaddle," Ardella said with a wide grin on her face.

The woman's words had Carmen wanting to run, but she stood her ground and made a quick decision. She had to believe that the man she once loved and whom she believed had once loved her would not do anything to embarrass her. She and Matthew would be civil to each other, even if it killed them. And then she would find out just why he was here. He owned the Hampton compound, but the divorce settlement gave her the right to stay there whenever she liked, as long as he remained in L.A. So why wasn't he in California? He seldom found time to come to New York.

"Carmen."

She felt his heat at the same moment she heard her name issue from his lips. Both affected her greatly. He was standing directly behind her and as much as Carmen didn't want to, she slowly turned around and feasted her gaze on her ex-husband.

Feasting was definitely the right word to use. No matter when or where she saw him, he looked as enticing as any man could. Dressed casually in a pair of tan slacks and a designer navy blue polo shirt, he was the epitome of success. And with a clean shaven head, skin the color of rich cocoa, a strong jaw line, dark piercing eyes and full lips, he had stopped more than one woman in her tracks.

Before branching out to become a director and producer, he had starred in a few movies. And when he'd been an actor, Matthew Birmingham had been considered a heartthrob. To many he still was.

Knowing they were the center of attention, she knew what she had to do, and so she did. "Matthew," she said, rising on tiptoe to plant a kiss on his cheek. "It's good seeing you."

"Same here, sweetheart."

From the tone of his voice she knew her kiss had caught him off guard, and now he was only playing along for her benefit. She felt anger beginning to boil within her at seeing him here, on her turf. This was a place he knew she enjoyed coming during the summer months, a place he conveniently stayed away from since work usually kept him on the west coast.

"I'm sure we can do better than that," he whispered.

He reached out and pulled her into his arms, claiming her mouth. His tongue slid between her parted lips and immediately began a thorough exploration. She heard the click of a cell-phone camera and figured Ardella was at work. Carmen was tempted to pull her mouth away and break off the kiss but she didn't have the willpower to do so.

It was Matthew who finally retreated, leaving her in a daze, unable to think clearly. When she saw they'd caused a scene and people were staring, she figured she had to do something before things got out of hand.

"We need to talk privately," she stated, hearing the tremble in her voice and trying to ignore the sensations in her stomach. She moved to leave the tent. As expected, he fell in step beside her.

As soon as they were away from prying eyes and extended ears, she turned to him. The smile she'd fabricated earlier was wiped clean from her face. "Why did you kiss me like that?"

He smiled and a dimple appeared in his cheek, causing a swell of longing to flow through her entire body. "Because I wanted to. And need I remind you that you kissed me first," he said in an arrogant tone.

"That was my way of saying hello."

He chuckled. "And the way I kissed you was mine."

She pulled in an irritated breath. He was being difficult and she had no time for it—or for him. "What are you doing here, Matthew? You heard the judge. I get to come here and stay—"

"As long as I remain in California," he interrupted. "Well, I'm embarking on a new business venture in New York. It was finalized today. That means I'll be relocating here for a while." His smile widened as he added, "Which means you and I are going to be housemates."

Matthew was tempted to kiss that shocked frown right off his ex-wife's face. Just knowing his words had agitated the hell out of her was the satisfaction he needed. If looks could kill, he would be a dead man.

Trying to ignore the tumultuous emotions that always overtook him whenever he saw her, he added, "Of course, you can always pack up and leave. I would certainly understand."

He knew for certain that that suggestion would rattle her even more. He was well aware of just how much she enjoyed coming here every summer to hit the beach and hang out at the polo matches. That was one of the reasons he'd purchased the compound in the first place. And if she assumed for one minute that he would allow her to sleep with her lover under the roof of a house he'd paid for, then she had another think coming.

"How dare you, Matthew."

He couldn't help but smile at that. There was a time she had loved his outrageous dares—especially the ones he'd carried out in the bedroom. "Careful, Carmen, people are still watching. You might want to continue to play the role you created for Ardella Rowe moments ago. I rather liked it."

She looked up at him with what everyone else assumed was a warm, friendly smile, but he could see the bared teeth. His gaze flicked over her features. She was still the most beautiful woman to walk the face of the earth. He'd come into contact with numerous glamorous women, but he'd known the first time he had set eyes on Carmen five years ago, when she'd read for a part in one of his movies, that her looks would stop men dead in their tracks. And on camera or off, she gave new meaning to the word *radiant*.

"We need to talk, Matthew."

He looked away, well aware that his demeanor was distant. She had wrapped him around her finger once but she wouldn't be doing it again. He would be the first to admit he was still having problems with the fact that she'd walked out on their marriage. That said, he was only human, and if he continued to look into the depths of her dark eyes, he would remember things he didn't want to. Like how her eyes would darken when her body exploded beneath him in a climax.

He pulled in a deep breath and met her gaze again when he felt his heart harden. "No, we don't need to talk, Carmen. When you left me, you said it all. Now if you will excuse me, the first match is about to begin."

And he walked off and left her standing there.

Chapter Two

Every nerve in Carmen's body tingled in anger as she drove off the grounds of the Seven Oaks Farm. After Matthew's kiss, no doubt rumors of a possible reconciliation would begin circulating again. Feigning a headache to several people, she had gotten into her car and left.

It was a beautiful July day and as she drove past the stables in her convertible sports car, she doubted if Matthew even cared that he'd ruined what would have been a perfect afternoon for her. He'd probably known when he'd shown up what would happen, which only proved once again what a selfish person he was.

Somehow he had lost sight of what she'd told him about her parents' marriage—how her father's need to be a successful financial adviser and her mother's drive to become the most prominent real-estate agent in Memphis had isolated them from each other, which eventually led to their divorce. She had wanted more from her marriage to Matthew, but in the end, he had somehow given her even less.

Glancing around, she admired the countryside and regretted she would have to leave though she'd just gotten here yesterday. Her summer vacation had been spoiled. She pulled in a frustrated breath, wondering just what kind of business deal he'd made that would take him from California. As her hair blew in the wind she decided she really didn't care. What he did was no concern of hers.

Moments later she turned down the narrow street that led to their estate and within seconds, the sprawling beachfront home loomed before her. She could remember the first time Matthew had brought her here, months after they'd married, promising this would be the place where they would spend all of their summers. She had come every summer after that, but he'd been too busy to get away. His work had taken precedence over spending time together.

As she parked in the driveway and got out of the car, she couldn't help wondering if Matthew had plans to bring Candy Sumlar here. Would he spend more time with his girlfriend than he had his wife?

The thought that he probably would annoyed the hell out of her. She fumed all the way to the front door and slammed it shut behind her before glancing around. When she'd walked through the doors yesterday evening upon arriving, she had felt warm and welcomed. Now she felt cold and unwanted.

She quickly went upstairs, determined to pack and be miles away by the time the polo match was over and Matthew returned. There was no way he would do the gentlemanly thing and go somewhere else. It didn't matter one iota that she had been here first.

Entering the bedroom, she stopped. He had placed his luggage in here, open, on the bed. Had he been surprised to find she was already in residence? He'd wasted no time finding her to let her know he was here. And he had kissed her, of all things. She placed her fingers on her mouth, still able to feel the impression of his lips there.

Shaking off the feeling, she went to the closet and flung it open. She sucked in a deep breath. His clothes were already hanging in there, right next to hers. Seeing their clothes together reminded her of how things used to be, and her heart felt heavy and threatened to break all over again.

She pushed his clothing out of the way and grabbed an armful of hers, tossing it on the bed. She was glancing around for her luggage when she suddenly felt stupid for letting Matthew ruin the summer she had been looking forward to for months. Why should she be the one to leave?

She was tired of running. For a full year following her divorce, she had avoided going to places where she thought he would be, and had stayed out of the limelight as much as she could. She had practically become a workaholic just like him, and now she wanted to have some fun. Why was she allowing him to rain on her parade, to make her life miserable when really she should be making *his* miserable?

Suddenly, she knew just the way to do it.

She hung her clothes back in the closet. It was time to give Matthew Birmingham a taste of his own medicine, Carmen style. She would work him over, do everything in her power to make it impossible for him to resist her, and then when he thought he had her just where he wanted—on her back, beneath him in bed—she would call it a wrap and leave him high and dry…and hopefully hard as a rock.

She smiled. The taste of revenge had never been sweeter.

Matthew walked into the house, closed the door behind him and glanced around. He'd been surprised to see Carmen's car parked in the driveway. He'd expected her to be long gone by now.

Ardella Rowe had sought him out during divot stomping to let him know of Carmen's headache. Of course, to keep his ex-wife's charade going he'd had to show his concern and leave immediately, though he knew she had used the headache as an excuse to slip away.

He heard her moving around upstairs and from the sounds of things she was packing. Now that she knew he was here, she wasn't wasting any time hightailing it back to wherever she'd been hiding the last few months. She was good at disappearing when she didn't want to be found.

Moving toward the stairs, he decided to wish her well before returning to the polo fields, hoping to catch the last match if he was lucky. His footsteps echoed on the hardwood floor as he walked toward the master suite. Her scent met him the moment he stepped onto the landing. It was an alluring fragrance that he knew all too well, and it was so much a part of her that he couldn't imagine her wearing any other perfume.

Jamming his hands into his pockets, he continued his stroll. This would be the first time he'd be here without her. He shook off the dreary feeling that realization had brought on. He was a big boy and could handle it. Besides, Carmen had done enough damage to mess up his life. He doubted he would ever forgive her for breaking his heart, for making him believe there was such a thing as true love and then showing him there really wasn't.

He'd stopped trying to figure out at what point they'd begun drifting apart. He would be the first to admit he'd spent a lot of hours working, but all those hours he'd spent away from her were meant to build a nice nest egg so they wouldn't have to work forever.

And although she was paid well for her movies, as her husband, he'd still felt it was his duty to make sure she got anything and everything she wanted in life. They had talked about having a family, but she hadn't understood that knowing he could provide for her and any child they had was important to him.

Her parents had had money and unlike him, she hadn't grown up poor. More than anything, he'd wanted to keep her in the lifestyle she'd been accustomed to. What in the world could be so terribly wrong about wanting to do that? To this day he just couldn't figure it out, and the more he thought about it, the angrier he got.

He had built his world around her. She had been the only thing that truly mattered and everything he'd done had been for her. But she hadn't appreciated that. So now, because of a decision she'd made without him, he was a man whose life was still in turmoil, although he fought like hell to keep that a secret. And he placed the blame for his shattered life at her feet.

He reached the bedroom's double doors and without bothering to knock, he pushed open the door.

And stopped dead in his tracks.

Chapter Three

Carmen swung around at the sound of the bedroom door opening and tightened her bathrobe around her. She threw her head back, sending hair cascading around her shoulders. "What are you doing in here, Matthew?"

For a moment he simply stood there staring at her, no doubt taking in the fact that she had just taken a shower and was probably stark naked beneath her short robe.

When he didn't answer, she said in a sharp tone, "Matthew, I asked you a question."

His attention shifted from her body and slid up to her face. "What do you think you're doing, Carmen?"

His voice sounded strained and his breathing shallow. "What does it look like I'm doing? I just finished taking a shower and now I'm putting on clothes. You should have knocked."

Carmen watched as something flickered in the depths of his dark eyes and a muscle clenched in his jaw. He took his hands out of his pockets, causing the material of his pants to stretch across the huge bulge at his center. It was quite obvious he'd gotten aroused from seeing her half-naked. She inwardly smiled. He'd taken the bait just the way she'd planned.

"I own this place. I don't have to knock, Carmen. And why are you still here? Why aren't you gone or at least packing?"

She crossed her arms over her chest and followed the movement of his eyes from her face to her breasts. She was very much aware that her curves were outlined through the silky material of her robe. It seemed he was very much aware of it, as well.

"I decided that I won't be leaving."

He pulled his gaze away from her chest. "Excuse me?"

"I said I won't be leaving. I'd assumed you would be in L.A. all summer, which is why I made plans to spend my vacation here. I don't intend to change that just because you've shown up."

A muscle clenched in his jaw again, making it obvious her statement hadn't gone over well with him. She wasn't surprised when he said, with an icy gaze, "You should have checked my plans for the summer. If you had, I would have told you this place was off-limits. I regret that you didn't. I also regret that you have to leave."

She inched her chin a little higher and declared, "I'm not going anywhere, Matthew. I deserve some peace and quiet. I've worked hard this year."

"And you don't think that I have?"

The sharpness of his tone had her gearing up for a fight. But she had to be careful what she said or he would toss her out and halt her plan. "I know you work hard, Matthew. In fact, you carry working hard to the extreme," she said bluntly.

His gaze narrowed and she wondered if perhaps she'd pushed him too far. But she couldn't help saying how she felt. The amount of time he'd spent away from her would always be a wound that wouldn't heal.

He began moving toward her in that slow, precise walk that could make women drool. She wished she didn't notice his sex appeal or just how potently masculine he was. She had to get a grip. Her objective was to make him regret ever taking her for granted, to give him a taste of his own medicine, so to speak. She intended to turn her back on him like he'd done to her.

Carmen swallowed when he came to a stop in front of her but she refused to back up—or down.

"You," he said with deep emphasis, "are not staying here. I think things were pretty clear in the divorce settlement. You wanted to end our marriage and so you did. Under no circumstances will we stay under the same roof."

Carmen saw the hardness in his features. This face that once looked at her with so much love was staring at her with a degree of animosity that tore at her heart.

"Then nothing is different, Matthew, since we seldom stayed under the same roof anyway. I'm not leaving. I was almost mobbed by the paparazzi getting here and they are probably hanging around like vultures waiting for me to leave. Your recent love life has caused quite a stir and they are trying to bait me into giving my opinion."

"The media isn't giving me any more slack than they're giving you. And your affair with Bruno Casey isn't helping matters, either. I'm sure if you return to California, he'll be able to put you up for the summer in that place he owns off the bay."

It was on the tip of her tongue to tell him nothing was going on with Bruno, but she decided it was none of his business, especially in light of his ongoing affair with Candy. She refused to bring the other woman up since the last thing she wanted was for him to think that she cared. Which she didn't.

"Bruno is shooting in Rome and this is where I want to be. I love it here. I've always loved it here and the only reason you didn't agree to let me have this place during the divorce was because you knew how much I wanted it. For spite, you were intentionally difficult."

"Think whatever you like. I'm leaving to catch the last of the polo matches. I want you gone when I return."

"I'm not leaving, Matthew."

His expression turned from stony to inexplicably weary. "I'm not going to waste my time arguing with you, Carmen."

"Then don't."

They stood there staring at each other, anger bouncing off both of them. Then, without saying another word, Matthew turned and walked out. Carmen held her breath until she heard the front door slam shut behind him.

Matthew decided not to return to the Seven Oaks Farm for the match. Instead, he went for a drive to clear his head and cool his anger. Carmen was being difficult—she hadn't behaved that way since the early days of their courtship.

He had pursued her with a single-minded determination he hadn't known he was capable of, and she had put up a brick wall, refusing to let him get close. But he'd known the first moment he'd laid eyes on her that he not only wanted her to star in his movie but he wanted her in his bed and wouldn't be satisfied until he got both.

She'd gotten the part in the movie, earning it fair and square. Getting her into his bed had proven to be difficult and before he got her there, he'd realized he had fallen in love with her. He wasn't certain how it had happened, but it had. He'd loved her so deeply, he knew he wasn't capable of ever loving another woman that way.

She'd stood before him in that church and promised to love him forever. So what if he worked long hours—didn't "till death do us part" mean anything to her? And if he hadn't worked so hard, he would not have earned the reputation of being one of the country's up-and-coming film producers.

A throbbing warmth flowed through his chest, which was immediately followed by a rush of anger that was trying to consume him. He had wanted so much for them and she had done something so unforgivable it hurt him to think about it. He had been absolutely certain she was the one person who understood his drive to build something of his own, the one person who would never let him down. His father had let him down by not marrying his mother when she'd gotten pregnant, and then his mother had let him down when she married Charles Murray, the stepfather from hell. Carmen had restored his faith that there was someone out there who wouldn't disappoint him. So much for that.

Matthew parked the car on the side of the road and just sat there, gazing at the beach. Walking into the bedroom and seeing her barely clothed had been too much. For a moment, lust had overshadowed his common sense and he could only think of how her breasts felt in his hands, how they tasted in his mouth.

With the sunlight streaming through the window, her nearly transparent robe had revealed the darkened triangle between her legs. It had taken all his strength not to cross the room, toss her on the bed and bury himself deep inside her body the way he used to after they'd argued and made up.

And they'd had to make up a lot since the amount of time he'd spent away from home had always been a bone of contention between them. But they'd always worked through it. What he'd tried so hard to figure out was, what had made the last time different? Why had she felt like throwing in the towel? She'd known his profession when she married him. As an actress, she of all people should have understood how things were on a set. Her filing for divorce had confused the hell out of him.

He remembered the night he hadn't shown up in Spain as planned. It had been a week from hell on the set. Wayne Reddick, the main investor for the movie he'd been producing at the time, had unexpectedly shown up on location. He and Wayne had butted heads several times and the man's impromptu visit had prompted him to cancel his plans to meet Carmen in Barcelona. The fate of his production, which had been behind schedule, was at stake and it had taken some serious talking for the man to agree to extend funds for the movie's completion. He had tried calling Carmen to explain things, but she hadn't answered the phone. The next thing he knew he was receiving divorce papers.

He tightened his hand on the steering wheel thinking that maybe he was handling the situation with his ex-wife all wrong. Since she was hell-bent on staying in the Hamptons, maybe he should just let her. It would give him the chance to extract some kind of revenge for the hell she'd put him through.

He glanced at his watch. A smile touched his lips when he pulled back onto the road and headed home, determined to return before she left. He needed to convince her that it was fine with him if she stayed, without making her suspicious of his motives.

He'd been an actor before becoming a director and producer. He would seduce her back into his bed and then make her leave. And he would go so far as to change the locks on the doors if he had to.

The more he thought about it, the more he liked the idea and knew just how he could pull it off. When it came to seduction, he was at the top of his game.

Chapter Four

"You're still here, Carmen."

Carmen drew in a quick breath before turning around where she stood in the kitchen. Matthew had said he was returning to the polo matches—she hadn't expected him back so soon. At least she'd had time to put on some clothes and start dinner.

"I told you that I'm not leaving, Matthew. I deserve my time here so I figure you can do one of two things."

"Which are?"

She was surprised he asked. "You can call the cops and have me arrested for trespassing, which should make interesting news this week. Or you can leave me be and ignore the fact that I'm here. This house is big enough for you to do that."

She studied his features for some clue as to which option he fancied. And then he said impassively as he leaned against the kitchen counter, "The latter will cause just as much ruckus as the former."

He was right about that. Ever since she had publicly thanked him when receiving her Oscar, the tabloids had claimed a reconciliation between them was in the works. The paparazzi had shadowed their every move, determined to find out if the rumors were true and the Hollywood darlings were ready to kiss and make up. And then her agent had come up with this idea to make things even more interesting by introducing Bruno into the mix. Plus there was the matter of his lingerie model.

"I'm sure when you explain things to Candy, she'll understand," she said with warm humor in her voice. Of course Candy wouldn't understand, but then Carmen really didn't give a royal flip. Candy had had her eyes on Matthew for years and hadn't wasted any time latching on to him after their divorce had become final.

He stared straight into her eyes when he asked, "And what about Bruno? Is he an understanding sort of guy?"

The heat of his gaze touched her in a way that she couldn't ignore. She knew he meant to be intimidating and not sexual, but that look was as sexual as anything could get and she wasn't happy about the surge of desire flowing through her. The memories of what usually followed such a look swirled all around her and touched her intimately. Bottom line, Matthew Birmingham could make her feel like no other man could.

"Must be pretty serious if you have to think about it."

She blinked upon realizing he'd been waiting for her response while she was thinking that he could still take her breath away. "Yes, he's an understanding sort of guy." She would let him ponder exactly what that said about the seriousness of their relationship.

Carmen turned to check the rolls she had put in the oven earlier. She was wearing a pair of jeans and a tank top. He'd always liked how jeans hugged her backside, and she was giving him an eyeful now as she bent over. She heard the change in his breathing and inwardly smiled. Poor baby, he hadn't seen anything yet.

"If I decide to let you stay," he was saying behind her, "there have to be rules."

She turned around and lifted a brow. "What kind of rules?"

"Bruno isn't welcome here."

She could live with that, since she hadn't intended to invite him anyway. "And what about *your* Miss Candy? Will you respect me as your former wife and keep her away while I'm here?"

It annoyed her that he actually had to think about his answer. Then he said, "I guess our plans can be rearranged."

A coldness settled in her heart. His response meant two things. He *had* intended to bring Candy here, and the two of them were sleeping together. The latter shouldn't surprise her since she of all people knew how much Matthew enjoyed making love. That was the one thing the two of them had in common.

"Does that mean you're okay with me staying, Matthew?"

"Seems you're hell-bent on doing that anyway. And like you said, the less the media knows about our business, the better."

She laughed. "You're concerned with the media? You? The same person who kissed me in front of a tent filled with people, including Ardella Rowe?"

"Like I said, you kissed me first." He looked over her shoulder at the stove. "So, what are you cooking?"

"Something simple."

"I didn't know you could cook at all." The amused glint in the dark depths of his eyes made her smile, as well. Matthew didn't smile often but when he did, it was contagious—and sexy.

"I started cooking after Rachael Ray had me on her show." And then, because she couldn't help it, she added, "I'd prepared a couple of meals for you when I thought you would be coming home. When you never showed up, I fed everything to the garbage disposal."

He looked at her as if he wasn't sure she was serious. "Here's another rule, if we're going to be here together. No talk of the past. You bailed out on our marriage and I'd rather not get into it—"

"I wasn't the one who bailed out, Matthew," she countered, lifting her chin. "You replaced me."

A fierce frown covered his face. "What the hell are you talking about, Carmen? I was never unfaithful to you."

"Not in the way you're thinking," she said, truly believing it. "But there *was* a mistress, Matthew. Your work. And she was as alluring to you as any woman could be. I couldn't compete and eventually stopped trying."

His frown deepened. "I don't want to hear it. I've heard it all before."

He'd heard, but he hadn't listened. "Fine," she said, "then don't hear it because personally, I'm tired of saying it."

"You don't have to say it. We're divorced now."

"Thanks for reminding me."

There was a moment of awkward silence between them, although the chemistry they shared was keeping things sizzling. She knew he felt it as much as she did, and wasn't surprised when he tried easing the tension by asking in a civil yet curious tone, "What are you making?"

She glanced over at him. "I've smothered pork chops with gravy and got some rice going along with homemade rolls and field peas."

"You prepared all that?"

"Yes. I made more than enough—you're welcome to dig in, too. Later we can toss for the bedroom."

He raised a brow. "Toss for the bedroom?"

"Yes, toss a coin to see which one of us will get the master suite, and who will have to settle for one of the guest rooms."

He shrugged. "Save your coin, I don't mind using the guest room. I'm going to wash up."

Carmen watched him walk out of the kitchen, thinking that while revenge might be sweet, she needed to watch her step where he was concerned, especially since all she had to do was look at him to remember how things used to be between them—both in and out of bed. But for some reason she was reminded more of how things were in bed than out. It didn't take much for sensuous chills to flow through her body whenever he was near, even during those times she found him infuriating.

A wave of uneasiness washed over her. It was too late to question whatever had possessed her to take him on since it was too late to back off now. And the one thing she did know was that she would not go down in defeat.

"I never got the chance to thank you for mentioning me at the Academy Awards during your acceptance speech," Matthew said, glancing across the table at Carmen as they ate. "You didn't have to do that."

He hadn't expected her to give him any kind of acknowledgment when she'd accepted her award. He'd figured, considering how things had been during the divorce, that his name would be the last one off her lips that night. It had been quite a surprise. But then, she was always surprising him, like when he'd returned from washing up to find she'd set the table for two.

"Of course I did, Matthew," she claimed. "Regardless of how and why our marriage ended, I would not have taken that role if it hadn't been for you. You made me believe I could do it."

He didn't say a word as he thought back over that time. He'd known she could do it and along with Bella Hudson-Garrison, who was cast as the lead, Carmen had given a stellar performance. Bella had walked away with an Oscar for best actress, and Carmen won best-supporting actress.

He had arrived at the Kodak Theater and walked the red carpet alone, surprising many by not having a woman on his arm. His manager, Stan, had tried convincing him to bring a date, since chances were Carmen would be bringing one. But he hadn't taken Stan's advice. And when he saw Carmen had also come alone, he'd been happy, although he'd tried convincing himself he didn't give a damn.

He'd felt bitter that night, knowing she should have strolled down the red carpet on his arm. And she'd looked absolutely radiant; her gown had been stunning. On that night for a brief moment, he had placed his anger aside and had rooted for her getting the award she truly deserved. And when she had unselfishly acknowledged him as the driving force behind her taking the part, the cameras of course had switched to him, to gauge his reaction. His features had remained emotionless but on the inside, he had been humbled by what she'd done.

"So, Matthew, what's this new business venture you're involved with here in New York?"

He blinked, and realized he'd been staring at her like a fool. He quickly glanced down at his wineglass to get his bearings and recoup his common sense. When he felt pretty sure he had done both, he responded, "You know that although I enjoy doing features, it's always been my dream to make a documentary."

Carmen had known that. While married, they had talked about his dream many times.

"Well, earlier this year I learned that New York is gearing up to celebrate the one hundred and twenty-fifth anniversary of the Statue of Liberty's dedication, and that the city is looking for someone to film a documentary highlighting the event. The last big documentary was directed by Ken Burns back in 1986, and it was nominated for Best Documentary Feature."

She nodded. "That was a while ago."

"My name was given to the committee, and I've met with them several times over the past year. I learned yesterday that I was selected. They've requested that I use a New York–based film crew, and I don't have a problem with that. It only means I need to be here for preproduction, not in L.A. It's important that I get to know the people I'll be working with and they get to know me and my style."

She knew just what he was talking about. Matthew was an outstanding director, dedicated to his work and he expected those who worked with him to be dedicated, as well. She'd been in two of his movies and both times had been in awe of his extraordinary skills.

A sincere smile touched her lips. She was happy for him. In fact, she was ecstatic. God knows he'd worked hard to prove himself in the industry, which was one of the reasons why they were sitting across the table from each other not as husband and wife but as exes. Still, she would put the bitterness aside and give him his due.

"Congratulations, Matthew, that's wonderful. I am truly happy for you," she admitted, standing and carrying their plates to the sink.

"Thank you," Matthew said, leaning back in his chair, steepling his fingers together as he watched Carmen move across the room with more grace than any woman he knew. There was a jaw-dropping sexiness to her walk that had the ability to turn on any man, big time—especially him.

It hit him just how much he missed seeing her and spending time with her. The last time they'd been together had been in the judge's chambers, ending their marriage with their attorneys battling it out to the end.

"So, you're committed to being here all summer then?" she asked, turning around, leaning against the counter and meeting his gaze.

He smiled, wondering what she would do if she knew he was practically stripping her naked with his eyes while thinking of all the naughty things he wanted to do to her body. "Yes."

"Working?"

"Basically."

"Which means I'll rarely see you."

Matthew flinched. She knew how to say things that could make him grit his teeth. She made it seem as if he'd never given her any attention while he worked. Well, that was about to change. He was on a mission to seduce her and then kick her out on that hot little behind of hers.

"Maybe you will and maybe you won't. There will be days when I'll be working from here."

She shrugged. "It doesn't matter, Matthew. Work drives you no matter when and where you're doing it. That's all you ever think about."

He could tell her that wasn't true since at that very moment, he was thinking about how he wanted to make love to her once he got her back in his bed. "If that's what you want to believe."

She laughed shortly. "That's what I know. Now, if you don't mind, I intend to go to bed."

He shot her a confused look. "Bed? Don't you think it's kind of early? The sun's still up," he pointed out.

She lifted a brow. "And your point?"

My point is that I can't very well seduce you if you are making yourself scarce. "There's still time to do things tonight."

"I agree, which is why, after putting on my pj's, I plan to sit out on my bedroom balcony with a good book and watch the sun set over the ocean. I might go for a swim in the pool later tonight, but you shouldn't be concerned that I'll be underfoot. Like I said, this house is big enough for both of us. See you later."

She turned and left the kitchen. He watched her go, admiring her body, remembering her touch, more determined than ever to get her in his bed.

Chapter Five

Carmen curled up on the chaise longue on the private balcony off the master suite. If she were going to seduce Matthew, the last thing she needed to do was appear too accessible, too anxious to be in his presence. That was the reason she'd decided to go to her room first rather than straight to the pool.

A cool breeze was coming in off the ocean. She recalled making love with Matthew on this very balcony one night that first year he had brought her to the Hamptons. She had been concerned that their neighbors would see them, but Matthew had assured her that they had total privacy. The house had even been built in a no-fly zone, which kept the overzealous paparazzi from taking to the skies.

She glanced at the book she'd placed on the table, a romance novel she had been trying to get through for the last couple of days. It's not that it wasn't a good book—it was—but it was hard to read about someone else's fantastic love life when hers had gone so badly.

Instead of resuming the book, she decided to close her eyes and conjure up her own love story with her and Matthew in the leading roles. Things between them had been romantic during the early days of their marriage, especially that first year when he hadn't wanted her out of his sight. They had been in bed more than they had been out. Matthew was something else in the bedroom—he'd been able to reach her on a level that went deeper than any man ever had—and a part of her knew that no other man ever would.

From the moment they'd met, something had passed between them that was instinctive, and primitive. She was surprised she'd been able to read her lines during the audition session. That day, for the first time in her life, she'd discovered how it felt to truly desire a man.

She had gotten the role because Matthew had seen something in her. He thought she was good, and was going places. Although the temptation to become his lover during filming had been great, she had been determined to keep things professional between them.

After they'd wrapped the movie, they had their first date. He had taken her someplace simple—his favorite bar and grill for hamburgers, fries and what he'd claimed was the best milk shake she would ever taste. He'd been right. That night had practically sealed her fate. They'd dated exclusively for six months and then that Christmas, he'd asked her to marry him and she'd said yes.

The media had kept tabs on their budding relationship, referring to them as Hollywood's Darlings—Matthew, the staunch bachelor who claimed he would never marry, and she, the woman who'd stolen his heart. Their courtship had been as private as they could make it, but that hadn't stopped the paparazzi from stalking their every move and painting them as the couple whose marriage was most likely to succeed in Hollywood. Boy, had they been wrong.

Nearly five years later and here they were, no different than most other Hollywood couples—divorced and blaming the other for what had gone wrong. She drew in a deep breath, not wanting to think of how she'd felt being replaced by his career. The loneliness and pain had nearly swallowed her whole. Although by that time she'd had success as an actress, as a wife she felt like a total failure—a woman who couldn't compete against her husband's workaholic nature, who couldn't entice him away for a smoldering-hot rendezvous.

More pain settled around her heart as she remembered she'd lost more than her husband's attention in Barcelona. She'd also lost the child they had made together. Had she gone full-term, their little girl or boy would have been almost four months old by now.

She felt her lip trembling and fought back tears. She wanted to recall the good things about their marriage. She wanted to remember how well they'd gotten along in the beginning, how she would respond to just about anything when it came to him. His soft laugh, his touch, the sound of his breathing…that look he would give her when he wanted to make love.

She had seen that same look in his eyes today in the kitchen. She didn't know what racy thoughts had been going through his mind, but her body had responded and a rush of sensations had flowed through her. Her hormones had surged to gigantic proportions and it would have been so easy to cross the room, slide onto his lap, curl into his arms and bury her face in the warmth of his chest. Then she would have kissed him the way she used to. Kissing him had the ability to make her all but moan out an orgasm. In fact, a few times she had done that very thing.

She had the satisfaction of knowing he wanted her. Although she was woman enough to admit she'd desired him, too. What she had to do was keep her desires at bay while continuing to stir up his. That was her game plan and she intended to stick to it. She would not get caught in her own trap.

But there was nothing wrong with getting wrapped up in memories while lying stretched out on a chaise longue with the breeze from the ocean caressing her skin. Memories were a lot safer than the real thing. With her eyes still closed, she vividly recalled the night when she and Matthew had come out here, naked and aroused, with only one thing on their minds.

They had gone to a polo match and returned home, barely making it up to their bedroom to strip off their clothes. And then he had swept her off her feet and carried her to the balcony. Even now she could recall how fast her heart had been beating and how her pulse had throbbed. Pretty similar to how she was feeling now, just thinking about it.

He'd reached out to touch her breasts and her stomach had automatically clenched in response. Then she had watched in heated lust as he'd leaned forward and used his tongue to capture a nipple between his lips and—

"Carmen? Why didn't you answer when I knocked?"

She found herself staring into a pair of dark, sensuous eyes. His lips were so close to hers that it wouldn't have taken much for him to lean in just a little closer and taste her. And then there was his scent—aftershave mingled with man—that began manipulating her senses in a way that could be deemed lethal.

Her eyes narrowed as she felt a warming sensation between her thighs. Matthew was crouched down over her. She fought to ignore the sensual currents that were rippling through her.

"What are you doing here?" she asked, her voice sounding strained to her own ears.

His gaze continued to hold hers. "I knocked several times and you didn't answer."

The heat of his breath was like a warming balm to her lips. She was tempted to lick the fullness of his mouth from corner to corner. It didn't exactly surprise her that she was thinking of doing such a thing, considering what she'd been thinking about just moments ago.

She slowly pulled herself up in a sitting position, causing him to move back, for which she was grateful. The last thing she needed right now was to be in close proximity to him. The temptation was too great. "And why were you knocking on the bedroom door when I told you I would be out here on the balcony reading?" she asked.

"I need to get my things moved to the guest room." He paused a moment and said, "I noticed you were sleeping, but figured I could get my things without disturbing you. But then…"

She lifted a brow. "But then what?"

A sensual smile touched the corners of his lips when he said, "But then I heard you say my name in your sleep."

She faltered for a minute, then quickly fought not to show any emotions as she swung her legs to the side to get up, causing him to back up a little more. She stared at him, exasperated, not sure what she should say. She decided not to say anything at all. What was the use in denying such a thing? It probably hadn't been the first time she'd said his name in her sleep and more than likely it wouldn't be the last. After all, he'd once had the ability to make her come just by breathing on her. In fact, he probably still could.

"Go ahead and get your things, Matthew. I'm awake now," she said, breaking eye contact with him to stand and gaze toward the ocean. He could think whatever he liked about hearing her say his name. She figured all kinds of thoughts were running through his mind—he was probably trying to figure out the best way to get into her panties right now.

She glanced back at him and her nipples immediately hardened when she noticed how he was staring at her outfit. She had changed into a strapless terry-cloth romper and it fit real tight over her backside. She knew just how much he enjoyed looking at that part of her anatomy.

He also used to compliment her on what he said was a gorgeous pair of legs. And now he was scanning her from head to toe, and concentrating on the areas in between. He wasn't trying to hide his interest.

"Is there a problem, Matthew?" she asked, watching his gaze shift from her legs to her mouth. Seeing his eyes linger there ignited a burning sensation low and deep in her belly.

His survey then slowly moved up to her eyes. A flash of

panic ripped through her when she recognized the *let me make you come* look in his eyes. She felt her body succumbing without her consent.

"There's no problem, if you don't think there's one, Carmen," he said throatily, her name rolling sensuously off his tongue.

"I don't," she replied, easing back down on the chaise longue, knowing he was watching her every move. She stretched in a way that caused his attention to be drawn to her backside and legs once again. "I'm sure you don't need my help packing up your things."

Too late she realized she'd said the wrong thing. His expression went from hot to furious. She knew he was recalling the last time she'd said those very words to him, when he was moving out of their home in Malibu.

"You're right, Carmen. I didn't need your help then and I don't need it now."

Chapter Six

As Matthew began opening drawers to collect his clothes, he had to keep reminding himself there was a reason he hadn't yet tossed his ex-wife out on her rear end.

When she hadn't opened the bedroom door, he'd figured she had fallen asleep on the balcony. He thought he could be in and out without waking her. But when he'd heard her moan his name, not just once but several times, nothing could have stopped him from going on that balcony.

He had found her stretched on the chaise with her eyes closed, wearing a hot, enticing outfit that barely covered her. Seeing her resting peacefully had tugged at his heart, while her clothing and her words had tugged on another part of his anatomy. He'd stood there, thinking about all the things he'd love to do to her while getting harder as the seconds ticked by.

And he had been tempted to kiss her, to make love to her mouth in a way that would not only leave her breathless but tottering on the brink of a climax. When she had awakened and looked into his eyes, he had seen a need as keen as any he'd ever known from her. And then she had ruined the moment by reminding him that they were no longer husband and wife, and wouldn't be sharing the same bedroom or bed.

But not for long.

He was looking forward to reminding her just what she'd been missing this past year. And the way he saw it, she was definitely missing something if she was moaning his name in her sleep.

As he pulled the briefs and socks out of the drawer and tossed them into the bag on the bed, he glanced to the balcony where Carmen now stood with her back to him, leaning against the rail and gazing out at the ocean again. At that moment, intense emotion touched him and nearly swelled his heart while at the same time slicing it in two.

He had loved her and he had lost her. The latter should not have happened. She should have stuck by him and kept the vows they'd made to each other. But when the going got tough, she got going.

He pushed the drawer closed, deciding to put his plan into action. She had pushed a few of his buttons—now it was time for him to push a couple of hers.

Carmen felt Matthew's presence before he'd even made a sound. She felt a unique stimulation of her senses whenever he was near. She had felt it earlier today when he'd entered the tent at the polo match. She'd known he was there. Just like she knew he was here now.

Biting her bottom lip, her fingers gripped tight on the rail as her breathing quickened, her pulse escalated and heat flowed through her. He didn't say anything. She couldn't stand another second of silence and slowly turned around.

The sun had gone down and dusk had settled in. Behind him she saw the light from the lamp shining in the bedroom but her focus was on him. She studied him, not caring that it was obvious she was doing so. His eyes darkened and she felt his desire. And as she stood there, she couldn't help but relive all the times he had held her in his arms and made love to her.

He had been the most giving of lovers, making sure she enjoyed every sexual moment they'd shared to the fullest. Her body was tingling inside, remembering how it felt to have his mouth to her breasts, or how his lips could trail kisses all over her body, heating her passion to the highest degree. It had been her plan to get him to the boiling point, but she was ashamed to admit he had her there already.

She pulled in a deep breath. "Are you done?"

"Not quite."

And then he slowly crossed the distance separating them. "I came to say good-night."

The husky sound of his deep voice sent sensuous shudders running all through her. Total awareness of him slid down her spine. She forced her gaze away from his to look out at the ocean to say something, anything to keep her mind off having her way with him.

"I love it here, Matthew. Thanks for agreeing to let me stay." She glanced back at him and saw he'd come to stand directly beside her. "You didn't have to, considering the terms of our divorce," she decided to add.

He stared at her for a moment and then said, "It was the right thing to do. At the very least, we can be friends. I don't want to be your enemy, Carmen."

His words nearly melted her, but she had to remember that she wanted him to regret the day he began taking her for granted, to realize that when she'd needed him the most, he hadn't been there for her. She had been alone while grieving their loss.

"What are you thinking about, Carmen?"

She glanced up at him. "Nothing."

"Maybe I should give you something to think about," he said softly, in a deep, rich voice. And then he wrapped his arms around her waist and lowered his mouth to hers.

She saw it coming and should have done a number of things to resist, but it would have been a waste of time and effort. Every part of her turned to mush the moment his lips touched hers. When his tongue began mingling with hers, she moaned deep in her throat.

Carmen hadn't known how much she'd missed this until now. She had tried burying herself in her work so she wouldn't think about the loneliness, the lost passion, the feel of being in the arms of the one man who could evoke sensations in her that kept her wet for days.

I miss being with the one man who can make me feel like a woman.

He deepened the kiss and she felt the rush of sexual charge. And when he lowered his arms from her waist to cup her backside, bringing her closer to him, she felt the hardness of his huge erection pressing into her. On its own accord, her body eased in for a closer connection.

Their mouths continued to mate in the only way they knew how, a way they were used to. But regardless of the number of kisses they had shared in the past, she was totally unprepared for this one. She hadn't expected the degree of desire or the depth of longing it evoked, not only within her but within him, as well. She could feel it in the way his tongue dominated her mouth as if trying to reclaim what it once had, and was entitled to. He was not only taking what she was giving but going beyond and seizing everything else he could.

Then he began slowly grinding his body against her. She felt the hot throb of his erection between her legs as if the fabric of their clothing wasn't a barrier between them. His body rubbing against hers electrified her senses in a way that felt illegal. And how he fit so perfectly between her legs reminded her of just how things had been with them, whether they were standing up or lying down, in a bed or stretched out on top of a table. They'd always made love with an intensity that left them with tremors of pleasure that wouldn't subside for hours.

Everything around her began to swirl wildly, and as his large hands continued to palm the cheeks of her backside, pressing her even closer to him, an ache took over in the pit of her stomach and began spreading through every part of her.

He slowly released her mouth but didn't stop the movement of his body as he brushed kisses across her cheekbones and chin. She pulled in a deep breath and then released a whimpered sound of pleasure from deep in her throat as he licked a path from one corner of her mouth to the other.

Blood rushed through her veins and it took everything within her to keep from begging for more. But nothing could stop the waves of pleasure and the tremors that began to shake her. She closed her eyes and reveled in the sensations rushing through her, bit by glorious bit. And when he began nibbling on her lips and then proceeded to suck those lips into his mouth, she was literally thrown over the edge. She pulled her mouth from his and cried out as intense pleasure shook her to the very core while he continued to grind his body against hers with a rhythm that had her rocking in sensuous satisfaction.

"That's it, sweetheart, let go," he murmured against her moist lips. "You are totally beautiful when you come for me. So totally beautiful. I miss seeing that."

And she missed feeling it, she thought, as the orgasm that had ripped into her slowly began receding and returning her to earth after a shuddering release. And when she felt the heat of his tongue lap the perspiration from her brow, she slowly opened her eyes.

"Matthew."

His name was a breathless whisper from her lips. As if he understood, he leaned down and kissed her, tenderly but still with a hunger she could feel as well as a taste she could absorb.

He slowly pulled his mouth away and with a sated mind, she met his eyes. The gaze staring back at her was just as intense and desirous as earlier, making it obvious that although she'd easily managed a climax fully clothed, he'd maintained more control over his aroused state.

"Matthew, let me—"

He placed a finger to her lips to halt whatever she'd been about to say. "Good night, Carmen. Sweet dreams."

She watched him leave, thinking that thanks to him, her dreams tonight would be the sweetest she'd had in a long time. She had to admit that this was not how she had planned for things to go with Matthew. He had deliberately tapped into one of her weak spots, which was something she hadn't wanted to happen. Was he gloating that he'd gotten the upper hand?

Carmen drew in a deep breath as her body hummed with a satisfied sensation. A flush heated her cheeks when she remembered how he had kissed her into an orgasm; she was feeling completely sated. The chemistry between them was just as it had always been, explosive.

She leaned back against the rail and knew, even though the sexual release had been just what she needed, she had to regroup her priorities and continue with her plans. Everyone was entitled to get off the track at least once, but the important thing was to get back on. And she was confident that after a good night's sleep, she would be back in control of her senses once again.

Chapter Seven

Pulling off his shirt, Matthew headed for the bathroom, needing a shower. A cold one. Just the thought that he had brought Carmen pleasure had nearly pushed him over the edge. While kissing her, he had been overtaken with a raw and urgent hunger. The sensation had been relentless, unyielding, and for him, nearly unbearable.

As soon as his lips had touched hers, the familiarity of being inside her mouth had driven him to deepen the kiss with a frenzy that had astounded him. And each time she had moaned his name, something deep inside him had stirred, threatening to make him lose all control.

It didn't take long after she'd bailed out of their marriage to realize that she was the only woman for him. Any time he held her in his arms, kissed her, made love to her, he'd felt like a man on top of the world, a man who could achieve and succeed in just about anything. He had worked so damn hard to make her happy and in the end all of his hard work had only made her sad.

He stripped off his clothes, filled with a frustration he was becoming accustomed to and a need he was fighting to ignore. He stepped in the shower and the moment the cold water hit, shocking his body, he knew he was getting what he deserved for letting a golden opportunity go by. But no matter the torment his body was going through, he was determined to stick to his plan, and at the moment he was right on target.

His goal was to build up a need within her, force her to remember how things were between them, and how easily they could stroke each other into one hell of a feverish pitch. And then when she couldn't handle any more, when she was ready to take things to another level, instead of sweeping her off her feet and taking her to the nearest bed like she would expect, he would show her the door.

He stepped out of the shower and was toweling himself dry when he heard his cell phone ring. Wrapping the towel around his middle, he made his way over to the nightstand to pick it up. Caller ID indicated it was his manager, Ryan Manning.

"Yes, Ryan?"

"It would have been nice if you'd given me a heads-up that you and Carmen were back together."

Matthew frowned. "We're not back together."

"Then how do you explain the photograph the *Wagging Tongue* plans to run of the two of you kissing? Luckily I have a contact over there who thought I'd be interested in seeing it before it went to press. They plan to make it front page news that the two of you have reconciled your differences and are remarrying. The papers hit the stands tomorrow."

Matthew rolled his eyes. The *Wagging Tongue* was one of the worst tabloids around. "Carmen and I are divorced, nothing has changed."

"Then what was that kiss about?"

"It was just a kiss, Ryan, no big deal. People can read into it whatever they want."

"And what about Candy?"

"What about her?"

"What will she think?"

Matthew drew in a deep breath and said, "Candy and I don't have that kind of relationship, you know that."

"But the public doesn't know that, and this article will make her look like a jilted lover."

He had no desire to discuss Candy or their nonexistent bedroom activities. Ryan knew the real deal. Candy was trying to build a certain image in Hollywood, and Matthew had agreed to be Candy's escort to several social functions, but only because he had gotten sick and tired of hanging around the house moping when he wasn't working. Ryan and Candy's agent felt it would be good PR. He'd known the media would make more out of it than there was, but at the time he hadn't given a damn.

"And where is Carmen now?" Ryan asked.

"In bed." He smiled, imagining the erroneous vision going through his manager's mind.

"Dammit, Matthew, I hope you know what you're doing. Her leaving almost destroyed you."

A painful silence surrounded him. No one had to remind him of what he'd gone through. "Look, Ryan, I know you mean well, but this is between me and Carmen."

"And what am I supposed to tell the media when they can't contact you and then call me?"

"Tell them there's no comment. Good night, Ryan."

Matthew breathed a sigh of relief as he ended the call. Ryan could be a pain in the ass at times, especially when it came to the images of his clients. But then he could definitely understand the man's concerns. His separation and subsequent divorce from Carmen had left him in a bad way for a while. But that was then and this was now. He could handle things. He could handle her. Pride and the need for self-preservation would keep him from falling under her spell ever again. He felt good knowing that although he'd given her some sexual release, she would still go to bed tonight needing even more. There was no doubt in his mind she would be aching for his touch.

He smiled. This sort of revenge was pretty damn sweet.

* * *

The next morning Carmen was easing out of bed when her cell phone rang. She reached over and picked it up. The sunlight pouring through the window was promising a beautiful day.

"Hello?"

"Girl, I am so happy for you. When I saw that article and picture, I almost cried."

Carmen recognized the voice of her good friend Rachel Wellesley. Rachel was a makeup artist she'd met on the set of her first movie. The close friendship she and Rachel had developed still existed to this day.

She knew what Rachel was referring to and decided to stop the conversation before her friend went any further. Carmen was well aware that Rachel probably said a special prayer each night before she went to bed that Carmen and Matthew would reunite. Rachel liked taking credit for playing matchmaker and initially getting them together.

"Chill, Rachel, and hold back the tears. No matter what you've heard, seen or read, Matthew and I aren't getting back together."

There was silence on the other end of the line.

"But what about the kiss that's plastered all over the front page of the *Wagging Tongue* this morning?" Rachel asked, sounding disappointed. "And don't you dare try to convince me it's a photo that's been doctored."

Carmen didn't say anything as she remembered the kiss and the effect it had on her. "No, it's not a photo that's been doctored, although a part of me wishes that it were. It started when I ran into Ardella Rowe at the polo match yesterday and she mentioned something about Matthew and me being enemies. I firmly denied it and went further, painting a picture of the two of us as friends, regardless of what the tabloids were saying. Well, before I could get the words out of my mouth,

Matthew walked into the tent and all eyes were on us. To save face, I greeted him with a kiss on the cheek. Of course he decided to take advantage of the situation by turning a casual kiss into something more."

"From the photo, it looked pretty damn hot, if you ask me."

It was. But it was nothing compared to the one they'd shared last night on the balcony. She felt heat rise to her face as she imagined what he'd thought of the fact that she'd climaxed from his kiss.

"You should talk to him, Carmen, and tell him the truth. You know what I think about you not telling him about losing the baby."

Carmen pulled in a deep breath. Rachel was one of the few people who knew about what had happened that night. When she'd found out about her pregnancy, she'd been so excited she had wanted to share it with someone. Rachel had actually been the one who'd come up with the idea of making a surprise video telling Matthew of her pregnancy.

While curling up in his arms on the sofa in the villa, she had planned to suggest that they watch a few video pitches for possible projects that directors had sent her. Instead, unbeknownst to him, she would play the video of her first ultrasound, even though the baby was just a tiny speck in a sea of black.

But things hadn't worked out that way.

"Yes, I know how you feel and you know how I feel, as well. Matthew should have been there with me." He'd always had legitimate excuses why he was late arriving someplace or not able to show up at all because of some last-minute emergency on the set. But for once he should have placed her above everything else, and he hadn't.

Knowing that Rachel would try to make her see Matthew's side of things, reminding her that he had no idea what was going on, she quickly said, "Look, Rachel, let me call you back later. I'm just getting up."

"Sure. And where's Matthew?"

"I have no idea. We spent the night under the same roof but in different bedrooms, of course. Knowing him, he's probably gone by now. He has this new project here in New York, so I'm sure he's left already to go into the city."

"The two of you will be living there together all summer?" Rachel asked.

Carmen could hear the excitement in Rachel's voice. She knew it would be a waste of time telling her not to get her hopes up because it wasn't that kind of party. The guest room Matthew was using was on the other side of the house, and considering his schedule, their paths would probably only cross once or twice while they were there.

"Yes, for the most part, but this house is so big I doubt I'll even see him."

After ending her conversation with Rachel, Carmen got up and went into the bathroom. She planned to go swimming in the pool and then head down to the beach after breakfast.

Even though things had started off pretty rocky between her and Matthew yesterday, thanks to him she'd slept like a baby last night. An orgasm brought on by Matthew Birmingham never failed her. Whenever she'd had a tension-filled day on the set, he would make love to her to calm her frazzled nerves.

But upon waking her greedy body wanted more. It was as if she'd suddenly developed an addiction to Matthew's touch, a touch she had managed to do without for more than a year but was craving like crazy now.

An intense yearning and longing was rolling around in the pit of her stomach and although she was trying to ignore it, doing such a thing wasn't working. Now that her body recognized the familiarity of his touch, it seemed to have a mind of its own.

She frowned while stripping off her nightgown. She wondered if Matt had deliberately set her up for this—she wouldn't be surprised to discover that he had. He of all people knew how her body could react to him. So, okay, she would admit that he had bested her this round, but she was determined not to lower her guard with him again.

Chapter Eight

"**I** thought you had left to go into the city." Matthew glanced up and nearly swallowed his tongue. Carmen was standing in the kitchen doorway dressed in a two-piece bathing suit with a sheer, short sarong wrapped firmly around her small waist that placed emphasis on her curvaceous hips and beautiful long legs. Her hair was pulled up into a knot displaying the gracefulness of her neck, and even from across the room he could smell her luscious scent.

He felt a flash of anger with himself that she could still have this kind of effect on him. But last night had proven just how things were between them. Of course sex had never been the issue—her inability to believe she was the most important thing in his life had been. What he resented most was her not giving them time to work anything out. And once the media had gotten wind of their problems, they had made a field day of it, printing and stating things that hadn't been true.

But seeing her now almost made it impossible to recall why there were problems between them. She was the most beautiful, desirable woman he had ever laid eyes on.

He lowered his head and resumed eating. It was either that or do something real stupid like get up from the table, cross the room and pull her into his arms.

"I figured since you have business to take care of in Manhattan, you would have left already," she explained, looking genuinely surprised to see him.

He wondered if she'd actually been hoping their paths would not cross today, and he knew that was a pretty good assumption to make. Sighing, he picked up his coffee cup. "Sorry to disappoint you, but I'll be doing most of my work from here."

"Oh," she said. He continued to watch her as she crossed the room to the stove.

"I take it you're spending the day on the beach?" he asked, wondering why she had to look so ultra-feminine and much-too-sexy this morning. But then she always looked good, even when she'd just woken up in the morning. He'd so enjoyed making love to her then, stroking the sleepiness from her eyes as he stroked inside her body.

"Yes, that's my plan, after taking a dip in the pool first," she said, pouring a cup of coffee. She took a sip and smiled. "You still make good coffee."

He chuckled as he leaned back in his chair. "That's not the only thing I'm still good at, Carmen."

Carmen swallowed hard, thinking that he didn't have to remind her of that.

Her heart began pounding in her chest and she felt breathless when he stood. All six feet three inches of him was well built and dangerously male. And she thought now what she thought the first day she'd laid eyes on him: Matthew Birmingham had the ability to ignite passion in any woman.

Focus, Carmen, focus. Don't get off track here. You need to win back the upper hand. Remembering her call from Rachel, she asked, "Has Candy Sumlar called you yet?"

He pushed his chair under the table and went to the sink, pausing for a moment to glance at her. "Is she supposed to?"

Carmen shrugged. "Don't be surprised if she does. Someone took a picture of us yesterday and it made the front page of the *Wagging Tongue*."

He turned toward her after placing his cup in the sink. "I know. It could cause a problem or two, I suppose."

He took a few steps toward her until Carmen had to tilt her head back to look up into his face. "Then why did you kiss me?" she asked.

"Because I wanted to."

His words, precise and definitely unapologetic, gave her a funny feeling in the pit of her stomach. Sexual tension filled the room and for a moment, she was mesmerized by his gaze— those extraordinary dark eyes could render a woman breathless if she stared into them for too long.

So she broke eye contact and moved away. "Doing things that you want to do without thinking about the possible outcome can get you in trouble."

"And who said I didn't think about it?"

Carmen fell silent. Was Matthew insinuating that he'd kissed her knowing full well what he was doing? That he would have done so anyway, even if she hadn't made a move first with that kiss on the cheek? She ignored the tingle in her stomach at the mere thought that this was more than a game to him. That perhaps he had wanted her and initiating that kiss had been just the thing to push him over the edge.

Umm. The thought of that had her nipples feeling hard and pressing tight against the bikini top. She drew in a deep breath and as her lungs filled with the potent air they were both breathing she felt her nipples grow even more sensitive. He was leaning against the counter, his eyes roaming up and down her body. She wanted him to check her out good and assume that he could get more from her than just the hot-and-heavy kiss they'd shared last night. Then she would gladly show him how wrong that assumption was. If he was playing a game, she would show him that two could play.

She moved toward the table to sit down, intentionally swaying her hips as she did so. She took a sip of her coffee as she felt heat emitting from his gaze.

"There are some muffins in the refrigerator if you want something else to go with your coffee," he said.

"Thanks, I'm fine."

"There's another polo match tomorrow. Do you plan on going?" he asked.

"I do," she replied.

She knew why he was asking. By tomorrow, a number of people would have read the article and all sorts of speculations would be made. The main question was, how would they handle it?

The room got quiet. He finally broke the silence by asking, "What about Bruno? Will he get upset when he hears about the article?"

Carmen looked over at him and plastered a smile on her lips. "No, because he knows he has nothing to worry about." She knew that comment irked him. Back in the day when he'd been a movie star, Matthew and Bruno had been rivals as Hollywood heartbreakers. The two never developed a close friendship and even now merely tolerated each other for appearance's sake.

"Good. I wouldn't want to cause friction between the two of you."

"You won't." Seeing she would not be able to drink her coffee in peace while he was around, she stood and announced, "I'm going to the pool."

Matthew watched her leave, irritated by what she'd said about Bruno knowing he had nothing to worry about. The very thought that the man was that confident about their relationship didn't sit well with him. A sudden picture of her in Bruno's arms flashed through his mind and he felt anger gathering in his body, all the way to his fingertips.

He drew in a deep breath and then let it out slowly, wondering what Bruno would think if he knew his girl had gotten pleasured by her ex last night. Although they hadn't made love, Matthew knew her well enough to know that that orgasm had been real and potent. In fact, if he didn't know any better, he'd think it was the first she'd had in a while, which meant Bruno wasn't taking care of business like he should.

But the thought of that man taking care of business at all where Carmen was concerned had steam coming out of his ears and a tic working in his jaw. Deciding it was time to rev up his plans of seduction a notch, he left the kitchen to go upstairs to change.

Carmen opened her eyes when she heard footsteps on the brick pavers. She took one look at Matthew and wished she'd kept them closed. He was walking toward her wearing a pair of swim trunks that would probably be outlawed if worn in public.

Her gaze settled on his face and the intense expression she saw there, before lowering her eyes to the sculpted muscles of his bare chest and then sliding down to his midsection. The waistband of his trunks hung low and fully outlined a purely masculine male.

She stiffened slightly when she felt a deep stirring in the middle of her stomach and fought to keep perspective. She sat up on the chaise longue and held his stare, wishing her heart would stop beating so rapidly.

And wishing she still didn't love him like she knew she still did.

That stark realization had her moving quickly, jumping out of her seat, nearly knocking over a small table in her haste. "What are you doing here, Matthew?"

He came to a stop in front of her. "Why do you always ask me that like I'm out of place or something?"

Silence hung heavy between them. Then she lifted her chin and said, "Probably because I feel like you are. I'm not exactly used to having you around." She then moved toward the pool.

Matthew didn't say anything, mainly because he was focused on the pain in her voice—as well as the realization that she was right. This *was* the longest they had been together in the same place in a long time—including when they were married.

Suddenly, he couldn't even fortify himself with the excuse that all those hours he'd been away working had been for her. Because in the end, he'd still failed to give her the one thing she'd wanted and needed the most: his time.

He had missed this—her presence, the connection they'd shared in the beginning but had somehow lost in the end. How could he have been so wrong about what he thought she truly wanted and needed? He had wanted them both to find happiness, but they sure as hell weren't happy now. At least, he wasn't. His stomach clenched at the thought of just how unhappy he was. His plan for revenge didn't taste as sweet as it had yesterday, and he had no idea what to do.

He watched as she stood by the pool, untying the sarong from around her waist and dropping it to the ground. And then she dove in, hitting the water with a splash. He stood watching her, remembering when all he'd wanted was to make her his wife and to have children together one day. He had loved and wanted her so much.

And I still love her and want her.

The admission was like a sharp punch to his gut. Nothing mattered at that moment—not the humiliation he'd felt when she left, nor the anger or frustration he'd suffered when she chose to file for a divorce. What he was sure about more than anything was that he wanted her and if given the chance to repair the damage, he would handle things differently. What he was unsure about was whether or not she wanted another go with him. There was one way to find out.

It was time he was driven by a different motivation, not of revenge but of resolution. He moved toward the pool and dived in after her.

It was time to get his wife back.

Chapter Nine

Carmen surfaced when she heard a big splash behind her. Seeing Matthew in the water, she decided it was time to get out of the pool and began swimming toward the other side.

She eased herself out to sit on the edge and watch him, studying his strokes, meticulous and defined, and the way he was fluidly gliding through the water. He was an excellent swimmer, of course—after all, he had attended UCLA on a swimming scholarship.

He swam toward her until he was right there, treading water between her legs. And before she could catch her next breath, he reached up and pulled her into the water.

"Matthew!"

Carmen wrapped her arms around his neck so she wouldn't go under, but that ended up being the least of her worries as he tightened his hold on her and pressed his mouth to hers. She whimpered when his tongue grabbed hold of hers, stroking it hungrily. And when he deepened the kiss, she automatically wrapped her legs around his waist, feeling the strength of his thighs and his hard erection through his wet swim trunks.

She returned the kiss, realizing that she was powerless to resist this intense interaction, this outburst of sexual chemistry and reckless behavior. Heat and pressure were building up inside her. The feel of the water encompassing them captivated her, making her all too aware of the way he knew exactly what to do to her.

He began licking and nibbling around her lips, and she knew instinctively that this was a man with outright seduction on his mind. The only thing wrong was that she was supposed to be seducing him, not the other way around.

She couldn't resist the urge to clamp her mouth down on his, needing the feel of his tongue tangling with hers. She could truthfully say she'd never enjoyed kissing a man more— she had missed this intimate foreplay tremendously. Though she hated to admit it, being here with him was long overdue and she needed it like she needed to breathe.

When he began wading through the water toward the steps, she saw they'd somehow made it to the shallow end. Pulling his mouth from hers, he shifted her body in his arms as he walked up the steps from the pool. Cool air brushed across her wet skin and her entire body shuddered in his embrace.

She didn't ask where they were going. It didn't matter. She was overwhelmed by the way he was staring down at her with every step he took. And when he placed her on the lounger, she reached out, not ready for him to release her.

"I'm not going anyplace," he whispered in a deep husky tone, running his hands along her wet thighs. "I'm just grabbing a couple towels to dry us off."

He only took a step or two away from her but Carmen instantly felt desperate for his touch. The loneliness of the past year loomed over her and she felt a stab of regret, wishing she had handled things between them differently.

She had known from the first that Matthew was a proud man, a man who'd had to work hard for anything he'd ever had in life. That was the reason he was so driven. When they'd married, he had vowed to take care of her and in his mind, working hard was the only way to do that. And although she'd told him over and over that all she wanted was him, he hadn't been able to hear her, mainly because he was who he was—a man determined to take care of his own.

At that moment, something in her shifted and she felt something she hadn't felt in a long time—peace and contentment. When he returned to her with the towels, she reached up and touched his face, tracing his lips with her fingertips before leaning in and kissing him softly on the mouth.

She felt his hold tighten and she detected the raw hunger within him, but he let her have her way. Knowing he was holding back caused a surge of desire to flood every part of her body.

She released his mouth and he wrapped her up in one of the towels, wiping her dry. She moaned in total enjoyment over the feel of the soft terry cloth against her flesh. He slid the towel all over her body to absorb the water from her skin, leaving no area untouched. She knew she was being lured into a temptation she could not resist.

He dried himself off, as well, and she watched, enjoying every movement of the towel on his body, looking at his chest and shoulders and legs. He was so well built—watching him had to be the most erotic thing she'd witnessed in a long time.

Tossing the towels aside, he leaned down and covered her mouth with his once more while stretching out to join her on the lounger, her body under his. He broke off the kiss and used his teeth to lift her bikini top. Before she could utter a sound, his mouth was at her breasts, sucking the hardened tips of her nipples between his lips.

Matthew had always enjoyed her breasts and that hadn't changed. Carmen could tell that he refused to be rushed while cupping the twin globes in his hands, using his mouth to tease them one minute and lavish them the next.

And then she felt him tugging at her wet bikini bottoms, removing them from her body and tossing them aside. He stepped back and began lowering his swim trunks down his legs.

She shifted on the lounger to watch him like she'd done so

many other times. Her breath caught at what a fine specimen of a man he was in the raw—she had always enjoyed seeing him naked. And at that moment she was filled with a need to pay special tribute to his body the way she used to.

When he moved toward her, she sat up and her mouth made contact with his stomach as she twirled her tongue all around his abs. She felt the hard muscles tense beneath her mouth, and her hands automatically reached out to clutch his thighs as the tip of her tongue traced a trail from one side of his belly to the next, drawing circles around the indention of his belly button.

He moaned her name. Pressing her forehead against his stomach, she inhaled the scent of him. She then leaned back, her face level with his groin. She reached out and grabbed hold of his shaft, feeling the aroused member thicken even more in her hands.

The dark eyes staring down at her were penetrating, hypnotic and displayed a fierce hunger she felt all the way in the pit of her stomach. Although he wouldn't verbally express his desires, she knew them. She had been married to him for three years and she knew exactly how to pleasure him in a way that would give him the utmost gratification.

She opened her mouth and leaned forward, her lips and tongue making contact with his erection. She heard his tortured moan as she greedily licked him all over, focusing on her task as if it were of monumental importance—and to her, it was. He was the only man she'd ever performed this act on, and she derived just as much pleasure giving it as she knew he was getting from it.

"Carmen."

Her name was a guttural groan from his lips and when she felt his fingers plunge into her hair, she slid his erection inside her mouth and went to work, just the way he'd taught her, the way she knew that could push him over the edge. She so enjoyed watching him fall.

The thought that she was driving him crazy was a total turn-on for her. As her mouth continued its torment, she could feel his pleasure heightening. Soon, the same heat and passion consuming him began taking hold of her. He was the only man who could make her bold and daring enough to do something like this, the only man who made lust such a significant thing.

Was it wrong to desire her ex-husband so much? He was the very man who had broken his promise to make her the most important thing in his life, to cherish her forever....

She pushed those thoughts to the back of her mind, not wanting to dwell on all the things that had gone wrong. Instead she wanted to dwell on him, on making love with the most irresistible man to walk the face of the earth.

"Carmen!"

The throaty sound of her name on his lips—the instinctive response of a man reaching extreme sexual pleasure—pulled her back to the here and now. When the explosion she'd been expecting happened, she was overwhelmed by her own passion and the depth of her love for him.

And then she felt herself being lifted into his arms. When he crushed his mouth to hers, she knew there was no stopping either of them now. Their wants and desires were taking over and they wouldn't deny themselves anything.

She wrapped her arms around his neck as she felt herself being carried up the winding stairs. She knew exactly where he was taking her—to the master suite, their bedroom, their bed.

She pulled in a deep breath when they reached their destination and he eased her out of his arms and onto the bed. Before she could draw in another breath, he was there with her, reaching out to her and pulling her back into his arms.

His hands touched her everywhere, and where his hands stroked, his mouth soon followed. He moved from her lips down past her neck to her chest where, after cupping her breasts in his hands and skimming his fingertips across them, he used the tip of his tongue to lavish the twin mounds and hardened tips.

Matthew then glided his hands down her hips and between her legs to cup the warmth of her womanhood. And then his mouth was there, pressing against her feminine folds, as if needing the taste of her on his tongue.

"Oh, Matthew."

She rocked her body against his mouth and he responded by plunging his tongue deeper inside of her. The sensations he was evoking were so intense she could only cry out in a whimper once more before pleasure erupted within her, spiraling her into a shattering climax, the intensity of which brought tears to her eyes.

"You liked that?" he asked moments later when he slid back up her body and began licking her neck.

Unable to speak, she nodded her head. His mouth claimed hers again. Moments later he straddled her body with his arms, inching her legs apart with his knees. When he released her mouth, he peered down at her. "You sure about this, baby?" he whispered hoarsely before moving any farther.

She hadn't been more sure about anything in her life. "Yes, Matthew, I'm sure."

That was all he needed to hear. He continued to hold Carmen's gaze as his body lowered onto hers, his thick erection moving past her feminine folds and deep into the core of her. Her inner muscles clutched him and he groaned her name. He had missed this. He had missed *her*. He wanted to close his eyes and relish the feeling of being inside her this way, but he kept his eyes open. He held tight to her gaze as he continued moving deeper and deeper inside of her as she lifted her hips to receive all of him.

And when he'd buried himself in her to the hilt, he let out a rugged growl as pinnacles of pleasure began radiating through him starting at the soles of his feet and escalating upward. He felt every single sensation as he moved, his strokes insistent as he thrust deep, fully intent on driving her wild, over the edge and back again.

"Matthew, please…"

The longing in her voice revealed just what she was asking for and his strokes increased to a feverish pitch, giving her just what she wanted. He understood her need, comprehended her desires since they were just as fierce as his own. He thrust deeper still as they moved in perfect rhythm.

She tightened her legs around his back when he groaned, triggering an explosion that ripped through their bodies. As he spilled into her, he lowered his mouth to hers and took her lips while an earth-shattering release tore through them.

He sank deeper and deeper into her as a pulsing ache took control of his entire body and he felt himself swelling all over again inside her. Moments later, another orgasm slashed through him, drowning him in waves after waves of intense pleasure.

The moment he released her mouth, she cried out for him. "Matthew!"

As she gazed up at him, he knew their lovemaking had proven what they'd refused to admit or acknowledge up until now, this very moment.

Divorce or no divorce, their life together was far from over.

Chapter Ten

Depleted of energy, Carmen lay still with her eyes closed, unable to move, her body still intimately connected with Matthew's. She could feel the wetness between her thighs where their bodies were still joined.

She slowly opened her eyes. Matthew's face was right there. He was asleep, but still holding her in his arms, his leg was thrown possessively over her, locking their entwined bodies together. It was as if he'd deliberately chosen that position so that he would know if she moved the slightest bit.

She glanced at the clock on the nightstand and saw that it was close to two in the afternoon, which meant they had spent the last five hours in bed. Closing her eyes again, she thought that she had never experienced anything quite like the lovemaking session they'd just shared, and she could still feel remnants of sexual bliss simmering through her.

Her body quivered at the memory of his mouth between her legs, and of his tongue lapping her into sweet oblivion. She hadn't made love with another man since their divorce and now she knew why—her body didn't want anyone other than Matthew.

Suddenly, she felt him starting to swell inside her. She opened her eyes to stare right into the darkness of his. They lay there, gazing at each other while his shaft expanded into a huge, hard erection.

"Oh my goodness." The words slid from her lips as she felt him stretching her inside. Her inner muscles clamped tight and wouldn't let him go.

He leaned forward and kissed her, moving in and out at a slow pace. His unhurried strokes eased the tremendous ache between her legs and matched the rhythm of his tongue as it mingled with hers. She couldn't help moaning with each thrust into her body as she was overtaken with desire. He was so painstakingly thorough it nearly took her breath away.

Moments later she pulled her mouth from his when her body erupted into an orgasm so intense she screamed in ecstasy, totally taken aback at the magnitude of pleasure ripping through her. And then Matthew followed her into the thrill of rapture as his body exploded, as well. As he drove harder and deeper, she could actually feel his release shoot right to her womb.

"Matthew…"

She moaned his name from deep within her throat and when his mouth found hers again, she continued to shudder as her body refused to come down from such a rapturous high.

"I can't believe I feel so drained."

Matthew glanced over at Carmen and smiled. They had just arrived at Ray's Place, a popular hangout on the Hamptons. She was leaning against his car and, dressed in a pair of jeans and a cute pink blouse, she was looking as breathless as she sounded. "I wonder why," he said.

She laughed and gave him a knowing look. "Oh, you know exactly why, Matthew Birmingham." She raked a hand through her hair and laughed again before saying in a somewhat serious tone, "You're pretty incredible."

His smile widened. "You're pretty incredible yourself. Come on, let's go grab something to eat to feed that depleted soul of yours." He took her hand in his and they headed toward the entrance of the establishment.

The one thing he'd always enjoyed about Ray's Place was that it was private and the paparazzi were not allowed on the grounds, which was probably why a number of people were there tonight, many of whom had ventured to the Hamptons for the polo matches.

Another thing he liked abut Ray's Place was the excellent service, and he appreciated that they were seated immediately. He glanced over at her and thought he didn't mind being guilty of making her tired. Making love to her most of that day had been the most erotic thing he'd done in a long time, and because it was her and no other woman, it had been special.

"Umm, so what do you think we should order?" she asked, looking at the menu.

He leaned back in his chair. "Whatever can fill me up. I'm starving."

She rolled her eyes. "You're famished and I'm exhausted. Go figure."

"My friend Matthew Birmingham and his lovely wife, Carmen. How are you?"

Matthew glanced up and smiled. "Sheikh Adham, I heard you were a guest this year at the Polo Club. How are you?" he asked, standing and shaking the man's hand. He had met the sheikh over ten years ago when, as a college student, the sheikh had visited the United States and participated in a swimming competition at UCLA. They had become good friends then.

"I am fine, Matthew." And he leaned over and kissed Carmen's cheek. "And you, Carmen, are as beautiful as ever."

"Thanks, Sheikh Adham," Carmen said, smiling.

The man then gestured to the woman by his side. "And let me introduce my wife, Sabrina. Sweetheart, Matthew and Carmen are friends of mine."

The woman smiled as she greeted them. Matthew fought not to show the surprise on his face. Adham married? The woman was certainly a beauty. But he'd spent some time with Adham just last year while working on a historical piece in the Middle East when he'd claimed marriage was the furthest thing from this mind. Matthew couldn't help wondering what had happened to make him change his mind.

"Would you and Sabrina like to join us?" Matthew heard Carmen ask.

Adham shook his head. "We appreciate your kindness but we've already eaten and were just leaving. Hopefully, we can get together soon after one of the polo matches."

"Carmen and I would like that." They chatted for a few more minutes before the couple left.

"Wow, I can't imagine Adham married," Carmen said, speaking aloud what Matthew's thoughts had been earlier. Matthew returned to his seat, remembering it was well-known that Adham used to have a wild streak and be quite a womanizer.

"They look happy," Carmen added.

Matthew wasn't so sure about that. For some reason he didn't quite feel that happiness that Adham and Sabrina were trying so hard to emit.

"I can't believe I ate so much," Carmen said when they returned from dinner.

She glanced over her shoulder and saw Matthew grinning as he tossed his car keys on the table. "And just what do you find so amusing?" she couldn't help but ask him.

He leaned back against the door. "I have to say I don't ever recall seeing you eat that much. You ate your dessert and mine."

Carmen chuckled as she dropped down on the sofa. "Only because you didn't seem as hungry as you claimed you were. I, on the other hand, was not only exhausted, I was hungry."

He nodded. "Are you full now?"

"Yes, pretty much so."

"And your energy level?"

She lifted a brow, wondering why he wanted to know. "Good. Why?"

"Keep watching, you'll figure it out."

And she did. First went his shirt, which he removed and tossed aside. His shoes and socks came next and Carmen watched fascinated. When his hand went to the zipper of his jeans she shivered in anticipation. The man had a body that could make her tremble while waiting for it to be bared.

Determined not to be undone, she eased off the sofa and began removing her own clothes. By the time she had tossed her last article of clothing aside, he was slowly moving toward her. "You're slow, Carmen."

She grinned. "And you look hard, Matthew."

"You're right," he said, pulling her into his arms. She groaned out loud with the feel of his naked body against hers.

"Haven't you gotten enough yet?" she asked, smiling.

"No. Have you?"

She wrapped her arms around his neck. "No."

And then he pulled her back down on the couch with him.

Matthew gazed up at the ceiling. If anyone had told him that he would be spending a good part of his entire day making love to his wife—his ex-wife—he would not have believed it. Even now, while lying flat on his back, trying to regain his strength and listening to her moving around in the bathroom, he was still somewhat stunned.

Their lovemaking had been off the charts as always, but something had been different—he'd detected another element in the mix. An intense hunger had driven them to new heights, making them fully aware of what they'd gone without for twelve months and just how much they longed to have it back.

He had assumed leaving the house awhile would wean some of their sexual hunger, but it hadn't. No sooner had they returned, they were at it again. He could not get enough of her, and they had gotten it on every chance they got. Without any regrets. At least there certainly hadn't been any on his part and he hoped the same held true for her.

What if she was not feeling the same way that he was? What if it had been lust and not love that had driven her to sleep with him, and now that she had, nothing had changed for her?

Shifting positions, he lay on his side with his gaze fixed on the bathroom door. Carmen was an actress, and a damn good one, but when it came to certain emotions, he could read her like a book. At least he used to be able to.

But today she had made love with him as if they hadn't just spent an entire year not talking to each other. He wished he could let the matter go, but he couldn't. Their love had been too strong for him to just let things continue as they had before. He didn't want revenge anymore. What he wanted more than anything was an explanation as to why she had ended their marriage. As far as he was concerned, they could have worked it out if she'd just given him a chance, if she'd just communicated with him.

He drew in a deep breath as he waited for his ex to come out of the bathroom. It was time for all cards to be placed on the table. It was time for her to be honest with him and for him to be honest with her, as well. He wanted his wife back, and it was time he told her so.

Carmen stood at the vanity mirror after her shower, staring at her face, hoping that Matthew would still be asleep when she left the bathroom. She was not ready to see any sign of regret in his eyes. It had probably just been lust driving him to make love to her like that, and now that it was out of his system, it would be business as usual with them. He would remind her, in a nice way of course, that they were still divorced and nothing had changed.

Boy, was he wrong. Something had changed—at least it had for her. She could no longer deny that she still loved him. And she had to tell him about the baby—it wasn't fair to keep it a secret anymore.

At the time, she had been so hurt that all she'd wanted to do was wallow in the pain without him. She'd blamed him for not being there that night and had even gone so far as to tell herself that if he had been there, things might have been different. She hadn't wanted to believe what the doctor had said—that a large percentage of women miscarry a baby at some point during their reproductive years. According to the doctor there was no reason for her not to have a normal pregnancy when she was ready to try again. But at the time, she hadn't wanted to think about another pregnancy. She'd only wanted to mourn the one she'd lost.

She wished she'd handled things differently. She should have called Matthew and let him know what happened. She knew deep down that there was nothing, work or otherwise, that would have kept him from hopping on the next plane to Barcelona to be with her.

He would have held her while she cried, kissed her tears away and told her everything would be okay, that as soon as she was ready they would make another baby. He would have meant every word.

And when she'd been able to travel he would have taken her home and cared for her, pampered her and shown her that no matter how many hours he spent away from her, she was the most important thing in his life.

He had told her that many times but she hadn't wanted to hear it even though she, of all people, knew his family history and knew that taking care of her was important to him. But what she had done was turn her back on him and without telling him the full story, she had filed for a divorce. She hung her head, ashamed of her decision. He probably hated her for doing that, and their relationship could be beyond repair at this point.

She lifted her face to stare at her reflection again. Yesterday, she'd wanted to seduce her ex-husband in the name of revenge, but today she knew she needed him in her life. She loved him and wouldn't be happy until they were together again.

Somehow she needed to make him fall in love with her all over again. But first she had to tell him the truth. She had to tell him about the baby.

Matthew held his breath when the bathroom door opened and the moment Carmen appeared in the doorway his heart began pounding deep in his chest. The sunlight pouring in through the windows seemed to make her skin glow.

Silently he lay there and studied the way her short silk bathrobe clung to her curves. He had every reason to believe she was naked underneath it. There was a damp sheen to her brown skin and her hair was tied back away from her face, emphasizing her eyes and mouth. As he continued to watch her, that mouth he enjoyed kissing so much slowly curved into a sexy smile.

There were no regretful vibes emitting from her and he let out a relieved breath as they stared at each other. They'd done that a lot lately, staring at each other without saying anything. But what he saw in her gaze now nearly melted his heart. She loved him. He was certain of that. He might not ever hear her say the words to him again but he could see it—it was there on her face, in her eyes and all around those delectable lips.

He intended to do whatever had to be done to remind her of what they'd once had. More than anything, he wanted her to accept that there was nothing the two of them couldn't work out together. That was the one thing he was certain about. Two people couldn't love each other as deeply as they did and still stay apart. In his book, things just didn't work out that way.

He watched as she slowly moved across the room toward him and he sat up to catch her when she all but dived into his arms. And then she was kissing him with a hunger and need that he quickly reciprocated. He fought for control, his body burning with a need that was driving him off the deep end. He wanted to do nothing more than bury himself inside her body.

Moments later, she ended the kiss and leaned back. Her robe had risen up her thighs and the belt around her waist was loose, giving him a glimpse of a tantalizing portion of her breasts and the dark shadow at the juncture of her legs. The scent of her was drawing him in, making him remember how he'd felt being inside of her.

Unable to resist, he reached out and slid his hands beneath the silk of her bathrobe and began stroking her breasts, letting his fingertips tease the hardened nipples. When he began moving lower, she whispered, "Matthew, let's talk."

He agreed with her. They should talk. He wanted to start off by telling her how he felt, but the moment he opened his mouth to do so, he realized he wasn't ready after all. He didn't want to revisit the past just yet. Instead, he wanted to stay right here, right now. "I'm not ready to hash out the bad times, Carmen. Right now I just want to forget about what drove us apart and only concentrate on this, what has brought us together."

He held her gaze, knowing as well as she did that there was no way they could totally forget. If this was about nothing but sex, then that was one thing, but deep down he knew it wasn't. The love between them was still there, which meant there were problems they needed to address. Had his long hours been the only thing that had driven her away from him? He was certain she knew he hadn't been unfaithful to her.

She nodded, and he drew in another deep breath. Eventually they would talk, and he meant really talk. Because now that he had his wife back in his arms, his heart and his bed, he intended to keep her there.

Chapter Eleven

Carmen had agreed to postpone their conversation at Matthew's request, and they had spent an amazing week together, enjoying each other. They were both fearful that an in-depth discussion of the state of their affairs would put them back at square one. And they weren't ready to go back there yet.

Instead they'd opted to spend time together, living in the present and not venturing to the past. At the polo matches, everyone was speculating as to what exactly was going on between them. And the *Wagging Tongue* wasn't helping matters. More than one snapshot of them together had appeared in the tabloid, and she and Matthew didn't have to work hard to figure out the identity of the person passing the photos to the paper. Ardella Rowe was the prime suspect. They had seen her at dinner the same night they'd run into Sheikh Adham, and she had tried pestering them with questions, which they'd refused to answer.

At one polo match, she and Matthew had stuck to "no comment" when a mic was shoved in their faces by a reporter wanting to know whether or not they'd gotten back together. The fact of the matter was, they couldn't exactly answer that question themselves.

One paper she had seen claimed they were having a summer fling with no chance of reconciliation while another had announced they'd remarried at a church on Martha's Vineyard. A third had even reported the real Carmen Akins was in Rome with Bruno and the woman Matthew was spending time with in the Hamptons was only a look-alike, a woman he'd taken up with who closely resembled his ex-wife. She could only shake her head at the absurdity of that.

Carmen stood at the huge window in the library, looking out upon the calm waters of the Atlantic.

This past week had been the best she'd known. And it hadn't bothered her in the least the few times Matthew had gone into Manhattan on business, even when one of those meetings had extended well into the late afternoon.

Now she could truly say that although she'd blamed him for the breakup of their marriage, a good portion of the blame could be placed at her feet. She of all people knew how demanding things could be for a director at times, dealing with temperamental actors, overanxious investors and too-cautious production companies. On top of that, there were a number of other issues that could crop up at a moment's notice. And because she'd known all of that, was aware of the stress, she could have been a lot more understanding and a lot less demanding of his time.

The sad thing about it was that she'd always been an independent person and had never yearned for attention from anyone, yet during that time she'd needed Matthew's. Or she'd thought she did. And when she'd lost the baby, she couldn't stand the thought of a future in which Matthew was never there for her, not even when she needed him most.

She selected a book of poetry and was sitting down in one of the recliners when she heard Matthew's footsteps on the hardwood floor. She glanced up the moment he walked into the room, surprised. He had taken a ferry to Manhattan that morning and she hadn't expected him back until much later.

The moment their eyes met, a sensation erupted in the pit of her stomach. And then the craving began.

She placed the book aside as he walked toward her with that

slow, sexy saunter. She knew exactly what he had on his mind. Because it was on hers, too. But she also knew it was time for them to talk. They couldn't put it off any longer.

Carmen rose from her seat. "I think it's time for us to talk now, Matthew. There's something I need to tell you."

Matthew had a feeling he knew what Carmen wanted to talk about but he wasn't ready to hear it. The last thing he wanted to discuss was that she was beginning to feel as if there were nothing but sex between them. Given that they'd made love multiple times during the day for seven straight days, he could certainly see why she thought that.

But what she'd failed to take into consideration was that every time he was inside her body, his heart was almost ready to burst in his chest. And each and every morning he woke up with her in his arms made him realize just how much he loved her. What she didn't know was that making love to her was his way of showing her with his body what he hadn't yet been able to say out loud.

He knew things couldn't continue this way between them. Time was running out and they would have to talk sometime, would have to rehash the past and decide what they would do about their future. But not now, not when he wanted her so much he could hardly breathe.

"Matthew, I—"

He reached out and pulled her into his arms, and within seconds surrender replaced her surprise. This is what he wanted. What he needed. He deepened their kiss, intending to overtake her with passion, to overwhelm her senses.

He closed his arms tightly around her and lifted her just enough to fit snug against his crotch, needing to feel her warmth pressed against him. The feel tormented him and he pulled his mouth away, turning her around so her back fit solidly against his chest.

"Hold on to the table, baby," he whispered.

Carmen felt the warmth of his breath on her ear and knew Matthew was trying to take her mind off her need to talk. And for now, she would let him. Her insides began to quiver and she pressed against him. Emotions she couldn't hold at bay consumed her entire being.

"I want you so much I ache," he added in a deep husky voice that had her body shivering. She loved him and wanted more between them than this. But she would settle for this for now. She didn't want to think about what would happen when she told him about losing their baby. Would he understand the reason she hadn't told him?

He slid his fingers into the elastic of her shorts and pulled them down her legs, leaving her bare. The cool air hit her backside and when he began using his hands to caress her, molding her flesh to his will, she couldn't help but moan even more.

She heard the sound of his zipper and then he tilted her hips up to him. She closed her eyes to the feel of the warm hardness of his erection touching her while his fingers massaged between her legs.

She tightened her grip on the table as he placed the head of his shaft at her womanly folds. The feel of him entering her from behind sent her mind spinning and when he pushed deep, she cried out as sensations tore through her. In this position she felt a part of him, enclosed in his embrace, in the comfort and protection of his body.

He began moving and her body vibrated with every stroke inside her. She closed her eyes, relishing the feel of something so intimate and right between them. He ground his hips against her, going deeper and deeper—she wondered if they would be able to separate their bodies when the time came to do so.

When he slid his hands underneath her top and began fondling her bare breasts, she threw her head back. She loved the feel of his hands on her breasts, the tips of his fingers tormenting her nipples.

The way he was mating with her, the hot warmth of his breath on her neck as he whispered all the things he planned to do to her before the night was over—all of that stirred heat and stroked her desire to a feverish pitch she could barely contain any longer.

She let go, sensations ripping through her. She began quivering in an orgasm from head to toe. Those same sensations overpowered him and he tilted her up toward him even more and drove deeper inside of her. He groaned her name as she felt his hot release. She felt it. She felt him. And before she could stop herself, she cried out, "I love you, Matthew."

She couldn't believe she'd said it, and part of her hoped that he hadn't heard it. Slowly, he turned her around and gave her the most tender, gentle kiss she'd ever had from him. But he didn't say anything. Not a word.

Matthew glanced around the bedroom as he leaned against the closed door. The last thing he had expected was for Carmen to admit to loving him, and as soon as he could escape her presence, he had. He should have told her that he loved her, too, but for some reason he hadn't been able to do so. Not that he didn't, but because he loved her so much. Had he confessed it at that moment he probably would have lost it—to know that she still loved him after all this time was more than he could handle. He needed to pull himself together before facing her. Before pouring his heart out to her and letting her know just how miserable his life had been without her in it.

He'd enjoyed being here with her for the past week and was looking forward to the rest of the summer. And he was doing a pretty good job balancing the work and spending time with her. They'd spent a lot of hours on the beach and had gone to several polo matches. And of course the media was in a frenzy trying to figure out what was going on between them.

Even with all the gossip floating around, things between them were almost like they'd been in the beginning. But not quite. He knew his time was running out. Given what she'd just said to him, they had to talk. And they had to talk today. He would take her for a walk on the beach, and they would finally hash it all out.

He opened a drawer and searched around for his sunglasses, smiling when he found the case buried at the bottom. He was about to close the drawer when he noticed a DVD case labeled, "For my Husband." And it was dated the day he was supposed to meet her in Spain.

Curious about the video, he took it out of the drawer. After inserting the DVD into the player, he sat on the edge of the bed.

He smiled when Carmen appeared on the screen in what looked like a spoof of his very first job as a director, which was for a game show called *Guess My Secret.* She was talking to the camera, to him, daring him to discover her secret. The only clues she gave were a plate and a small clock. Soon she added a number of other clues into the mix—a pair of knitting needles and a jar of cocoa butter.

He was still scratching his head and laughing at her when she added more hints. Breath was sucked from his lungs when she placed two additional items on the table—a baby bottle and a bib. With a shaking hand, he reached over to turn up the volume while she smiled into the camera.

"Very good, Matthew. Since you're a smart man, I'm sure you now know my secret. We are having a baby! That's why I wanted to make our time here in Barcelona so special."

"Oh my God!" he groaned. Carmen had been pregnant? Then what happened?

"Hey, Matthew, I was beginning to think you got lost up here. What's going—"

Carmen entered the room and stopped talking in mid-sentence when she saw herself on the screen. Her gaze immediately sought out Matthew, and the pain she saw on his face tore at her heart.

"Is that true, Carmen? Had you planned to tell me that night in Barcelona that you were pregnant?"

She swallowed as she nodded. "Yes. I... I wanted to tell you in a fun way so..." Her words trailed off.

He nodded slowly and then asked the question she had been dreading. "What happened, Carmen?"

She lowered her head as she relived that night. The stomach pains that kept getting worse. Her not being able to reach him on his cell when she'd awakened that night, bleeding. Everything became a blur after that. Except the part about waking up and being told by a doctor that she'd lost the baby.

"Carmen?"

She lifted her head and met his gaze as her eyes filled with tears. And then she began speaking, recounting every single detail of that night. As she talked, she watched his expression. The shattered look on his face and the pain that clouded his eyes nearly broke her heart, and she felt his agony. A part of her was relieved to tell him the truth and no longer have the burden of keeping a secret on her shoulders.

"And you never told me," he said in a broken tone. "You never told me."

She pulled in a deep breath as tears threatened to spill down her face. "I couldn't. I wanted that baby so much. Losing it, and then not having you there with me to share my pain, made me bitter, unreasonable. I tried contacting you first and when I didn't get you, all I could think about was that I needed you and you were at work, away from me. In my emotional state, I blamed you."

He bent his head and when he raised his eyes to her again, the pain in them had deepened. "And I blame myself, as well," he said in a hoarse tone. "I blame myself because I should have been there with you. I don't know if I can ever forgive myself for not being there."

She saw the sheen of tears in his eyes and quickly crossed the room to him. As they clung to each other, tears she had held back since that night flowed down her face. She had cried then but it hadn't been like this. Her shoulders jerked with sobs she hadn't been able to let go of until now, until she was with him.

"I'm so sorry, Carmen. Now I understand. I had let you down by letting you go through that alone. I know I won't ever be able to forgive myself for that."

She leaned away from him, wiping her eyes. "You can, Matthew, and you must. It took me a while to see it wasn't your fault, nor was it mine. The same thing would have happened if you'd been there. And being here with you this past week made me realize I can't be angry at you for something you didn't know about, something that was not in your control. I had tried telling you several times over the past week, but you kept wanting us to wait. I'm sorry you had to find out this way."

She wiped more tears from her eyes. "The woman who owned the villa called her doctor and made arrangements for him to take care of me there, figuring that I would want to keep it from the media. With her help, I was able to avoid the circus that could have taken place. The doctor said I can try again," she said, leaning up against him, holding tight. "But I so wanted that one," she whispered brokenly, burying her face in his chest.

Matthew swept her off her feet and carried her over to the settee. He sat down with her cradled in his lap. He bent his head, and felt his wet cheek against hers.

"It wasn't your fault, Matthew. It wasn't my fault. It was just something that happened. We have to believe that so we can move beyond it. There will be other babies."

He lifted his head to meet her gaze. "But will there be other babies...for us, Carmen? For you and me?"

Carmen knew what he was asking. He'd once told her that he didn't want any other woman to have his child but her. And from the look in his eyes he still wanted that. He wanted to know if their relationship would ever get back to the way it was, when he was her whole world and she was his.

She shifted slightly in his embrace to wrap her arms around his neck. She wanted to make sure he heard what she was about to say. "I never stopped loving you, Matthew. The reason I wanted that baby so much was because it was a part of you, and a part of me. And the reason I hurt so much afterward was because I thought I had lost that connection. I thought the baby would bring us back together." She paused a second and then said, "But I've discovered that all it takes to bring us back together is us. Being with you here this past week has shown me there is still an us, and I want that back so badly. I was never involved with Bruno. It was all a publicity stunt. The only man I ever wanted to belong to was you. Can you forgive me for shutting you out of my life when I needed you most? Can you forgive me for running away? I will never leave you again."

"Oh, Carmen. I need you to forgive me, as well. I love you so much. I was so driven to give you the things you were used to having that I lost focus, I forgot about those things that truly mattered. You, and truly making you happy. I've been so lonely without you. And Candy, too, was just a publicity stunt. Hell, I was looking forward to spending time without her here. But when I arrived and discovered you, I wanted you to stay. At first I wanted revenge, to hurt you the way I was hurting, but I soon discovered it couldn't be that way with us."

She nodded. "I was going to make you want me and then leave again. Instead I ended up wanting you so badly I didn't know what to do."

"We're going to handle our business differently from here on out," he declared. "I've learned this week that I can balance my work and the rest of my life. Will you give me another chance to prove it?"

Carmen smiled up at him as he pushed back a strand of hair from her face. "I want that, too, Matthew."

"And will you marry me, Carmen?"

She felt more tears come to her eyes. "Yes, yes, I will marry you, and this time will be forever."

"Forever," he said, bending down to kiss her. And the kiss they shared was full of promise for a brighter and happier future. Together, knowing what they now knew about each other, they would be able to do anything.

Moments later he broke off the kiss and stood with her in his arms. She recognized the look he was giving her. "What about the polo match?" she asked.

He chuckled as he crossed the room to the bed. "There will be others."

Carmen knew he was right. Being in his arms and making love to him was what she needed. They were being given another chance at happiness and were taking it.

"It will be me and you together, Carmen, for the rest of our lives."

She reached up and caressed the side of his face. "Yes, Matthew, for the rest of our lives."

Epilogue

Ardella rushed over to them the moment Matthew and Carmen entered the tent, and from the anxious look on her face it was evident she was looking for a scoop. This time Matthew and Carmen didn't mind giving her one.

"So you two, what are you smiling about?"

Matthew pulled Carmen closer to his side. "It's a beautiful day and we believe it will be a good polo match."

The woman gave them a sly look. "I think there's something else."

Carmen decided to take Ardella out of her inquisitive misery. "There is something else and you can say you heard it right from us. Matthew and I have decided to remarry."

The smile on the woman's face appeared genuine. "I am truly happy for you two, but you know everyone will want details and facts."

Carmen threw her head back. "Sorry, but some things we plan to keep secret and sacred." She refused to spill the beans about their plan to have a private ceremony on the beach here in the Hamptons this weekend. The first person she'd called was Rachel who had been supremely ecstatic.

"Matthew, will Carmen star in any future Birmingham movies?"

Matthew glanced down at Carmen and chuckled. "Ardella, Carmen can do anything Carmen wants."

Ardella beamed. "I will take that as a yes."

"You do that," Matthew said. And, knowing that Ardella probably had her secret camera ready, with the profound tenderness of a man who was in love, he pulled Carmen into his arms and kissed her.

No one would understand the emotions flowing through him at that that moment. They were the heartfelt emotions of a man meant to cherish the woman he loved. A man who'd recently realized that he really was husband material.

Carmen's heart was just as full and later, as she and Matthew sat beside each other watching the polo match, she couldn't help but wipe a tear from her eye. They had talked and together had promised not to let anything or anyone come between them again.

"You okay, sweetheart?"

Carmen glanced up at Matthew and nodded. "I couldn't be better." She paused and, still holding his gaze, whispered, "I love you."

A smile touched his lips. "And I love you."

She leaned closer to him when he tightened his arms around her shoulders. She was happy about the future that lay before them. He wanted to try again for a baby and so did she. But right now she looked forward to being Carmen Akins Birmingham again.

She smiled, liking the sound of that and deciding to show him just how much when they returned home later. Life was good but being with the man you love, she decided, was even better.

* * * * *